A CHRISTMAS MURDER

MARY GRAND

Boldwood

First published in Great Britain in 2024 by Boldwood Books Ltd.

Copyright © Mary Grand, 2024

Cover Design: Head Design Ltd.

Cover Photography: Shutterstock and iStock

A CIP catalogue record for this book is available from the British Library.

Paperback ISBN 978-1-80426-922-0

Large Print ISBN 978-1-80426-919-0

Hardback ISBN 978-1-80426-923-7

Ebook ISBN 978-1-80426-921-3

Kindle ISBN 978-1-80426-920-6

Audio CD ISBN 978-1-80426-928-2

MP3 CD ISBN 978-1-80426-927-5

Digital audio download ISBN 978-1-80426-924-4

Boldwood Books Ltd
23 Bowerdean Street
London SW6 3TN
www.boldwoodbooks.com

To Rachel,
Thank you for all your friendship, encouragement, and support,
With love
Mary xx

PROLOGUE

Most of the guests in the manor house were asleep. Only the killer was aware of the snow falling in a heavy swirling mass outside. Layer upon layer of dense snow covered the ground, slowly cutting the manor off from the outside world. And only the killer was aware that one of the party was now dead.

Weeks of planning had culminated in the perfect murder, and now Duncan Fern was deceased. It had been quite thrilling: being God, deciding who lived and who died.

Of course, when light dawned on a new day, Duncan's body would be discovered. After the shock, suspicion and fear would set in. The guests would start watching each other, weighing up each word spoken, each look, no matter how insignificant. This was just the beginning, the killer knew that murder was simply the first move in the game.

1

THURSDAY, 22 DECEMBER

'What a nightmare!'

Seven o'clock in the morning was an unnerving time to get a phone call and, by the time Susan picked up the phone, a number of horrendous scenarios had flashed through her head, all involving close members of her family.

However, the voice she heard was her friend Robert's, and the emergency he went on to describe was of quite a different nature.

'Meera has had an accident. We got back from A and E at midnight. She's on crutches.'

Robert was working at the local manor house, Bishopstone Manor, which had recently been converted by the new owner, Meera Gupta, at great expense into an exclusive hotel.

'The guests are arriving later,' continued Robert. He hesitated, before enquiring, 'Just checking – are you still going to be on your own for Christmas?'

Susan was on the alert. She had a pretty good idea what was coming. She was also aware that her bedroom seemed lighter; there was a chill in the air.

Holding her phone, she got out of bed, opened the curtains, and gasped. When she'd taken the dogs for their final walk last night, she had felt a few gentle wet kisses of snowflakes falling on her face. She'd known more was forecast, but heavy snowfall was rare on the island. Susan had forgotten how you went to sleep in one world and woke in another. At night, snow worked in a silent, magical way. And so, this morning she stared in wonder at the sight of the whole village – houses, trees, cars – covered in a thick white dustcloth.

'Susan, are you still there?'

'Sorry. Yes, I was looking out the window. Um, yes, I am on my own for Christmas. Zoe is on her way to Edinburgh to be with Fay's family. I'm not worried, in fact I've turned down a few offers of Christmas dinner. I'm actually looking forward to my first Christmas Day on my own, snuggled up with the dogs; easy food, a book, TV and my knitting.'

'That's good but, well, I've a huge favour to ask. Would you be prepared to come here and help Meera out?' He added quickly, 'There wouldn't be any cooking or cleaning. Meera just needs a right-hand woman. Someone to meet and greet the guests, be the face to sort out problems. The job requires people skills, and you have plenty of those. There will be a small, exclusive group, only seven guests. Duncan Fern, the editor of *The Morning Flame*, and his adult family.'

'I can't stand that newspaper—'

'I know Duncan Fern is hardly your ideal guest, but he's a very influential man. Meera desperately needs this stay to go well. And there's not just him she needs to impress. There's his son Bryson, the crime writer, his wife, a renowned restaurant critic... I could go on. They're a high-maintenance lot and she needs everything to go without a hitch.'

Susan pressed her lips together hard, and then asked, 'How many nights would this be?'

'The guests are staying six nights.'

She glanced out of the window. 'I know the manor is only up the road, but the forecast is for a lot more snow.'

'I've thought of that. You can stay here in my flat, and the dogs would be welcome.'

Susan bit her lip. She'd never stayed overnight with Robert.

'There's a spare bedroom,' Robert added quickly. 'Please, Susan. It might even be fun. The food here is great. The dogs will have a wonderful time.'

Susan could feel herself weaken. Her Christmas dinner was simply a ready meal of nut roast and vegetables; that could go in the freezer. Robert would drop everything to help her. Maybe she should go?

'When do you need me?'

She heard the breath of relief from Robert. 'After lunch today? Oh, and one more thing. I told Meera you were musical. She wondered if you had any Tudorish instruments. Maybe you could play when the guests are eating? That kind of thing?'

The idea that she would have a stash of medieval lutes and hurdy-gurdies in a cupboard amused Susan, but she replied, 'I have a treble recorder and I can find some music to bring along?'

'You're a star. Thanks so much,' replied Robert.

Susan ended the call slightly in shock as it sank in what she had agreed to. She sent her daughter Zoe a text to let her know where she would be.

Susan quickly showered, dressed and went down to her cocker spaniels, Rocco and Libs. Rocco was her timid boy, a sable roan who she'd had since he was a puppy. Libs she'd adopted, a gorgeous black cocker, always sniffing and tracking scents. She opened the back door, and the dogs charged out, running around the garden, wagging their tails frantically.

They might be excited, but snow always had a strange effect on Susan. She found herself mesmerised by it. She'd read that snow absorbed a lot of sound. She could believe it that morning: everywhere was so hushed and still.

However, she had no time today for aimlessly staring at snow. She had a lot to do. She called the dogs back in. They all had breakfast, then she wrapped them up.

'Right, you two, your walk will be a visit to the village shop. As I do every year, I have run out of wrapping paper, and I still have Robert's present to wrap.'

She pushed open the front door. Rocco and Libs raised their noses, pulled on their leads, enthusiastic for their walk into this strange new world.

The ground snow in her close was completely unblemished. For a moment, Susan felt like an explorer stepping out into a new land. She glanced at the house next door, with the 'For Sale' sign outside. Tracy in the shop, who knew everything, assured her there had been a lot of interest, although Susan hadn't seen anyone looking round the house yet. She briefly thought about her previous neighbours, the tragic murder Susan herself had become involved in solving. Would the history of the house put people off?

At the end of the close, Susan entered the heart of the village, which had taken on a chocolate box quality. Snow coated the thatched roofs and iced the tops of the gravestones in the ancient churchyard.

Susan crossed the road to the village shop. Usually there were vegetables and fruit arranged on stalls, plants and bags of timber outside, but nothing had been laid out this morning. As always, the inside of the shop felt warm and welcoming, with

Tracy behind the counter. Her little black cocker spaniel, Lottie, came running out to greet Rocco and Libs.

'Morning, Susan. You're up early. Fancy us having real snow here on the Isle of Wight. I can't remember when we last had a white Christmas, or even serious snow.'

'Nor me. My two love the snow. What does Lottie make of it?' asked Susan, leaning over to fuss the little dog.

'Oh, she was up at five, going mad in the garden. Now, do you need me to put bread by for you on Saturday, Christmas Eve? We're going to open for a few hours in the morning of Christmas Day, but there won't be a delivery from the bakers, and bread will sell out, particularly with the weather. You wouldn't believe the way people have been stocking up.'

Susan thanked Tracy but said she was fine for bread.

'Now, you know the offer to come to dinner with us on Christmas Day still stands. I don't like to think of you on your own.'

'Actually, I won't be alone any more. I'll be up at the manor.'

The news naturally enthralled Tracy.

'Oh, you're off to the manor! Is this because of Meera's accident?'

Susan was amazed. Even for Tracy, this was impressive. 'How on earth do you know about that? It was only last night.'

'The mother of one of my papergirls works in radiology. She X-rayed Meera's ankle and hand. Poor thing: very nasty strains, very painful. I hear your Robert took her in. He's been very good, hasn't he, helping her out? I guess he's working over Christmas then?'

Susan chose to ignore 'your Robert' but did acknowledge that he would be there as well. She registered Tracy storing away this new nugget of information.

Tracy picked up a copy of *The Morning Flame*, which was

lying on the countertop with the other daily papers. 'This poor woman. Every day there seems to be a new story about her.'

Susan read the headline – 'Isabelle's heartbreak – the affair – the abortion' – which was accompanied by a full-page photograph of a young celebrity. She shook her head. 'I remember when she won the cooking competition. It was so exciting, and I really liked her. Why are they digging up stories like this? It's her private life, nothing to do with anyone else.'

'You can ask Duncan Fern about it when you see him.'

'You know he's a guest?'

'Yes, he used to bring his family on holiday here years ago. They rented that solitary house up by the Longstone on the downs.'

'Oh, I know the house you mean. I've often thought how exciting it would be to stay up there, particularly at night. Very atmospheric.'

'I wouldn't want to stay there. It's so isolated, no other houses around and pitch black at night. Anyway, they obviously enjoyed it. Duncan Fern brought his family to stay for nigh on ten years running apparently and, of course, this was their closest shop.'

'I hadn't realised.'

'This was before my time, over twenty years ago, when Alice still ran the shop.' Susan smiled at the mention of Alice, who was now in her nineties. They had only been friends a few years, having met under the highly unusual circumstances of solving a murder together.

Tracy continued, 'Now, Duncan Fern's daughter, Hayley, who is also a guest, rang us up, here at the shop, a few days ago. She used to come into the shop and chat to Alice. She wondered if Alice was still alive and, if so, was she still local. Hayley said there was something important she needed to talk to Alice about.'

'That sounds intriguing.'

'Doesn't it? I told her Alice was in the nursing home. I think Hayley was going to try and go and visit her.'

'Alice would love that. I'm going to visit her tomorrow. Maybe I'll be able to get the low down on what she remembers of Duncan and the family.'

Susan picked up a roll of Christmas wrapping paper from a stand next to the counter. 'I've some last-minute packing to do. Don't suppose I'll see you before Christmas now, so I hope you have a lovely day. Happy Christmas!'

'Thank you. Christmas in a Tudor manor sounds very romantic, and they say Meera has spent a fortune up there. I shall look forward to hearing all about it.'

Susan returned home and started to sort out some clothes to take to the manor. She assumed there wouldn't be any sort of uniform, so she would take her smarter dresses, which might be preferable to her usual denim skirt and jumper.

She was becoming increasingly concerned about the roads getting blocked and, after stocking up all the bird feeders in the back garden, she was glad to wrap herself and the dogs up and set off soon after lunch.

Fortunately, the gritters had been out, although she could see new snowfall was rapidly covering their work. Usually she loved the view on this drive, but today it was impossible to see the horizon between the white fields and the gravel-grey sky. She drove carefully, and slowly, with her windscreen wipers pushing away the flutters of snow, feeling the tyres pulling her slightly to one side.

Susan was relieved finally to turn off the main road and onto the unmade road that led to the large car park for the manor and the downs walk. Once she'd parked, she took the dogs out of the car. She decided they were quite enough to handle in one journey to the manor and she would return for her bags later. She threw her small cross-body 'dog-walking' bag over her head and zipped the car keys into it. With the dogs securely on their leads, she approached the steep flight of stone steps out of the car park. 'You two need to calm down. I don't want to fall,' she warned the dogs, pulling them closer, putting the leads in one hand and holding the metal handrail with the other. The flight of steps was broken up by a small concrete platform from which you could continue down to the manor or turn left and clamber up the public footpath that weaved around the perimeter of the manor grounds and led onto the downs.

Susan caught her breath, descended the final steps, then made her way through the stone archway which joined two old barns and out into the courtyard in front of the manor.

The gardens, to the left, had been open to the public for years and Susan loved visiting them. Although much smaller than gardens in some of the grand country houses, they were carefully laid out, with rose gardens, allotments, avenues of fruit trees and wildflowers, a small area of woodland, and a hedged-off area with a small shack and café area. Susan had wonderful memories of bringing Zoe and the foster children here, taking part in the Easter trails, and eating ice creams. On some visits they would leave the gardens through a small wooden gate and then climb up to the downs and the Longstone. The manor house had not been open to the public and so she had only ever been able to admire it from the outside.

Now that she was here, Susan was excited at the thought of going inside this elegant Tudor L-shaped stone building. Today it looked picture-book perfect, snow covering the tiled roofs, topping the tall chimneys, lacing the leaded windows, and coating the surrounding hedges and trees in the small courtyard.

'Susan,' a familiar voice called.

2

The sight of Robert always warmed Susan, and she smiled over at him.

She had been married to quiet bookish GP Steve for forty years, and they'd had a happy, companionable marriage. The ending, three years ago, had been sudden and brutal. Steve calmly explained one evening over tea that he no longer loved her and was leaving. Numb with shock, Susan had begun the difficult process of rebuilding her life. Moving to Bishopstone had been part of this fresh start.

Robert, widowed, sporty, and a retired detective, had offered friendship that Susan had been very grateful for through those early years of adjusting to a single life. However, he wasn't 'her Robert', whatever Tracy at the shop might think. They had certainly grown a lot closer lately, but Susan had been hesitant to dive into a new relationship.

Robert enveloped her, as he always did, in a bear hug. 'You made it.' He glanced over at the house. 'As a former history teacher, I'd expect you to know all about the history of this place,' said Robert, grinning.

'I know some of it. Apparently, it was originally a Saxon farmhouse. Did you know that it was engulfed by a landslip and buried for two hundred years?'

'Ah, Meera said something about that.'

'I've never been inside the house. I'm so excited to see what she has done.'

Robert smiled. 'You'll be impressed. Now, go on in. Give me your car keys and I'll get the rest of your stuff.'

Susan pushed open the ancient wooden door and entered a large stone-floored room with leaded windows, and wood-panelled walls. On these walls hung portraits and tapestries. Susan could easily imagine she had been transported back to Tudor times.

There was a very small reception area with a desk and laptop, but the room was dominated by an enormous roaring fire, leather chairs, bookshelves and a stone stairway leading upstairs. In addition, there were Christmas garlands of holly and ivy, mistletoe hung from beams and, slightly out of period, Meera had allowed a real pine Christmas tree, with subtle lights, which shone a gentle glow over the wooden walls and stone floor.

Robert returned with her belongings and two dog beds under his arms.

'Isn't it impressive?' he said. 'Meera calls this the library, rather than reception.' He pointed to the right. 'Through there is the Great Hall for dining, and the kitchens. We're heading down this side hallway to the left.'

Susan followed Robert, past Meera's office, along the corridor and finally to his flat. Before they entered, he nodded towards a door at the end of the hallway. 'That's one of the few exit doors. It's sometimes used at night when the front door is all locked up. Guests apparently will have a key, as well as staff.'

Robert pushed open a heavy door into the living room of his flat which was a rather strange juxtaposition of mismatched modern furniture, with stone floors and wooden panelled walls. This wasn't a room that had been lovingly put together, and there was a chill in the air, but Robert had brought cushions, added photographs and pictures in an attempt to make it homely.

He put down the dog beds and took Susan's case through to what she guessed was her bedroom.

Robert had two dogs of his own. Gem Gem was a beautiful liver and white pointer cross springer spaniel and Dougie was a velvet black cocker spaniel with a white flash on his chest. They came rushing over to greet their friends Rocco and Libs as Susan unclipped their leads.

'There's a small kitchenette for coffees, but we get main meals from the kitchen. The chef, Gary, is really good. He's an islander, actually, but worked in some of the best restaurants on the mainland. Meera is very pleased to have snapped him up. She has him creating something extra special for Christmas Day. These two are loving it here,' Robert continued. 'Gem Gem has been up hunting rabbits on the downs. Dougie has been finding all the rubbish visitors over the autumn have dropped and demanding I put it in the bin.'

Robert opened a patio door that led into a small courtyard surrounded by high walls. 'It's a nice safe area for them,' he explained. The cold air hit the room but the dogs, unconcerned, pushed past them and rushed out into the snow.

'All those paws to wipe down!' said Robert.

Susan laughed. 'They're loving it.'

'There's a little gate over in the corner, safely locked now, but we can go through to the garden that way.'

'Brilliant. So, how are you finding it over here? The manor is very different to your house in Ventnor.'

'You're right, but I wanted a change. I miss the sound of the sea at night. However, I do get to hear foxes and owls.'

'How much longer do you think you'll stay?'

'Until March. I want to be back home for the spring. Meera would like me to do out this flat properly for staff, so I will work on that next.'

'And are you refitting guest rooms at the moment?'

Robert grinned. 'I'm not allowed anywhere near the guest rooms. They're being refurbished by experts. My jobs are far more basic: maintenance, decorating the staffing and office areas. There's masses more to do, but Meera will take on more workers soon.'

'What's Meera like?'

She noticed Robert blush slightly. 'She's nice. I think you'll like her. We get on well. She has a good sense of humour, knows her mind, which of course she needs to when taking on a business like this. She has quite a strong Mancunian accent which some of the staff here find confusing – she grew up there after her parents moved over from India.'

Susan was aware of Robert rushing his words and looked at him more carefully. 'And is she single?'

'Recently divorced,' he replied quickly, then looked over at the dogs. 'They've sniffed enough out there. Let's get them in. I'll grab some towels.'

The dogs raced back in and, once their paws were wiped down, they mooched around the room.

'Let me show you your room.' Robert didn't catch her eye as he spoke but walked determinedly to a small bedroom off the living room. There was a pretty flowered duvet. Susan noticed a small vase of freshly cut holly and greenery.

'Sorry, there wasn't much around—'

'It's so kind of you, very Christmassy, thank you.'

Robert smiled shyly. 'I hope it meets with your approval. There's one problem. I'm afraid there's a security light that can be set off by people using the back door or by wildlife and it shines into the room. I hope it doesn't disturb you too much.'

'I'm sure I'll manage,' replied Susan. She picked up her bag. 'I'll leave this here. Um, I think I'd better change before meeting Meera.'

Robert tactfully left the room while Susan put on one of her dresses and a cardigan she had very sensibly packed.

'This will have to do,' she said, glancing at the mirror, then returning to the living room.

'You look lovely,' Robert said in that way that made her blush. She looked at Robert sideways, checking for any hint of sarcasm, but there was none. Embarrassed, she turned to the dogs. She had the kind of conversation that doggy people have with their pets, telling them to be good, they would be fine in their new home, and she would be back soon.

The dogs seemed to understand and made their ways to their own beds and settled down.

3

Susan followed Robert next door to the office. He knocked on the door. A firm voice invited them in.

The room was light and bright with classic prints and trailing house plants. Meera sat at a large wooden desk. She wore a smart black suit and white blouse and was typing awkwardly on her keyboard with one hand. She didn't turn immediately, but the decisive thump on a key announced that she had finished the task in hand.

Meera swivelled around in her office chair, carefully placing her bandaged foot onto a nearby footstool, nursing a bandaged hand on her lap. She greeted Susan with a broad smile.

'Ah, Susan. Thanks a million for coming. If I could stand, I'd get up and give you a proper hug.' Susan remembered Robert had mentioned Meera's strong Mancunian accent. She found it very warm and welcoming. 'I can't believe I've done this to myself!'

'Accidents happen.'

'No, this was my fault, rushing around. The hand is a minor strain, but the ankle is a lot worse. I was lucky not to break it.

Anyhow, grab a seat.' She glanced at Robert. 'We'll be okay. I expect you want to get on?'

Robert eyes twinkled. He took the hint and left.

Susan looked more carefully at the woman in front of her. She was probably in her early fifties, ten years younger than Susan, comfortably plump, with shoulder-length black silky hair. Her outstanding feature was her deep brown eyes. They were a beautiful olive, almost black, with spark and glow in them.

'First of all, I guess you want to know what you've let yourself in for?'

'I hope Robert explained that the last thing I am is a domestic goddess. I live in a mess and on ready meals,' said Susan, suddenly nervous about what she'd undertaken.

However, she was reassured as Meera gave a deep, uninhibited laugh. 'God, that's just how I'd be if I didn't spend my life in hotels. I don't know when I last made a proper meal or my own bed. Anyhow, all that side of things is taken care of. What I need is someone to handle the guests. There's also a fair bit of running around, checking people in, checking over rooms in the evening when they're finishing their evening meal. Also, I need you to be available for queries, anything really. Does that sound like something you'd be prepared to do?'

'As long as you're supervising me, I'm happy to give things a go.'

Meera gave a sigh of relief and a broad smile. 'Brilliant. The phone signal in the house is terrible, I'm afraid. We have Wi-Fi in all the rooms, but mobile signal is very unreliable. I've installed an internal phone system in the guests' rooms for them to contact me or the kitchen, but I'm afraid for an outside call on a mobile you need to go out to somewhere like the car park.'

'I should have brought my laptop to send emails and the like—'

'Don't worry. You're welcome to come in here and use the office computer.'

Meera opened the drawer of a small table close to her and took out a small device.

'Don't laugh, but these were Robert's idea. We used to call them walkie talkies when I was little, but they say two-way radios now. Actually, they've been brilliant here. I have one, so do Robert and Gary in the kitchen, and I'll give one to you. It means you can always get hold of me and, of course, I can always get hold of you.'

Susan took the radio, remembering that Zoe and her friends had something similar when they were young. She slipped it into her pocket.

'Right,' continued Meera. 'Let's get through the basic paperwork and then I'll fill you in on the guests.'

Meera was very efficient; everything was settled quickly.

She sighed. 'Honestly, we weren't even meant to be receiving guests yet. But then I happened to meet Duncan at an event in London at the end of November and was telling him about this venture. He suddenly asked if he could bring the family. He'd been unwell, wanted to get everyone together. He'd been to this area before, apparently. I reckoned we could get the place ready for them, and it's quite a coup. Getting good recommendations from Duncan Fern and family could put this place on the map.'

'Tracy in the village shop had told me Duncan Fern was coming.'

Meera laughed. 'I'm not surprised Tracy knows. I've only met her a few times, but I sense she has a kind of psychic gift for knowing everything that is going on in the village. So, we have seven guests: Duncan Fern, his wife Kristen, son Bryson with wife Victoria, daughter Hayley with partner Lewis and an associate editor from *The Morning Flame*, Antoine.'

'Oh, I thought it was just family—'

'I think that had been the plan, but Antoine couldn't get out to see his family in France. He and Duncan have worked together for years. I believe he's one down from Duncan at the paper so, anyhow, he's coming as well.'

Meera winced as she adjusted her leg. Susan guessed she would be a lot happier tucked up with Netflix on a sofa, but this was the price of running your own business.

Meera continued. 'The guests are staying until the Wednesday morning after Christmas, so that's six nights. The programme is flexible, particularly with this weather. Obviously, Christmas Day is the big one. On the day after Boxing Day, the 27th, we're holding a Twixmas party, inviting a few of the locals and others to a get-together, early evening, from six to nine. The family leave first thing on the 28th. Robert tells me you're free for the whole of this time?'

'I am but, weather permitting, I'd like to go and visit my friend Alice in a local nursing home and also pop back to check on the house from time to time.'

'Of course. Now, if I can manage it, I'd like to quickly show you the rooms.' Meera grimaced, reaching for her crutches, propped up on the desk next to her, and began her slow progress across the room.

Susan held the door open. 'Thanks. These things are so hard on my arms,' Meera complained.

They walked to the library. Susan wondered how Meera was going to tackle the flight of stairs.

'This is where I fell. I was rushing coming down, slipped and my ankle went right over. I was in agony. Anyhow, I'm not going to attempt them now. We have a small lift here. I've tried to make this place as disabled friendly as I can, but obviously there are constraints in a building of this age.'

Coming out of the lift on the first floor, Susan could see a door to her left and a long corridor to her right.

'My wing is behind that door; these are the guest rooms. We've five more to go.'

The guest corridor was clearly freshly decorated, with smart cream walls and plush carpets. Meera opened the door to the right.

'This is the master suite and will be Duncan's room. As requested, his wife, Kristen, has a separate room next door. Apparently, Duncan disturbs her, as he often wakes in the early hours, has a drink of whisky and reads.'

Duncan's bedroom had a large four-poster bed, dark wooden furniture, cream walls and heavy curtains. The bathroom had an enormous enamel bath, as well as a walk-in shower cubicle.

In one corner of the bedroom stood a small decorated Christmas tree, and on a table stood a bright red poinsettia.

Meera sighed. 'I'm restricted on size with these rooms. I can't provide the kind of suites they have at the Ritz, but we have this beautiful building and the atmosphere. Everything you can see is a genuine antique. I had people attend auctions, and the workmen who restored the walls were specialists. I've hidden away all the luxuries people expect: the fridges, smart TVs, charging points, coffee makers, etc. I didn't want to ruin the look of the rooms.'

'The renovations must have been very expensive.'

'They were, but I am proud of what we've achieved.'

'Good, it's stunning.'

Susan noticed a smart silver hip flask featuring an intricate array of Celtic knot designs on Duncan's bedside table. This stood next to a tall rectangular box inscribed with:

15-year-old single-malt whisky

In front of this stood a card, which she picked up.

Wishing you all a very Happy Christmas

'Are these courtesy gifts?'

'Gosh, no. Kristen has bought one of these hip flasks and a bottle of this single-blend whisky for each of the guests, well, apart from Bryson, who gets an alcohol-free spirit. They're her Christmas gift. She had them delivered here and asked me to have them ready in the rooms. They're beautiful. Look at the engraved silver hip flask. There's even a matching integral tot cup that screws on top of the lid. They're quite something.'

'Wow. They must have cost her a packet.'

'I saw the receipts. They did.'

Susan wandered over to the window, looked down on the courtyard. 'Well, with a fabulous room and that view, I'm sure Duncan Fern will be impressed.'

'Let's hope so.' They moved on to the room next door. It was very similar to Duncan's, only slightly smaller. 'This is Kristen's room. She made all sorts of requests. She's a bit of a prima donna, I think, or maybe as an American she doesn't trust the English to run a decent hotel. Among other things, she requested specially lit mirrors, which I have provided. They won't be staying – not in keeping with the hotel's aesthetic at all. She also requested a particular make of bottled water; she refuses to use tap water even for her teeth.' Meera raised her eyes to the ceiling as they carried on to the third on that side of the hallway. 'This is for Antoine, the journalist I mentioned. He only seemed concerned about the Wi-Fi. I'm guessing he's planning on working while he's here. I hope he doesn't get too narked about the mobile signal. I have warned him.'

They left Antoine's room and stood in the hallway while Meera explained, 'In the rooms opposite will be Duncan's children and partners. Son Bryson with Victoria is opposite Duncan, daughter Hayley with Lewis opposite Kristen. Bryson is a crime writer and his wife is the journalist and food critic Victoria Fern.'

'Victoria Fern? I've read her column,' interrupted Susan, 'but she's not with Duncan's paper, is she? Surely she's with *The Informer*?'

'That's right. Victoria is far more left wing than her father-in-law, so I hear. They must have some lively family gatherings. She asked for all these specialist teas that I've made sure are in her room. Hayley is a kind of freelance editor of novels. Her partner, Lewis, is a personal trainer. He wanted to check we have a gym. I explained we have a small room with gym equipment. I made sure the equipment is all top of the range but I'm sure his London gyms are far more sophisticated. I decided it was best to lower his expectations.'

They checked the other rooms quickly and, as they left the final one, Meera explained, 'I will come with you to greet the guests, but after that if you could take them to their rooms, see if they need drinks, etc., check they're happy with everything. This evening we will serve drinks at half seven, and then the evening meal. Robert tells me you're able to provide some kind of background music for the guests as they eat?'

'I've dug out my recorder and found some medieval tunes. It's nothing fancy—'

Meera flapped her hand dismissively, clearly not that interested in the music. 'That's fine. Your music will just add to the atmosphere and, of course, you will be able to keep an eye on things. So, once they've eaten, maybe you could go and check their rooms, just turn down the beds, that kind of thing. That should be it until the morning. Just ask me if there's anything you need or if there are any questions from the guests. I shall be around, smiling but not really being much more use.'

Meera paused. She had hardly taken a breath throughout the long speech. Her eyes were burning, nerves clearly underlying her words.

'I'm sure the holiday will be a success,' said Susan. 'Everything looks perfect. What a gorgeous way for them all to enjoy Christmas together.'

Meera smiled. 'I hope so. Mind you, they sound quite a dynamic family. I'm not sure how they will cope being hemmed in together. Christmas is notorious for family fall-outs – let's hope this goes well.' She faltered and looked at Susan. 'Robert told me you'd been involved in solving a few murders. I do hope we're not going to be embroiled in anything like that – not the image I want for the hotel.' She laughed nervously.

'Of course that won't happen. I'm sure it will be all peace and goodwill.'

'Let's hope so. Now, I need to get some painkillers. You go and settle in.'

However, Susan didn't have long in the flat before Meera contacted her on the two-way radio. 'A car is pulling up. Our first guests are arriving.'

4

As Susan approached the library, she could hear voices. When the room came into view, she saw Meera talking to a couple.

'How was your journey?'

'Exciting in this weather,' said the man, beaming. 'I was worried about cancellations, but we left on time. We were booked in the Signature Lounge, and I ate my money's worth of pastries. The drive was quite spectacular. I'd forgotten what a beautiful island this is and, in the snow, well, it's amazing.'

Meera caught sight of Susan. 'Ah, and this is Susan who will be looking after you this weekend. You also have a phone in your room to contact me, of course. Susan, this is Mr and Mrs Bryson Fern.'

'Oh, Bryson and Victoria, please,' interrupted Bryson. 'Good to meet you, Susan.'

Quite a short man, Bryson looked freshly kitted out in country gentleman attire: brand-new waxed jacket, tweed flat cap, and boots. His way of smiling was unusual. He tilted his head, widened his rather startling blue eyes, only moving half of his mouth: giving him a surprised rather than pleased appearance.

Susan smiled. 'Welcome to the island.'

'It's great to be back.'

'I understand you stayed close by as a child?'

'I did. I was only a kid when I first came and then we kept coming back every summer on the first Saturday in August until I was eighteen. Our last visit was twenty-five years ago, makes me feel old.' He looked at Susan, wide-eyed and childlike as if excited but also reaching out for approval.

His wife Victoria was searching around with a more critical eye. She turned to Meera, eyes looking with an almost frightening directness through enormous black-framed glasses. 'Comfortable, warm, well done,' she said in assertive, public-school English: the manor at least had passed its initial inspection.

Victoria had very short brown hair. In her dress, she matched her husband, with a long waxed jacket and hat, and leather boots. However, unlike her husband's brand-new outfit, her clothes appeared well worn, comfortable. Susan imagined Victoria had probably grown up in some old country house, with a range in the kitchen, rows of muddy Hunter wellies in the hallway and horses in the stables. Victoria carried a large 'organiser bag', the type Susan hated because, despite the name, she could never find anything in them. From her manner, Victoria, she was guessing, would not have that trouble.

'Looking forward to good food,' Victoria continued. 'I've experienced Gary Lowe's food before in London, at The City Hotel, classics with a twist. I get tired of foams, gels and drama. I'll be glad to return to basics.'

Susan smiled to herself, not sure Gary Lowe would find the description of 'basic' for his food particularly flattering.

Bryson chuckled. 'The joys of being married to a foodie.'

'I'll give you your keys,' continued Meera. 'This is the front door key; you won't be able to use that after twelve. This key is for a smaller back door at the end of the corridor past my office down there. If you come or go late, please make sure to lock up after yourselves.'

'Thank you,' said Bryson. 'Mind you, I can't see us stepping out much in this weather. Right, we've had a long cold journey, let's get to our room.'

'Let me get someone to help with your luggage.'

Bryson looked down at the smart luggage. 'We can manage. Seriously, we'll be fine.'

'If you're sure, then I'll leave you with Susan, but don't hesitate to contact me if you need anything.'

'Thank you. I hope my father's flight is okay in this weather. He managed to charter a private jet. I hadn't realised the island had any kind of airport.'

'There's just two small private airports, over to the east. No commercial flights.'

Susan escorted Bryson and Victoria Fern upstairs. Bryson chatted away easily, asking Susan about her work and the manor. However, once in the bedroom he walked to the window. Despite the fact that it was getting dark and the landscape was merely white and black shapes, he seemed to become fixated on the view, and fell silent.

Victoria headed straight to a bedside table and picked up the bottle of whisky and the card. 'From Kristen – she's out to impress. These hip flasks must have cost a bomb. Your father will approve.'

She picked up one hip flask, unscrewed the top cup and lid, filled the flask with whisky, then opened the other and filled the cup with the alcohol-free spirit.

She went to join Bryson and handed him his flask. 'Happy

Christmas,' she said. Bryson raised his flask to hers and they knocked back their drinks. He returned his cup to Victoria and went back to staring out of the window, as if the sight had hypnotised him.

Susan began to explain various features of the room. Victoria paid particular attention when she was shown the selection of teas.

'Good, just what I ordered. You may think I'm fussy but my husband insisted on bringing his own coffee beans and para-phernalia.' She threw an indulgent look his way.

Bryson, however, remained at the window.

Victoria frowned, walked over to him, slipped her arm through his. 'Is it strange to be back?'

He looked at her, smiled. 'A bit odd.'

'Hayley didn't want to come initially, did she? But I got a text from her last night saying she was glad to be coming.'

'She said that?' Bryson raised an eyebrow. 'Maybe she wants to share her holiday experience with Lewis.'

'It could be that. Your dad was determined to come whatever everyone felt. It seems a bit odd to me. It's hardly the glamorous holidays he's used to.' Victoria shivered. 'Shall we pull the curtains?'

As Victoria pulled the curtains, Bryson turned to Susan.

'Are you local?'

'I am. I live down the road in the village of Bishopstone. I understand you used to go to the shop in our village when you were on holiday here.'

He gave an amiable smile. 'We did. When we were driving here today, I was amazed to see it's survived. In fact, the village didn't look a lot different. Actually, Hayley has arranged for us to visit the lady who used to own it, Alice.'

'Tracy in the shop mentioned it. Alice will be thrilled.'

'I was amazed, to be honest, that Alice is still with us. She seemed a very old woman to me even back then. We're going to visit her in her nursing home on Boxing Day.'

'She'll be so pleased,' said Susan.

'Hayley sent her a copy of one of my books, but I don't know if she's up to reading now.'

'Oh, she is. I usually find her doing the crossword on her iPad. She'll be interested to hear all about what you're doing.'

'I'm glad to hear it. She always seemed to me a sharp woman: didn't miss a lot.'

'You'll be able to tell her that you will soon be a famous TV personality,' said Victoria to Bryson, then turned to Susan. 'Bryson is to have his own chat show soon, prime time. I know he'll be a great success.' She spoke with an almost maternal pride.

Bryson gave a self-conscious grin and said, 'I've you and your father to thank for opening that door.'

'Don't underestimate yourself. When my dad saw you on the book programme, he knew you were a natural. And he really approves of the way you've supported charities, used your experiences to help others.'

'I've only done what's right.'

Victoria kissed him on the cheek. 'And that is one of the reasons I love you.'

Bryson smiled shyly, then asked, 'Do you think I should check with my agent if the press should know about this visit to the nursing home?'

'They won't be interested in a visit to a local nursing home,' said Victoria, rolling her eyes.

Feeling sorry for Bryson, Susan added, 'I'm sure Alice and the other residents will be excited to see you. I hope you're comfortable in here. Now, I can bring you up hot drinks, or anything else, maybe mulled wine, champagne if you would prefer?'

Victoria once more took charge. 'I think champagne would be better than some excuse for masking cheap wine with some herbs and spices in. We could also do with some decent snacks.'

'Of course, I will go and get them.'

Susan set off to the cavernous kitchen, which retained the original floor and windows, with rows of pots and pans hung on hooks. However, the gleaming steel ovens and work surfaces showed it was a serious place of work. There were three members of staff there and, unlike those Susan had seen on television, everyone seemed calm and to be getting on with their jobs. At the centre was a short, balding dynamo of a man, who, while tasting a sauce, was clearly aware of every other member of his staff, occasionally commenting on their work. Susan guessed this must be Gary Lowe, a chef very much in charge of his kitchen.

He spotted Susan and, reluctantly leaving his sauce, walked over to her. When she explained that she had come for a tray for Bryson and Victoria Fern, she noticed his eyes widen.

'Ah, Victoria Fern has arrived. Good, right. I'll put this together.'

He had several plates of food prepared, and he carefully selected sandwiches, patisserie-style cakes, canapes, intricately iced mince pies, and miniature Christmas cakes.

'Goodness, I expected you to give me a mince pie and slice of cake.'

Gary stared, horrified. 'You know who Victoria Fern is? Everything I serve her has to be perfect. She can make or break a chef.'

'She's here on holiday.'

'A restaurant critic is never on holiday. She will judge every morsel of food and drink I present her with.'

Susan raised her eyebrows. 'Wow, no pressure then.'

Gary blinked fast. 'I have to get everything right with this group. It's not just Victoria, I need them all to be impressed. Nothing can go wrong.' He caught her eye, his shoulders relaxed slightly. 'Sorry. I haven't even asked your name. I'm Gary.'

'And I'm Susan. I've been shipped in to support Meera because of the accident. I live down the road in Bishopstone.'

'Oh, right. Welcome to the team.'

'Thanks. Oh, they asked for champagne—'

Gary grinned. 'Victoria doesn't trust me to make a decent mulled wine. She's wrong, but champagne it will be for now, and a good bottle at that.'

He carefully selected a bottle from the wine fridge, placed it in a silver ice bucket and handed Susan the tray. 'I'd take the lift, this is heavy.'

Susan carried the tray carefully, took the lift as suggested, and was about to knock on the bedroom door when she heard Victoria's voice.

'God, this weather! I won't stay banged up in here. I can't be imprisoned with your father day after day. One of us will end up killing the other.'

Susan smiled inwardly as she remembered Meera's words.

'Come on. He's mellowed lately,' responded Bryson.

'Rubbish. He hasn't changed a bit. Have you seen the head-line in today's *Morning Flame*? Your father will have sanctioned that. It's brutal. They won't be happy until that poor girl has killed herself,' said Victoria.

Susan, still in the hallway, quietly placed the tray on a small table, knocked, then took it inside just as Bryson was saying,

'Don't go rowing with Dad. We're here to celebrate Christmas, time for family.'

'More's the pity,' mumbled Victoria. Seeing Susan, she made no effort to smile, although Bryson switched on a grin and walked over to the tray.

'This looks splendid.'

Victoria glanced around the room. 'The manor would make a pretty good setting for one of your murders, Bryson. These panelled walls must hold some pretty dark secrets.' She looked at the tray, inspected the offering.

Susan was glad to leave them to their drinks and left the room. As she did, she heard the buzzing of her two-way radio and answered it. 'Come to the library,' said Meera. 'They're here.' Meera's voice was tight. It was clear to Susan who had just arrived.

5

As she reached the hallway, Susan saw a couple and a taxi driver struggling to get through the front door with a number of suitcases.

Meera was at the entrance, greeting the couple warmly.

Susan gave them a fleeting smile but walked past them to hold open the door for the taxi driver. He rolled his eyes. 'There's more to come.'

'Duncan, how lovely to see you again and to meet you, Mrs Fern,' enthused Meera.

Kristen's 'look' was old-fashioned Hollywood glamour, with tightly controlled long blonde waves, scarlet lipstick, large gold jewellery and expensive perfume that filled the library. Susan shuddered at the fur coat and matching hat. She had a horrible feeling there was nothing 'faux' about it.

Kristen held out a leather-gloved hand, shook hands with Meera, and spoke with a thick American drawl, 'Do call me Kristen, so pleased to meet you.' She waved her hand slightly dismissively around the room. 'Who wants to be in the Maldives when you can stay in a real Tudor manor?' Kristen forced a smile, but

Susan was pretty sure she would have turned around and taken a plane to sunnier climes in a heartbeat.

Duncan stepped slightly in front of his wife, between her and Meera. He was shorter than Kristen, wore a dark woollen coat, with an old-fashioned but beautifully made trilby hat. Susan guessed he was in his seventies.

He spoke gruffly from behind his cashmere scarf. 'We'll have an old-fashioned English Christmas here. They've even laid on snow. I've only seen the island in August when we brought the children... not always sunny, but of course, never snow. However, for all that, it all feels familiar, like going back in time.'

'How was your flight? Did the weather interfere with it?' asked Meera.

'God, I've never been in a plane like it. Some old tin can. I thought we were all going to die, crashing into the ocean,' said Kristen.

'The Solent isn't the ocean,' corrected Duncan. 'It was damned cold, though.' He gave a dry raspy cough, and his face went very red. Kristen frowned, but he shook his head before she could say anything. 'A few more hours and the flight would have been cancelled.'

'Well, I hope you will be very warm and comfortable here,' said Meera.

Kristen looked around with a slight air of confusion. 'I expect Elizabeth I to come and greet me.'

'We'd have to pay extra for that,' Duncan said gruffly, but there was the concession of a half-smile, and Susan could see the likeness between father and son. However, the same startlingly blue eyes on Duncan were screwed up, cold, measured, hinting at threat.

Meera gave an apologetic smile. 'I'm afraid I had a little fall, and so Susan here will be taking you up to your room. You have a direct line to me, of course, so anything we can do to make your stay even better, just call.' She handed Duncan the keys, then looked at the luggage piled high.

'I'll get someone to bring up your luggage,' said Meera, leaving them.

They began to walk towards the steps, but, glancing at Duncan, Susan gestured towards the lift and said quietly, 'We do have this if you'd prefer.'

He grimaced but stepped towards the lift. Kristen gave an encouraging smile. 'Well done, honey. We don't want you having another funny turn.'

There was room for the three of them, and as they travelled up, Duncan asked Susan, 'Has my son arrived? I didn't see any cars out the front.'

'Yes, he has arrived with his wife. Guests park up the steps in a car park.'

In the upstairs hallway, they followed Susan to Duncan's room.

'I trust I have the master bedroom,' Duncan said, again with that fixed smile so close to the cliff edge of falling into disapproval.

'You have. Kristen, yours is the next room along,' said Susan, opening the door to Duncan's room.

Two younger members of the kitchen staff came up with the bags. Kristen directed which went into which room then entered Duncan's room with him and Susan.

Susan began to point out the facilities but neither guest commented, which was rather disconcerting. She was glad to finish and offer them refreshments.

'I'll have a cafetiere of coffee, can't stand those machines, rare roast beef sandwich, English mustard, scones, jam.' Duncan broke off. 'Do you need to write this down?'

Susan shook her head.

'Hope you've got a good memory then – I expect the chef to choose an appropriate sweet selection. Kristen?'

'Oh, I'll have a green tea and vegetable smoothie: trying to detox before the Christmas binge.'

Susan sensed a curtsey was expected but simply left the room. In the hallway she met one of the members of kitchen staff carrying more cases. 'How long are they staying? I'll have to make another journey.'

Susan, wishing now she had written down the order, found herself frantically going over the list in her head until she reached the kitchen and was able to spill it out.

'For God's sake, a vegetable smoothie? Really?' said Gary. 'The first Mrs Fern wouldn't have ordered nonsense like that.'

'You knew Duncan Fern's first wife?'

'I did. I knew all the family from when they came here on holiday. Duncan's first wife, the mother of Bryson and Hayley, was called Nancy. She was a very nice woman. They used to come for meals at the Bishopstone pub where I was just a lowly sous chef. My dad was a mechanic, and he became friendly with Duncan. He sorted out Duncan's car the first time they came on holiday, and they bonded over cars. Dad asked Duncan to join their Saturday night quiz team next time he came, and he did. He joined in every year after that and we always did well. In fact, the last time Duncan came on holiday we won the cup.'

'I find it very hard to imagine Duncan Fern being that sociable.'

'To be honest, he wasn't that popular. People found him a bit condescending. Like he was doing us a favour mixing with us islanders. Even that night he paid for all the drinks till closing time when we won the cup, some said he was showing off, splashing the cash. But as I said, Dad liked him, and Duncan would drop in and chat to Dad at the garage, talk cars, share all his worries. Now, Nancy, Duncan's first wife, she really was friendly, very popular. It was sad her last holiday here was spoilt.'

'What happened?'

Gary frowned, waving the question away. 'Oh, it was one of those things best forgotten. Dad knew stuff, the worries about drinking but, well, so young. Poor Nancy. Anyway, I still buy Duncan's paper and I've also read some of Bryson's crime books. I like them. Still, let's make this damn smoothie.'

Tutting, he started to search around for the necessary ingredients.

Susan returned to Duncan's room with the tray. As she entered, she noticed Kristen had left and Bryson had arrived. Father and son were sitting opposite each other.

Noticing Susan, Duncan barked, 'My wife will be back in a minute. Put mustard in the sandwiches, cream before jam on the scones, and then pour the coffee.'

Susan resisted the urge to admonish him and instruct him to at least say please, and began to prepare the food.

Duncan lowered his voice, spoke with a gentleness that had been missing before. 'I'm worried about Hayley.'

Bryson smiled at his father. 'You always worry about Hayley.'

'She's so like her mother. If anything ever happened to me—'

'Nothing is going to happen to you but, if it did, you know I will always look after her.'

Duncan nodded. 'I know, son. Maybe you could have a word with her. She keeps delaying putting down that deposit I gave her for the flat, and I don't know why. I know the flat will be perfect for her, and it's just down the road from us.'

'She's thirty-five, not a kid any more. Maybe she doesn't want to be so close by. She may prefer to move in with Lewis.'

'I've a nasty feeling that could be on the cards. They haven't known each other two minutes. I don't trust him, reckon he's after her money.' Duncan's voice became firmer, louder. 'In any case, it would be better if she was close by while she's working for me.'

'Ah, the autobiography? How's it going?'

'Very well. As I told you, first draft is pretty much sketched out.'

'That's brilliant. Your book will be such an inspiration. You have a lot to share. You've been in the newspaper business for over fifty years.'

'I have, and I'm still successful. Despite the hacking nonsense, and online competition, we're thriving. We're still getting a readership other papers can only dream of. I want to share my journey, working my way up from being a cub reporter.'

'Of course, you have a lot to teach the next generation.'

'I have. And not only about the business. I've decided to make those changes I mentioned. I shall talk to Hayley about it this weekend.'

'Fair enough. As I said, that's your decision and I support you.'

Duncan fiddled with a large gold signet ring on his left hand. For the first time there was real warmth in his voice. 'Thank you, son. It will be good to put the record straight about your mother and acknowledge the part she played in all my success.'

He was very red as he moved to put his arm around Bryson. 'I'm forever grateful that I have one person who is resilient. You're a good son.'

Bryson smiled back at his father. 'Thanks, Dad. Now, you're not to worry about anything. I'm sure we'll have a wonderful Christmas together.'

Seeing this warmer side of Duncan, Susan started to think she might have misjudged him. However, he then barked over, 'Do a scone for Bryson.'

Bryson glanced at her, cringed an apology, but then looked fondly at his father.

Susan was less forgiving. How dare Duncan be so high-handed? However, for Meera's sake she kept her lips tightly closed and began to prepare another scone.

Bryson walked to the window. 'There'll be a good view of the courtyard in the light, Dad.'

Susan looked up as the door opened. Kristen entered and rushed over to Bryson; her arms outstretched. 'Bryson, how wonderful to see you. We're going to have a marvellous time together.' She leant forward and kissed him enthusiastically on both cheeks, adding, 'There's plenty of mistletoe downstairs. Don't you just adore Christmas?'

Bryson blinked, glanced at his father, and stepped back looking rather bewildered. 'Um, yes, it'll be good to be all together.'

Duncan had gone over to the bedside cabinet where he was standing with his back to them, examining the flask and whisky. He glanced over at Kristen. 'Very pleasing, well done.'

She approached him. 'I'm so glad you like it, honey. I hope the rest of the family approve. I think the hip flasks are classy. I got everyone the same, even bought one for myself. It was a good idea, thanks,' she said to Bryson, sending him a shy smile.

'I hope you got one for Antoine,' said Duncan.

Kristen rolled her eyes. 'Yes, I got one for him, but I've no idea why he's butting into our family Christmas. He's hardly the life and soul of any event. You'd think being French he'd have charm, but no, he's so dull. Don't you dare disappear into corners talking about work.'

'Of course not, and I had no choice. I couldn't leave him in London on his own.'

'I don't see why not,' said Kristen harshly. 'Anyhow, I'm now going to unpack your medicines, lay them all out, over here. Don't try and stop me. I don't want you forgetting to take them.' Kristen took a square tartan bag out of Duncan's case. She carried it to a small table and took out seven bottles.

'God, you're only on three types of pills, so why has he prescribed so many bottles?' asked Kristen. 'He's given you enough of these to last months.'

'He might increase the dose. Leave them be,' Duncan growled. 'I don't need you touching them and muddling them up.'

'Just make sure you take them.'

'Leave me to it.' Turning to Susan, he demanded, 'Is that coffee ready?'

Susan had just poured the coffee and added the cream. 'All done,' she replied and was grateful to leave.

Susan went back to her room to check on Rocco and Libs. They were curled up in their beds, but looked up, wagging their tails when they saw her. At that moment, Robert came in.

'How's it going?'

'What a family! Duncan is rude and entitled. Honestly, I didn't think people spoke to staff like that any more.'

Robert laughed. 'As long as you managed to be polite back, that's all that matters.'

'I did my best. His wife Kristen appears affable, you know, with her "Honey" this and "call me Kristen", but she expects to get her own way. I reckon she could turn nasty.'

'Gosh, they made a good impression!'

'The son Bryson looks a bit like his dad but at least he's polite. He's a crime writer, apparently. He'll be on telly soon. He's married to Victoria, a restaurant critic – good luck, Gary in the kitchen. Having read her columns, I don't think she would do a hatchet job on someone who was genuinely good, but who knows? I'm guessing she expects perfection.'

Robert shrugged. 'They sound pretty demanding, but then they were all cold and tired. They might unwind.'

Susan grinned. Despite his past in the police force, Robert always seemed to see the best in people. 'I hope so. I wonder what the daughter, Hayley, is like. Duncan seemed worried about her, didn't seem to think much of her new partner, this personal trainer. Of course there is the other journalist to come as well. I hope he's not another Duncan. I heard Kristen describe him as dull, which to be honest could be worse. So, what have you been up to?'

'Working on one of the staff rooms. Meera wants it finished soon.'

'There's still so much to do. It's non-stop.'

'I know, but if anyone can achieve their vision for the manor, it's Meera. I've never known anyone quite so dynamic.'

'She is, and good with people. I find her very friendly.'

'Yes, we get on well. We've got into a habit of playing Monopoly in the evenings. Meera had never played it before. I brought my game over, and now she's hooked. It's a great way to unwind: a game and a glass of wine, and the TV on.'

'Sounds cosy.'

'We both enjoy having the company.'

Susan put her head to one side. 'By the way, don't your family mind that you are here and not with them?'

'Not really. My son is with his wife's family, and my daughter has taken all the family abroad. She's fed up with the cold and wet. They were glad they didn't have to feel guilty about accommodating me, I think.'

'That's okay, then.' Susan glanced at her watch. 'I wonder when the others will arrive.'

'Well, it's nearly dark. I'll take my two dogs out for a walk. Shall I take yours with them?'

'Are you sure?'

'Of course, they're all pretty good. I'll keep them on leads, though, in the dark, don't want them escaping under the gate at the end of the garden, and up the woods.'

'That's brilliant. Thank you. I'll put their coats on. Rocco is fine, but Libs tries to hide when she sees hers.'

As she leant over, the radio fell out of her pocket.

Robert laughed. 'You have me to blame for that.'

'Thanks! I thought it would fit in my pocket, but obviously not. Ah, hang on, I have an idea.'

She went into her room and found her 'dog-walking' bag which contained her mobile and key.

'I can wear this all the time, keep my bits and the radio inside.'

'Yup, that works,' said Robert.

No sooner had she zipped up her bag when the radio buzzed, and Susan had to retrieve it again. The call was from Meera telling her that Duncan's daughter Hayley and partner Lewis had arrived.

6

Susan went to meet the final couple to arrive in the library. Hayley held the handle of a medium-sized case; Lewis had a rucksack on his back and a sports holdall with a Welsh dragon on the side.

Lewis was dark, good looking. He wore a padded ski jacket, and boots. He looked energetic and fit, an advert for his work as a personal trainer.

'Hiya, we're Hayley and Lewis,' he said. He spoke with a strong Welsh accent, which Susan always found so appealing.

'Welcome to Bishopstone Manor,' said Meera. 'So glad you've arrived safely. Bryson and Victoria were on an earlier ferry. They said it was very busy.'

'Ours was very hectic too,' said Lewis. 'Things are getting backed up with the weather. Ours left half an hour late. I wondered at one point if we were going to get over here. Makes you realise how difficult it must be to live on an island. Do you often get cut off?'

'I've not been here long,' said Meera. 'Susan is a proper islander. She can tell you more about that.'

Susan grinned. 'You certainly can get stuck. Still, being remote and separate from the mainland is part of the island's charm. Even in the summer you can find plenty of quiet beaches and deserted downland, and it's a cluster of quite close communities.'

'We have them up in the valleys,' said Lewis. 'I grew up in Cardigan Bay and had friends there who thought I was wild going to university in Swansea.'

As he chatted, Susan's eyes were drawn to the pale woman behind him. Hayley was short, had her father's and brother's blue eyes, and blinked owl-like from behind large round glasses. Apart from the eye colour, though, she seemed to bear little resemblance to them. She had long red hair, was very pale and thin, like a ghost of some pre-Raphaelite woman, and was wearing a purple maxi coat and hand-knitted scarf. Although Susan had heard Bryson say earlier that she was thirty-five, she appeared younger, lacking the confidence of her father and brother.

Susan instinctively gave her a reassuring smile. Hayley shyly held out a wreath of pinecones, red berries, and other natural winter décor. 'This is for you and, if it is okay, I would also like to bring in a Yule log on Christmas Eve. They will welcome good spirits to this home, ward off the bad.'

Hayley's voice may have been quiet, but she spoke with intensity. Her eyes darted around nervously, as if she was alert to some invisible threat.

'Thank you so much for the wreath,' said Meera. 'We have nothing on the front door. I will make sure the wreath is hung properly.'

From her bag, Hayley produced a smaller one. 'I'll find the right place for this inside, bring the good spirits into the room.'

'Hayley is into all things pagan,' explained Lewis. 'Even

watched the sunrise at Stonehenge yesterday for the winter solstice. Online, of course.'

'It was magical,' said Hayley. She looked around. 'And of course, there is the Longstone here. When I was young, I had no idea of its significance. Of course, there are two stones, aren't there? There's that enormous upright. Did you know there is a little chink at the top of it? We used to throw coins up, try to get them to land there. There's also the smaller flat stone. I used to take my teddy out there, have picnics. It was all so innocent then. I hadn't read *Tess of the d'Urbervilles*: that ending, but now I see it must have been a sacrificial stone, "solemn and lonely".' She took a breath, her face seemed to go even paler, as she asked quietly, 'I'd like to go there soon. Can we get up to the stones easily from the garden?'

'Oh, yes, in good weather it's a straightforward walk. You just follow the paths to the end of the garden, go out through the unlocked wooden gate and then climb up to the right. You come out by the stones and the house you used to stay in.'

'I'd like to go up there tonight.'

'You could, but you'll need to wear the right boots. The snow will make walking up there difficult and, of course, you'd be in pitch darkness.'

'It would better to wait until tomorrow,' said Lewis.

'I've brought a torch, but maybe I'll wait. I'm not sure I'm ready to go up there yet,' said Hayley.

Meera handed out their keys and offered help with the luggage.

'Oh, no,' said Lewis. 'We're travelling light. We'll be fine.'

Meera excused herself. Lewis took all the bags and ran up the stairs ahead of them, with Susan and Hayley walking behind.

'You're second on the left, next to Bryson and Victoria,' called Susan, and Lewis flung open the door.

'I was told there is a gym?' asked Lewis anxiously.

'Yes, just along the hallway.'

'Great.'

'Oh, look at this,' said Hayley, picking up the hip flasks and bottle of whisky and reading the card. 'God, this is from Kristen, clearly trying to get on our right side.'

Lewis glanced over, but didn't seem too impressed. 'Why spend all that money on a hip flask? Seems a waste to me. We're never going to use it.'

'Dad will think it's smart. I bet he gets us all to use them while we're here.'

'Well. I could do with a really good cup of coffee now and something to eat,' replied Lewis.

With this, Susan offered to fetch refreshments, and this was eagerly accepted by Lewis.

She went to the kitchen and returned with a tray full of food.

'Homemade mince pies,' said Lewis enthusiastically, as he started to dig into the food.

Hayley didn't touch anything, but was checking around the room instead. 'This manor has an incredible energy. It must be haunted.'

'I'm not the right person to ask,' replied Susan. 'I've never believed in things like that.'

Ignoring her, Hayley continued. 'I read that the manor was buried under a landslip for years.'

'That's right. When they started clearing away the debris, they were amazed at how well preserved all the Tudor walls and windows were.'

'But it's not surprising, is it? The past, the present and the future are interconnected, like on a continual loop. The manor, like the Longstone, holds onto the past. Unfortunately, people are not so good with the past. We get confused. We misremember.' She looked over at Susan. 'Mind you, there was one person I knew who I think I could always rely on. She owned the shop here.'

'Do you mean Alice from the shop in the village?'

Hayley's face lit up. 'Yes, do you know her then?'

'She's a close friend now.'

'I was so excited to find she was still with us. I'm going to visit her. When I talked to her on the phone she sounded as bright as ever.'

'Oh, she is. She doesn't miss much.'

'I'm so glad. I've a lot I want to talk to her about.'

Lewis came and put an arm around Hayley. 'Come and have something to eat. You've not had anything since breakfast.' His phone pinged a text and he wandered over to the window to reply.

'Anyone I know?' Hayley asked. In a beat it seemed the child-like innocence melted away. Her face was cold, her words laced with suspicion.

'Oh, just Mum checking in, letting me know how Dad is.' He turned to Susan. 'Dad had a stomach upset.'

'You said he'd had a fall,' said Hayley.

Susan suddenly felt the shaft of tension between them.

'Dad is having a bad run, that's all: a fall, a tummy bug. It's a shame. They've not had a holiday for ages.'

Hayley didn't respond to him but turned away. Sensing the growing tension, Susan left the room. As she descended the stairs, she received a radio call from Meera asking to see her, so she headed for the office. They chatted about how everyone was settling in. Meera explained that the final guest, Antoine, had let her know he would not be arriving until after the evening meal.

'The ferries sound in chaos. Heaven knows when he'll get over.'

'I know, and I bet he's no idea how difficult it's going to be. People who aren't used to coming over just assume everything will keep running whatever the conditions. Anyway, it might be a good idea for you to grab a meal now before the guests have dinner.'

'Robert said I go to the kitchen?'

'That's right, Gary will have something ready. It'll be good. I can promise you that.'

As she was leaving, Meera called over, 'And thank you so much, Susan, I don't know what I would do without you.'

Susan was nervous about disturbing what must be a very busy kitchen but was welcomed by Gary, who had worked out the perfect meal for her – a gorgeous plate of small parcels of vegetables in filo pastry with sauté potatoes and salad. She was even given a choice of puddings, and chose a panna cotta.

'I'm going to have to take the dogs for some pretty long walks after a few days of eating like this,' she said to Gary.

'Do you cook well for yourself?'

Susan laughed. 'I used to cook when I had my husband, daughter and other children living with me, but since I've been on my own, I seem to live on ready meals.'

He frowned. 'That's not good for you. You must look after yourself.'

'I know. Maybe it could be my New Year's resolution. Thanks for this, and good luck this evening.'

She left the kitchen and was pleased to shut herself in the flat to eat. Rocco and Libs came and sat at her feet. As she ate, she chatted to them as she would at home. 'You two are settling in well: manor life suits you.' She put down her knife and fork.

'But then you don't have to worry about being polite to rude men like Duncan Fern.'

She finished her meal and when she had returned her crockery, Susan took out her recorder to quickly practise. Her breathing was all over the place and she realised how uptight she felt. What was the matter? They were easy pieces she had played and taught pupils to play hundreds of times. Then she realised it was nothing to do with the performance: it was this family. They had brought a tension with them and it had affected her. The source of that tension was difficult to identify: it was hiding away in the shadows. Then Susan shivered. She now understood that feeling she had seen in the dogs when they started to whimper minutes before a storm, a nasty feeling that something terrible was going to happen.

Outside the window she saw the snow falling, heavy and relentless. By tomorrow, the snowploughs and gritters would be defeated. Roads would be impassable. Her heart raced; adrenaline rushed through her body. She felt a primeval call to flee, get away: soon there would be no escape.

7

Later that evening, Susan greeted the smartly dressed guests in the library. Her earlier feelings of panic seemed ridiculous. She needed to stop her imagination running away with her like that. This was simply a group of friends and family, gathered to celebrate Christmas together. It felt both cosy and luxurious. All sat around a roaring fire, sipping fine wines and cocktails while making their choices from the menu.

Duncan was wearing a suit and white shirt that the buttons were straining to hold together. Kristen appeared dressed for a formal banquet, in a white sequined dress, diamond earrings that twinkled from behind her blonde locks, and her perfume again managed to hang in the air around her. Victoria, in contrast, wore a stylish tartan skirt, black cashmere jumper, gold earrings and necklace and, of course, carried her enormous handbag. While the others gave the menu a cursory glance, she read it with the serious air of someone studying a scientific journal.

Hayley arrived late; she was wearing a long purple velvet

dress. 'Sorry, Lewis is just finishing his shower, after the gym,' she said.

Duncan scowled but didn't comment. Fortunately, at that moment Lewis joined them, looking slightly uncomfortable in tidy trousers, jacket and tie.

Victoria commented that she needed to find her reading glasses and disappeared upstairs.

They continued to chat, until a waitress came to usher them to a long table in the Great Hall.

'I'll go and see what's keeping Victoria,' said Bryson. 'You carry on.'

Susan followed the remaining guests into the Great Hall where the wonderful smells coming from the kitchen were breathtaking.

The room was lit solely by the flames of beeswax candles and a large log fire. The table was decorated with holly and greenery, which wound itself around the candles as the crystal glasses twinkled.

Bryson and Victoria returned just as the others were sitting down and Duncan gestured to Bryson to sit next to him, Victoria next to Bryson. Kristen sat to the right of Duncan, and next to her were Hayley and Lewis. Duncan sat at the head of the table like Henry VIII holding court.

Susan took her place in a corner and started to play, and as she did, she was able to observe the group at the table.

Along the centre of the table were arranged sharing plates of warm olives, monkfish and sesame toasts, cuttlefish ink crackers and bruschetta. Each guest was offered wine and a handful of waiters remained standing ready to refill glasses.

As the guests tucked into the platters, the first courses were brought in. Beautiful dishes of locally caught crab and lobster and island garlic with vegetables were presented to the guests.

Victoria inspected her plate, rotating it before eating. She removed her glasses in a dramatic way, smelt the dish, replaced them, and finally picked up her knife and fork. It was more a performance than someone simply tucking into a meal.

Duncan dominated the conversation. He talked at length, mainly about his invitation to the palace, lunch at Buckingham Palace, and his hopes of a knighthood one day.

The family were compliant, Bryson particularly encouraging his father. 'Of course a knighthood will come your way. You've been the inspiration for generations of journalists and, whatever the current difficulties, you've been at the vanguard of journalism in this country for over twenty years.'

Duncan graciously nodded, accepting the words.

Once the starters were finished, the waiters cleared the table and the next courses were served. Plates of thick island beef steaks, roast lamb, lobster, hake and mushroom gnocchi were handed out, and for a moment conversation stilled as the family took in the feast before them.

Lewis, apparently oblivious to the tension in the room, turned to Bryson. 'Hayley tells me you're all set up for this new TV show. That's exciting.'

'Yes. The first programme will be on at Easter. We have some great guests lined up; the producer has done well. It's all a bit chicken and egg with chat shows. The top names come on if top names are already appearing, if you know what I mean. The problem is getting the first popular guests to take the risk. After that, the show kind of runs itself and agents start putting their clients forward.'

'I wish you all the best,' said Lewis.

A sharp buzz indicated a mobile phone. Lewis picked his out of his pocket, glanced at the screen, quietly left the table and exited to the library. Duncan scowled. He turned to Hayley. 'You

need to remind Lewis that in this family we do not bring phones
to the table.'

'He says his father is not well—'

Duncan raised an eyebrow cynically. 'Does he now? He's
never off that phone. When I looked over his shoulder the other
day, the screen didn't suggest family to me.'

Kristen laughed nervously and put her hand over Duncan's.
'Leave Lewis alone. He's a different generation to us.'

Susan glanced over. Kristen was clearly at least twenty years
Duncan's junior. Susan guessed this was a not particularly subtle
form of flattery, which Duncan was happy to accept. Kristen
continued, 'My sister's children in the States are never off their
phones. Even when I'm on Zoom with them, they're still texting
away.'

'You must find the English Christmas very different to back
home,' said Victoria.

'Yes, very different. I suppose for us everything kicks off with
Thanksgiving and ends on Christmas Day. Over here, you keep
going right up to New Year. I'd honestly never heard of Boxing
Day. And, of course, we have Santa, not Father Christmas. I'd
never had a Christmas cracker until I came here, and don't get me
started on those pantomimes: they're just weird.' She laughed.
'Still, as Duncan says, I've got to get used to your Christmas. He
tells me a lot of your traditions come from the Victorians.'

Hayley coughed and then spoke. 'Actually, many are much
older and come from pagan times. Imagine what it was like for
most people back then trying to survive the long hard winters.
No wonder they marked the shortest day, used holly and
greenery to remind themselves that spring, warmth and light
were on their way.'

'You're really getting into all this, aren't you?' commented

Bryson. 'I hope you're not going to get into black magic and start cursing us all.'

Hayley clenched her fists. 'Don't trivialise something I believe in. I'm trying to get in touch with nature, our roots. I'm searching for the truth.'

Bryson gave a slightly embarrassed grimace. 'Um, sorry. I wasn't mocking you.'

'On more practical matters,' interrupted Duncan, 'you need to get on and put the deposit down on that flat. We'll lose it otherwise.'

Hayley met his gaze. 'I know. I'll do it soon.'

'I transferred the money to your account weeks ago,' Duncan said, his tone gentle with his daughter. 'Oh, by the way, I had an email from your cousin up on that Scottish island on Monday. Your Aunt Betty has died. She said Betty had been in touch with you. I wondered why she had done that. I know your mum was close to her sister, but I haven't spoken to Betty since the funeral, over twenty years ago.'

Hayley took a sharp intake of breath. 'Oh, I'm so sorry she has passed on, although I knew she was very ill. She rang out of the blue a week or so ago. I was so surprised. Like you, I hadn't spoken to her since the funeral. I had the feeling she was ringing because she knew she didn't have long. There was something she had decided she needed to tell me—'

'And what was that?' demanded Duncan.

Hayley glanced around the table. 'I need to talk to you about it, Dad, but not here, not now, later.'

Lewis returned and slipped into his seat next to Hayley. Susan thought he looked anxious, but Duncan spoke gruffly to him. 'Lewis, how is your business doing? What with Hayley and now Kristen training with you, my house has more equipment than the local gym. When are you going to get your own premises?'

Lewis grinned. 'Sooner than you think.' He shot a knowing look at Hayley, who gave a whisper of a shake of her head.

Kristen rested her hand on Duncan's. 'I like to keep in shape for you.'

He glanced at the diamond ring on her finger. 'Don't you go losing that one as well. It cost more than the last.'

She kissed him on the cheek. 'You spoil me. Thank you.'

Victoria adjusted her glasses, lowered her head and looked down her nose at the ring. She frowned. 'What happened to the last ring?'

Kristen shrugged. 'I lost it in the bathroom. I was devastated.'

'You lost your watch as well, didn't you?' asked Victoria.

Before Kristen could reply, Duncan interrupted. 'Don't you all go worrying about your inheritance. Kristen has insisted she is left out of my will.'

Kristen placed her hand on his shoulders. 'Don't even talk about that. Honey, you know I can't imagine my life without you. Enough. It's Christmas. This food is simply divine.'

Susan was sure those words were said purely for dramatic effect. In the same way as she'd returned the first course untouched, Kristen had only picked at some of the fish on her plate. She felt sorry for Gary seeing the plates as they came back to the kitchen but maybe he would guess whose they were.

Having finished the piece she was playing, Susan was about to turn the page of her music when she became aware of voices in the library. She realised Meera was greeting someone and quietly laid down her instrument and went to see how she could help.

8

Susan saw Meera greeting a heavy-set man who was shaking the snow off the arms of his navy wool coat. After welcoming him, Meera asked if he would like a meal.

Glancing through to the Great Hall and seeing the family, he replied, 'I'll join the family to eat.' His words were spoken in the rushed, direct way of a man in a hurry.

'Of course.' Meera turned to Susan. 'Could you pop along to warn the kitchen and pick up a menu while I go through the keys with Mr Corbin?'

Susan left them heading quickly to the kitchen through the Great Hall, attracting a quizzical look from Duncan. 'Mr Corbin has arrived,' she explained and carried on to the kitchen, where she saw a variety of sumptuous desserts, cheese boards and sorbets ready to be taken to the guests. Susan asked for a menu. Gary groaned but said, 'I had a feeling this would happen. Okay, well, I guess he can choose what he likes. Can you get his order to us quickly?'

Susan returned to the library and escorted Antoine to his

room. He took little notice of the room, simply throwing his bags on the bed, and his coat on the chair.

'How was your journey? You were lucky there were still car ferries.'

'I couldn't believe the chaos that greeted me. Nothing's running to time now. I sat in a queue, just waiting to be let on anything that was sailing. I'd looked up local hotels over the other side, in case I got stranded. Once I was this side it wasn't much better. Thank God I brought the Range Rover. No one seems to have touched the roads.'

'I'm pleased you managed to make the crossing.'

'I had to. Some things need to be said face to face,' he said, cool anger bubbling behind his words.

Susan held out the menu and he scanned it. As he did, she looked more closely at him. He must have been in his mid-fifties, his hair scraggy, his face broad, dominated by a large squashed 'boxer's nose', but what struck her most was the energy coming off the man: it was arresting.

'Steak, blue, chips, salad. Followed by the tarte aux pommes for dessert. Right, I need to go and join everyone.' As the words for dessert tripped off his tongue, Susan heard the first hint of a French accent.

'Of course,' said Susan. 'I'll get this order down to the kitchen.'

As she left the room, she saw Antoine had quickly unzipped his suitcase, flung it open and was pulling on a jumper.

In the kitchen, Gary was pleased. 'Nice and straightforward. He'll do justice to the beef, at least,' he said approvingly.

By the time Susan had returned to her post playing her recorder, desserts were being handed out and Antoine had arrived in the Great Hall.

Duncan asked Hayley to move along in order for Antoine to

sit next to him and gestured to the waitress to serve Antoine a glass of wine.

After a brief preamble about journeys and crossings, Antoine turned to Duncan. Lowering his voice, he said, 'We need to talk about today's front page. I've been fighting fires all day. My understanding was that we'd agreed not to run this story.'

A silence descended on the table, everyone alert to the gathering storm in Antoine's voice.

'I'm the editor-in-chief. I made the decision last thing. It was the correct one.'

'People don't like it. Even our most loyal supporters are saying this was a step too far. We know about her family being Catholic. We shouldn't have gone there.'

'This is a bloody good story: the fact you've been putting out fires is brilliant. We're relevant, we've got people talking and that means sales.'

'I assume you're talking about Isabelle?' Victoria's words shot, bullet like, through the air, reached their target, and Duncan glared at her, his eyes sharp pieces of flint. A less confident person would have retreated, but not Victoria. Instead, she pointed her finger in an accusing way at Duncan. 'You should hang your head in shame. How dare you reveal Isabelle had an abortion? This information was of a highly sensitive and personal nature. You had no right to splatter it all over your front page.'

Susan's mind went back to the front page of *The Morning Flame* which she had seen in the village shop and her discussion of it with Tracy. She had to agree with Victoria: the story had been disturbing and cruel.

'Furthermore,' said Victoria, drumming her fingers on the

table, 'I'm betting you used your dark arts to get hold of Isabelle's confidential medical records.'

Susan saw a look shoot between Antoine and Duncan. Victoria spotted it too. 'I thought so.'

A waiter arrived with Antoine's meal and placed it in front of him. He cut into the steak, the blood oozing out onto the plate.

Duncan glared at Victoria. 'I testified under oath that I knew nothing about the hacking in the past. I would swear again that I would never sanction the stealing of someone's confidential records.'

'Your oaths and promises mean nothing. When you testify, you manipulate words to hide lies, not to reveal the truth. But your days are numbered. Times have changed. Carry on like this and you and all those associated with you will end your days in prison,' said Victoria.

The whole room froze. No one dared breathe as Duncan drew himself up. Any warmth of passion in that angry glare became white fury. It was vindictive, full of hate.

How Victoria held his gaze, and hadn't run from the room in fear, Susan had no idea. But she did. Duncan looked surprised, but spat out his reply, 'Your hypocrisy is staggering. That Zac Ledger story. What was so transparent about that with all your anonymous sources? And be warned.' Releasing the crystal goblet, he tapped a large gold watch on his wrist. 'I have photographs on my business phone that could ruin you.'

Victoria rolled her eyes. 'Oh, God, not the famous black phone business. Don't you realise that's a standing joke now?'

'You think you have control over everything in your life. You're so ignorant. Little by little, I could destroy your so-called perfect life.'

Bryson sat forward. 'Stop. Leave Victoria alone. You know everything she's doing for me.'

Duncan's eyes narrowed in challenge. 'And you need to remember what I've done for you. I made you and your writing career. I can just as easily break you.'

Victoria let out an exasperated groan. 'You think you're some kind of godfather figure, don't you, Duncan? But you're not. You're an old man who's past his prime, and I'm not scared of you. In fact, you're the one who should be worried.' She held his gaze for a second, then looked away, but not in the manner of someone defeated.

Duncan shook his head, and also took a drink. Bryson sat forward, smiling awkwardly. 'Let's put our professional differences aside for Christmas.'

Neither Victoria nor Duncan responded, but there appeared at least to be a silent truce for now.

Antoine nodded to the waiter for more wine as his plate was also taken away, before his dessert was brought in.

Duncan looked at Antoine, lips curled in his strange half-smile. His voice was cold, the rage from his conversation with Victoria clearly still simmering beneath the surface. 'I hope you found your hip flask and whisky, Antoine; they were a very generous gift from Kristen.'

'I appreciate it. Thank you, Kristen,' said Antoine. The polite thanks were perfunctory rather than heartfelt.

'They were for family,' said Kristen stiffly, 'and as you were joining us, of course you're included.'

Duncan looked around the table. 'Everyone will bring your hip flasks to the main meals on Christmas Eve and Christmas Day. It will be a new family tradition to share a toast.'

Everyone nodded, but there followed an awkward lull in the conversation until Bryson took it upon himself to fill the gap. He asked Lewis about his life as a personal trainer, asking questions about the best exercise for the average, unfit man. He had that gift of giving the appearance of hanging on the speaker's every word. Susan could imagine him doing well in the chat show.

Without explanation, Duncan stood up, nodded to Antoine, and they left the table, heading towards a small lounge room off to the side, leaving the others sitting around the table.

The conversation between Duncan and Antoine sounded heated. The rest of the guests moved into the library where they were served coffee and handmade chocolates. They tried to chat quietly but there was no ignoring the raised voices from Duncan and Antoine carrying from the small lounge. Things seemed to come to a head when Antoine shouted, 'My God, Duncan. You can't carry on as if nothing has changed. If this gets out, they will ruin you this time, and I'm not getting dragged down with you.'

There was a pause, then the conversation continued in far more muted tones, too quiet to decipher.

The family returned to chatting and Susan decided this would be a good time to go to check over the rooms before anyone wanted to retire. She headed quickly upstairs and decided to start with Duncan's room. Trying the handle, she realised the door had been left unlocked, and guessed the other guests had done the same. Everything was very neat and tidy, clothes hung away. On his bedside table lay two mobile phones. One was in a distinctive black leather wallet-type case with gold edging, the other a silver iPhone. There was also a hip flask and bottle of whisky. She fluffed up the pillows and turned back the bed sheets, went into the bathroom, neatly arranging the towels.

Kristen's room had the overwhelming smell of rich perfumes, her dressing table covered with exotic bottles. Antoine's was as he had left it. In the short time they had been there, Hayley and Lewis had managed to create havoc in their room, with clothes and towels strewn everywhere. Bryson and Victoria's room in contrast was tidy, everything hung up and put into drawers, piles of books and newspapers neatly stacked next to their beds.

The checks didn't take long, and Susan was about to go back downstairs when, to her surprise, she saw Meera coming out of the lift. 'I was coming up for a break. How are the rooms?'

'All done.'

'Excellent, thank you. Why don't you come and have a drink?'

Susan followed Meera to her room. This was naturally a lot more comfortable than Meera's office. Susan sank into a deep red sofa, covered in brightly embroidered cushions. There were a lot of photos of people. 'They are all my extended family in New Delhi. I get over about once a year. They were a bit shocked at my divorce but are getting used to the idea. Let me pour you a drink. Red or white?'

Susan accepted a glass of red wine and looked over at the small, tastefully decorated Christmas tree.

'I love the tree,' said Meera. 'In fact, I love everything about Christmas. Even though my parents were Hindu, we had a great time. Of course we have Diwali, a while before, but the Hindu idea of truth includes love, peace: a lot of the concepts that are prevalent at Christmas.'

'I can understand that.' Susan glanced at a small framed quotation sitting on a side table and read it aloud. 'Even if you are a minority of one, the truth is the truth. Mahatma Gandhi.' Susan nodded, adding, 'I like the idea of truth being something solid, tangible. I'm not comfortable with the idea that truth is subjective.'

'That's very philosophical,' said Meera. 'You've obviously thought a lot about this.'

'I have. The truth matters a great deal to me.'

'And to me. In fact, my marriage ended because of it. I shall tell you the story one day. However, for now, let's talk about food. Robert tells me you're vegetarian, like me?'

'I am.'

'Great. I have asked the chef, Gary, to make us my family Christmas dinner, Pav Bhaji – bread rolls and vegetable curry.'

'Sounds fabulous, thank you.'

'So, tell me, how are our guests doing?'

'They're an interesting lot. Duncan is very much in charge. Kristen, as you said, is quite fussy. She hardly ate anything at dinner. Bryson is pleasant, easy-going, but his wife, Victoria, is more critical. Gary is anxious about cooking for her but, so far, she appears happy enough with the food.'

'Good. Receiving a good review from her would be fantastic for the hotel. So, is everything going okay?'

'I think so, although there are family tensions, particularly as you anticipated between Duncan and Victoria. Oh, and I heard a row between that new journalist who arrived, Antoine, and Duncan. So, well, a few issues.'

Meera flapped her hand. 'Let's hope they all settle down. Oh, how is the daughter, Hayley?'

'Okay, I think. Her partner Lewis has already used the gym.'

Meera laughed. 'I knew he would. Well, we'll do our part, keep them comfy, feed them well, give them a good Christmas. Here's to a successful few days.'

They were raising their glasses when there was a gentle knock at the door and Robert entered.

'There you are, Susan. Someone told me you'd come up here. I was going to take the dogs out?'

'Oh, right. I wouldn't mind getting out.'

'The joys of owning a dog – out in all weathers,' laughed Meera. 'You go on, Susan. That's fine.'

'Is there anything else needs doing tonight?'

'About twelve, could you lock the front door? The key's hanging on the wall next to it, so that if someone is up early, they can let themselves out, but I like them to use the back door between twelve and around six. Anyway, when you lock the front door, you don't need to worry about locking anyone out as they can come in the back way.'

'Fine, I can do that.'

As they left the house with the dogs, Susan had a feeling again of stepping into a new world, emerging to a different version of Narnia each time she left the security of the manor. The freezing air hit her face; she was reminded that it could never apparently be too cold for snow.

'God, it's freezing out here,' she complained.

'You're right, the temperature has dropped.'

They let the dogs off and began to crunch their way up the garden. Soon Susan could feel her feet going numb with cold, and they returned, glad to be inside again.

Robert wanted to check on some work he 'd done earlier, leaving Susan to finish clearing up. Susan could see large puddles forming under the boots. Opening the patio door, she held up the boots to bang them together and rid them of the excess snow. However, before she could do this, she was aware of voices in the darkness, coming from behind the wall that divided the patio from the garden. She was surprised anyone was out in this weather. She couldn't be sure who was talking as the whispered voices were muffled by the snow, but when she heard the mention of Duncan, she assumed it was one of the guests. However, it was the reply that really caught her attention. Although she had no idea who was speaking, she would never forget what they said, or the intonation behind those words, for they were soaked in poison and hate.

9

'If only he could die.' The words were hissed out with such venom that Susan felt her stomach turn over. This person, whoever they were, hated Duncan, she was sure of that and with all their heart wished he was dead. Who was speaking? The words were spoken barely louder than a whisper, with a breathy intensity that made identifying the speaker impossible. She was aware of the acrid smell of cigarette smoke – which of the guests smoked?

The conversation outside ceased abruptly. Susan heard the sound of scrunching through the snow as the people disappeared into the darkness.

Susan cleaned off the boots and went back inside but she couldn't forget those words. The words had been spoken with such ferocity that they frightened her. Who would say such a thing? Her mind went back to the meal. She'd observed tension among the family, seen the row with Antoine, but nothing that suggested violence.

Of course, Duncan was a very rich man. Maybe whoever had spoken was simply thinking about the money they or their partner might inherit one day? If only she could rid herself of the urgency, the intensity of the voice, she would happily accept that explanation.

Realising there was little she could do about it that night, Susan decided it was time to unwind. However, looking at her watch she saw it was nearly quarter past twelve. She needed to lock the front door.

As Susan approached the front door, Bryson was standing, holding it open.

'Okay?' Susan asked.

'My wife went out for a walk. I thought she was mad, but she insisted. The snow is worse now, though. I'm worried about her.'

Feeling the freezing air forcing its way into the house, Susan understood his concern. The security light over the front door meant she could see into the courtyard. The falling snow sparkled like glitter: a snow globe world.

'The weather is shocking, isn't it?' continued Bryson. 'Maybe I should go out and find her?'

Fortunately, they both heard the crunching of footsteps and could slowly make out Victoria approaching from the garden and, separately, Antoine coming from the direction of the car park.

'Oh, thank God,' said Bryson. 'I was about to send out a search party for you.'

'You should have come for a walk. Good to get some fresh air before bed,' said Victoria. She flung out an arm towards the garden. 'I know it's small compared to a lot of country homes, but I enjoyed walking around, even in this weather.'

Antoine stepped forward, addressing Susan. 'I've just had to go to the car park to make a call. It's very inconvenient the signal in the house being so unreliable. I hadn't realised it was going to be this bad. I noticed Lewis was out in his car doing the same. Isn't there anything that can be done?'

'I'm sorry. I'll talk to Meera, but I understand she did warn you about the situation. You do have Wi-Fi, though.'

'But I use my phone a lot. I hadn't expected things to be so different over here, with the lack of signal and the mess with the ferries. I'd intended to commute for the next two days. In theory, the journeys aren't that bad, but I was shocked at the state of things coming over. If this weather continues, I'm assuming the situation will get even worse?'

'I'm afraid so. The ferries all have live updates. Keep checking them, but they could well start cancelling them.'

'So, we could get stranded here?'

'I'm afraid so.'

'Oh, God, what a nightmare.' Antoine pressed his lips together in frustration and then turned to Bryson. 'I'm going to speak to your father.'

'Sorry. I don't think you can, not this late,' said Bryson, his voice quiet but firm.

'But—'

'Sorry. Hayley stopped me when I tried to go in just now. She said Dad's very tired after all the travelling and has just settled. I guess we'd better listen to what she says.'

Antoine's eyes burned: he was clearly a man used to getting his own way. 'I don't see why I should listen to her but, as I'm stranded here, I'm prepared to let this wait till the morning. God, what a mess.'

He pushed past Susan into the house.

Susan was just wondering what to do about Lewis still being out when she saw him approaching through the archway.

'Sorry to hold you up,' said Lewis.

'That's okay. I'll lock up now.'

Susan located the key, locked the front door and hung the key back on its hook.

Bryson and Lewis headed off towards their rooms and Susan returned to the flat.

She was surprised that Robert was not back. She wondered if he'd gone to see Meera, and tried to ignore the slight niggling of discomfort that thought gave her. Of course there was nothing going on between them, she told herself quickly and, in any case, it wasn't really any business of hers if there was.

As she got ready for bed, her feet felt the cold of the freezing floor, and she quickly got under the duvet. After reading for a while, she turned off the light and settled down to sleep.

Sleep was elusive at first. It was darker here. There were no streetlights, and it was quieter, no comforting hum of the odd car along the village high street.

Susan lay listening to the odd creak coming from the walls, and from above. She was reminded of Hayley's talk of ghosts. Had she just imagined a sudden chill in the air? If any manor was going to be haunted, it had to be one like this. Susan turned over: this was foolish; she needed to get some sleep.

No sooner had she drifted off than she was disturbed by the security light coming on. Susan glanced at her watch. It was 1.20. She got out of bed and peeped through her curtains. The path at the side of the wall sloped upwards and she caught a glimpse of someone's blonde hair. She was sure it was Kristen. The snow was much heavier now, large clusters falling rapidly, swirling around. Why on earth was Kristen going out in this?

She watched as Kristen walked away from the light, out into the garden. Where was she going?

Susan climbed back into bed. Her mind was still racing, but she needed to get some sleep. It was just as she was finally starting to relax that she was disturbed again by the security

light flashing. Groaning, but unable to resist checking, Susan
clambered out of bed, peeped out and was in time to catch sight
of Kristen returning to the house. Glancing at her watch, she
saw it was quarter to two. What had Kristen been doing out
there for nearly half an hour?

Susan became aware of a shuffling noise in the living room
and was not surprised to see Libs padding into the bedroom.

'Sorry, did I disturb you?' she asked. As expected, Rocco
followed Libs in. She smiled, gave them both a fuss but said
firmly, 'Come on, back to bed now.' She led them back to the
living room.

Glancing at Robert's room, she noticed that the door was
open, and his bed empty. She didn't think he'd be working now.
Maybe he was with Meera? The thought unnerved her, although
she told herself crossly she had no right to mind what he was up
to. Susan was about to go back again to her room when she was
startled by a thumping sound coming from along the hallway in
the direction of the library. Looking down, she saw the ears of
the dogs pricked up: she hadn't imagined it. Maybe she should
go and check everything was okay?

Susan grabbed her dressing gown and made her way to the
library. She was surprised to see the glow from one of the side
lights close to the fire. Next to the light was a large armchair
turned away from her. It was deathly quiet in here now, the rest
of the room in darkness. Susan had assumed she was alone, but
then someone leaned out of the chair, reached out to the fire and
replaced a log that had fallen. They then sat back down and
disappeared from view. Susan's imagination ran riot: was this
one of the ghosts Hayley had been so sure would still be living
here?

She crept forward and approached the edge of the chair. It

was only when she saw who was sitting there that she let herself breathe.

'Are you okay?' she asked, her voice shaking.

Hayley looked up. 'I'm sorry. Did I disturb you? I hope it's all right for me to be sitting down here.'

Susan sat down in the chair opposite Hayley. 'Of course. You gave me a bit of a fright, though.'

'Ah, you thought I was a ghost?'

Susan shrugged. 'I don't know. Everything feels different in the dark. Your mind goes berserk.'

'I agree. It's not who's sleeping you worry about, but who or what might be awake.'

'Talking of those who are awake, have you seen anyone come in through the back door and go upstairs since you've been down here?'

Hayley shook her head. 'No, but I've had my back to the stairs. Why?'

'I thought I saw someone, that's all. So, why are you down here? Couldn't you sleep?'

'Lewis keeps disturbing me. He came in late after supposedly talking to his parents and some clients, but even then, he wouldn't settle. He's so on edge all the time.'

'He was speaking to clients?'

'According to Lewis, they pay good money and expect twenty-four-seven access to him.' She gave a cold laugh. 'Good job I'm not one of those jealous girlfriends or I'd be checking his phone. I've been to the gym, seen some of those gym babes who are his customers. Good job I trust him.' The words sounded weak. Susan was pretty sure Hayley didn't mean them. 'Anyway, I couldn't cope any more with his tossing and turning in bed, so I came down. But I'm sorry to disturb you.'

'Don't worry. I was awake. I heard a noise, thought I'd come and check—'

There were two books on the floor beside Hayley's chair. 'I'm re-reading my brother's books. We're going to republish them all, make big changes to the cover. It's exciting.'

'I didn't know you were involved with your brother's books.'

'Oh, yes. I've been editing his books since he started. I enjoy it. Have you read any of them?'

'Sorry, no.'

Hayley gave a half-smile. 'You can tell you're not in our family. It's a novelty to meet someone who hasn't read the books.' She leant down, picked up a book titled *Buried at Sea* and handed it to Susan. There was a picture of a young woman lying on the beach. 'I think you should give this a go. It's the first in the series.' She took a long swig from her water bottle. 'Lewis is always telling me to drink more water,' she explained.

At the sound of creaking floorboards from above, they both looked up.

'What was that?' asked Hayley. She held her breath, stared at the ceiling. There was another sound. Susan was sure it was footsteps now.

Seeing the fear on Hayley's face, Susan said, 'Don't worry. These old houses make lots of strange noises. But why don't I just go up and check everything is okay?'

She left Hayley and made her way upstairs, aware of how much colder the house was away from the fire. The night lights from the hallway above enabled her to make her way up the stairs. As she climbed them, she was aware of the portraits on the walls. They seemed to come alive at night: they watched her, whispered to each other. She was glad to get to the top of the stairs, where the lights were a little brighter.

Susan pushed open the door to her left, which led to Meera's flat. She could see lights coming from under Meera's door, and hear the television. Quietly closing the door, she looked back down the guests' hallway. Initially it appeared deserted. The bedroom doors were all tightly closed. She assumed everyone except Hayley was asleep in their beds. In a way it was reassuring but in another she couldn't help but wonder where the sound of those footsteps had come from. She again forced herself to dismiss the idea of ghosts. She was about to depart back down the stairs when she heard a door opening. Susan quickly stepped to the side and watched as a figure left Duncan's room. Through the gloom she could make out Victoria's hands in the pockets of her dressing gown and her bare feet. Victoria didn't look her way but, head down, scuttled across the hallway, and disappeared back inside her own bedroom.

Susan slowly released the breath she hadn't known she'd been holding in. What was Victoria doing in Duncan's room at this time of night? It seemed odd. She waited a few minutes to see if anything else transpired. As no one else came out of their rooms and there were no sounds, Susan decided to return downstairs.

'Everything okay?' asked Hayley.

'I think so—' Susan began.

Before she could explain any more, Hayley picked up another of Bryson's books. 'I was thinking you should have this as well. You'll get a proper feel whether the books are for you. I really like the central character, the detective. He's a kind of Columbo-type figure, someone everyone underestimates, but he knows much more than everyone thinks. His background is interesting.'

Hayley continued to talk about the books and Susan was

struck by the passion and insight she showed. However, as much as she loved chatting about books, Susan realised it was now very late, so she said goodnight to Hayley and went back to bed.

10

FRIDAY, 23 DECEMBER

Despite the lack of sleep, Susan woke early the next day. Picking up her phone, she noticed a missed call from her ex, Steve. She felt a wave of panic: had something happened to Zoe or the family? The call had been at four that morning. She immediately assumed the call had to be about an emergency of some kind. She tried to text back, but the signal failed. She would have to get out to the car park to try from there. She quickly threw on some clothes, put her phone in the bag with her radio and left her bedroom. To her surprise, she found Robert was already up, sitting in the living room.

'Oh, I didn't expect to see you,' he said. 'I was thinking of taking all the dogs out, once I'd had a coffee.'

'I've missed a phone call from Steve – I can't get a signal. I need to go up to the car park.'

Robert frowned. 'I hope everything is okay.'

'He's got me worried. I'd better get going.'

Susan left the flat and walked quickly to the manor house's front door. She was surprised to see Bryson turning the key in the lock.

'You're up early,' she said.

He turned. 'Good morning, Susan.'

Susan smiled. 'I'm on my way to the car park.'

He opened the door, saying, 'And me. It's rather a nuisance to have to go out there, but I've missed a call from my publisher in Australia in the night, and there's no signal.'

'Same for me, although my missed call wasn't from a publisher.'

Ahead, Susan saw Lewis coming through the archway looking rather dishevelled. Bryson passed Susan the wet key and greeted Lewis.

'Oh, hi,' he said. 'Been to the car to make a call. Glad the front door is open now. See you at breakfast.'

The snow was a lot deeper this morning. The steady fall had added to the layers. As Susan trudged across the courtyard with Bryson, she saw Robert making his way up through the garden with the dogs and gave him a wave. The dogs were bounding around in the snow, having a wonderful time.

Susan climbed the steps to the car park carefully. It was impossible to see the edges of the steps today. In the car park, the cars were completely covered in snow. Despite this, Susan and Bryson both stood next to their cars. Susan soon heard Bryson speaking. He had obviously got through quickly, and was talking about publication dates, while she stood waiting for Steve to answer. His phone went through to voicemail, which worried her even more, and she left a rather frantic message asking him to call her. She was wondering whether to phone her daughter Zoe but was in two minds as it was so early, and the emergency might be nothing to do with her.

As she went to leave, a pinging alerted her to an incoming text. This had been delayed and had actually been sent by Steve shortly after the call. She scanned it quickly.

Sorry, call was made by mistake. I meant to send this text. Don't worry. All is well. There's something important I need to chat to you about. It's personal, not Zoe and family. I'll phone in the next day or two, but if we don't catch each other, Happy Christmas.

Relief was replaced with irritation. What the hell was he doing even trying to send her a text in the early hours, which could have woken her up? She understood that from years of being on call as a doctor Steve had very little understanding of time, but all the same. He should be more careful. She read the text again and, calmer now, started to wonder what he needed to talk to her about. Maybe he and Hester, the woman he had left Susan for, were getting married? That had to be a possibility, although last time she had spoken to Steve he'd been wondering if he had made a mistake. Susan tutted to a robin frantically trying to pull the bright red fruit off a snow-covered holly bush and watched as a tiny berry fell like a drop of blood onto the pristine white snow below.

'What a pain that man is,' she said aloud. The robin sensibly ignored her.

As she made her way towards the path, she saw that Bryson had also finished his call.

'Everything okay?' he asked.

'Just my ex being a nuisance.'

Bryson gave a sympathetic smile. 'I'm sorry. I can't say my call was any more urgent. The publishers over there have no notion of the time difference. Come on, let's get back in the warm.'

Back inside, Susan took a long refreshing shower, and was dressed by the time Robert returned with the four dogs.

Rocco and Libs, wet and cold, came running to greet her.

'Thanks so much for taking them out,' she said.

'I stayed in the garden, let them off. They just go manic out there, don't they? Dougie's tail was literally spinning around. Rocco and Libs went chasing off, and Gem Gem was absolutely fascinated by the snow. Now, I have something interesting to tell you. You know where they have the outside café in the summer and where that shack is?'

'I know where you mean. The shack is amazing. Have you been inside? The architects who were renovating the manor years ago constructed it to live in while they worked. Despite looking like a garden shed, it's like a Tardis. Inside are beds, a shower, toilet—'

'Yes, I know all that,' said Robert quickly, clearly impatient to get on with his story. 'Listen, you know it's raised up off the ground and has steps leading up to it? Well, this morning there were snowy footsteps leading to the door. The top step had been completely cleared of snow. I'm guessing in order to open the door.'

'But who would be going in there at this hour and in this weather?'

'That's what I wondered, so I went in to check, closely followed by the dogs, of course, who thought this was very exciting. But the shack was empty, just some melting snow on the floor, so no great surprise. I just thought it was curious.'

'I wonder if that was where Kristen was off to in the early hours?'

'Kristen?'

'Duncan's wife. I was woken by the security light you warned me about, looked out the window, and saw her going out. It seemed most peculiar. I couldn't think where on earth she was off to, but I saw her return. She wasn't out that long. If you saw the footsteps, that might explain where she went, but I've no idea why.'

'I'm guessing that if you kept being woken by the security light, you didn't sleep that well?' asked Robert.

'Not really. I was disturbed again later too, but not by the light that time. I heard a noise from the direction of the library, went to investigate, and found Hayley in there reading. She said she'd been disturbed by Lewis. She's a bit strange, you know.'

'No one seems to have got much sleep last night.'

'I noticed you weren't in your room either.'

She waited to see his response.

'I was with Meera. We had a game of Monopoly to finish off and then watched some TV. Mind you, I kept dozing off. I didn't mean to stay that late.'

He spoke in his usual open way and Susan felt she should believe him, but, well, how to be sure?

'Right, we can feed this lot and then go and get some breakfast.'

They headed to the kitchen through the Great Hall, and Susan saw staff busy laying out the buffet of fresh fruits, pastries and cereals. While she helped herself to croissant and granola, Robert went into the kitchen to order a full cooked breakfast.

Susan then joined him at a wooden table in a small room off the kitchen.

'I love this weather,' said Robert. 'Real snow is particularly special on the island. It's so rare.'

'To be honest, I like snow for about a day and then would be happy for it to go away. I want to go and visit Alice tomorrow, but I'm concerned about this weather. I wonder if they're clearing the roads yet.'

'When the snow is falling as heavily as this, I'm not sure

what they can achieve. You should try and enjoy a white Christmas while it lasts.'

Meera came in as they were eating. 'Morning, all.' Addressing the kitchen staff, she said, 'Thank you so much everyone for getting into work. The radio is saying the roads are all snowed up.'

'My dad let me bring the Land Rover,' said one of the younger girls. 'It was pretty bad, though. No way would an ordinary car get through.'

'I'm very grateful you're here,' said Meera. She turned to Gary. 'We're very fortunate you only live down the road, and thank you so much for the crazy long hours you've been putting in.'

She went to sit with Susan and Robert. 'We're going to have to keep things local with the guests today. The roads between here and Osborne are impossible. I was going to suggest a walk up on to the downs for anyone who wants it. What do you think?'

'Sounds great. I'll go with them,' said Susan.

'I could join in,' said Robert. 'Give the dogs another walk.'

'Great. Susan, could you tell the guests to assemble in the library about eleven?'

Susan was on her way through the library when she realised someone was pushing open the front door. She rushed over to see if they needed a hand and found Antoine trying to hold the door open and bang the snow off his feet before entering.

'I rang and checked the ferries. You were right. It's chaos. Even if I could get over to the terminal, there's no getting off the island today. I even checked that airport Duncan used, but that's only private planes and nothing could fly in this weather. I'm finding it very hard to take in, but we really are stuck here, aren't we?'

'I'm afraid so. To get to the mainland we're totally dependent on the ferries, and they, in turn, are dependent on the weather. I've missed appointments, meeting up with people, had to leave get-togethers early on the mainland in order to get back, all because of bad weather.'

'So, it's not just snow?'

'Oh, no. Storms and gales can be just as bad, and then of course one of the ferries may break down.'

'I don't know how you live like this. Why don't they build a bridge? The distance over the Solent can't be that far.'

'The shortest distance, between Colwell Bay and Hurst Castle, is only just over a mile. However, I don't think there's the financial incentive to build a bridge. In any case, a lot of islanders don't want it; the whole place would change.'

'I can imagine that. That walk I had this morning was spectacular. I saw the sunrise, and the air was so clean. At least we're stranded somewhere pleasant.' He tried to clean the worst of the snow off his boots, gently knocking them against the wall of the manor and using the old boot scraper. Susan was pleased he at least seemed to have reconciled himself to being here.

The snow was falling heavily again. Susan looked down to her left to see a blackbird was attacking the holly bush. She noticed the snow behind the bush was churned up and guessed some hungry animal, perhaps a fox, had been rummaging as well.

Antoine eventually seemed content his boots were clean enough and entered.

'Right, I need to change before breakfast and then, fingers crossed, I may get a signal and be able to settle down to some work.'

After a brief return to the flat, Susan was going to head into the Great Hall but found Bryson and Victoria in the library, clearly waiting for the others to come down. Both dressed in country tweeds, they sat in leather seats, against the background of the wood panels and roaring log fire. They looked like a photo shoot for *Country Life*.

'Good morning again, Susan,' said Bryson. 'Great to see a fire blazing and smell the bacon. I'm starving.'

Victoria gave a restrained nod, her attention returning to a magazine she had picked up from a side table.

Hayley and Lewis arrived, followed by Antoine. However, no one went through to the Great Hall. They were all clearly waiting for Duncan and Kristen.

Before she could suggest they made their way to breakfast, Susan was startled by a scream, a door slamming and then Kristen appeared, running down the stairs. She was dressed, but white-faced and clearly distressed.

'It's Duncan. Oh my God—' She burst into tears.

Bryson stepped forward, put his hand on her shoulder. 'What's happened?'

Meera appeared from her office, hobbling, clearly having heard the kerfuffle. She indicated with a glance for Susan to go upstairs.

With great trepidation, Susan hurried up to Duncan's room and nervously pushed open the bedroom door.

11

————————

Duncan was lying very still in the bed, his lifeless eyes fixed on the ceiling, his hands by his sides. Susan approached him and touched his right hand. Any vestige of warmth was quickly leaving his body: it was clear he was dead.

Glancing at his bedside table, she noticed the hip flask and matching silver tot cup, with the remains of some whisky. There was a copy of yesterday's *Morning Flame* folded so that the photograph of Isabelle was showing. She shivered and realised there was a breeze in the room coming from a window that was slightly ajar.

She turned as the rest of the guests followed her into the room.

Kristen was still crying, now gently dabbing the tears, desperately trying to stop her make-up from running down her face.

Hayley looked over at her father, grabbed Lewis's arm and started to shake violently. He put his arm around her, trying to steady her.

Bryson walked over to the bed, and shook his head. 'Oh,

Dad. I never said goodbye,' he said, and tears fell down his cheeks.

'No!' said Hayley, who started screaming as if she was in pain, her eyes wide, tears falling down her cheeks.

Lewis gathered her in his arms, and she buried her head into his shoulder, shaking, her sobbing now muffled.

Then Meera appeared, bringing Robert with her. With a quiet air of authority, Robert walked past the guests and approached the bed. Leaning over Duncan, he quickly scanned the body, checked briefly for a pulse, then turned to Bryson, who was standing close by.

'Could you go outside, dial 999, explain we urgently need the ambulance and police services.'

Bryson wiped the tears on his face roughly away with the back of his hand. 'Um, yes, of course.' He clenched his hands purposefully, appeared relieved to be given something to do, and left the room.

Kristen stepped towards the bed, but Robert blocked her.

'I'm sorry, you can't touch anything.'

She complied, but stood, staring at Duncan's body. 'He was so excited to come to the island. Last night, before I left him, he was talking about trying to get up to see those stones up on the downs. I was worried about the hike, what with the snow and everything.' She sniffed. 'I'm sorry he never got there.'

'You say you left him,' interrupted Robert. 'Meera mentioned you slept in separate rooms?'

'Yes, we both decided it was best. Duncan is a restless sleeper, usually wakes and has a tot of whisky in the early hours.' She shook her head. 'I suppose that wasn't a good idea, but, well, he wouldn't listen. Anyway, he knew he could phone or call me if he needed anything.'

'Did he call last night?'

'No, nothing. I'd have come straight in, of course. I hope that means he went quietly, you know, in his sleep—'

Robert glanced around the room and focused on the open window.

'Did your husband usually sleep with the window open in the middle of winter?'

'Never,' said Kristen, her voice shaking. 'He hated being cold. When I came in this morning just before half past eight, I noticed it, but then I saw him and panicked. I ran downstairs.'

'Has anyone else been in here this morning?'

There was no response. 'So, when was the window opened? Kristen, when did you last speak to Duncan?'

'Before I went to bed, about half past eleven. The window was definitely shut then.'

Susan was alert to Robert's sharp questioning. Did he have a sense something wasn't right or was he simply getting information to hand on to the officials who would be arriving?

She glanced at Duncan, who looked very peaceful, but the conversation she had overheard, 'If only he could die,' resounded in her head. The words had been spoken by someone last night, and now he was dead. However, the words had been so dramatic that, if they had foreshadowed murderous intent, she would have expected to find a gunshot wound, or Duncan splayed across the Longstone, a medieval sword protruding from his chest, scarlet blood staining the crisp white snow. The reality of this scene couldn't have been less theatrical. Duncan lay with every appearance of an old man who had died peacefully in his sleep. And yet Susan couldn't dismiss the words, and neither could she understand that open window. Kristen said Duncan hated being cold, so why was it open? She glanced at the bedside table and, for the first time, noticed that while there had been two mobile phones on there the night before, now there was only one. Did that matter?

She heard footsteps running along the corridor. Bryson burst in. 'They're sending someone as soon as they can. Obviously with the weather it's not easy, but they'll be as quick as they can.'

Robert nodded. 'Good. Right, we all need to leave the room now. I suggest everyone goes down to the library while we wait for the emergency services. Kristen, I expect they will want to know your husband's medical history, what medication he was on. Would you be able to tell them about that?'

'He was rather secretive, but I'll tell them what I know.'

'Thank you.' He turned to Meera. 'I will secure the room and wait up here. Let me know when the police arrive.'

Susan led the way downstairs, followed by Bryson, Victoria, Hayley and Lewis. They walked in a close-knit huddle as if they were frightened to separate. Antoine walked with Kristen at the back and, as they entered the library, Susan noticed him talking quietly to her.

He seemed to sense Susan watching him, because he suddenly looked over and gestured back upstairs, saying, 'I'm just going to get my laptop,' and he raced back up the stairs.

Everyone sat together on the leather chairs in the library. They were soon joined by Antoine with his laptop. Kristen had stopped crying but was holding a scrunched-up tissue. Hayley's face was frighteningly pale. She'd stopped crying but sat staring, frantically tapping the sides of her cheeks with long thin trembling fingers. Lewis sat next to her, his hand on her knee, stunned. Bryson clenched his hands, but sat upright, as if ready to speak.

However, before he did, Meera took charge. 'I am so sorry for your loss. This must be an awful shock for you all. I and all the staff are here for anything you need. While we wait for the emergency services, the kitchen staff will help you all with food and hot drinks from the buffet,' said Meera. 'This could all take some time. If anyone would like a cooked breakfast, please ask one of the waiters, otherwise it might be more comfortable to sit here around the fire.'

Meera stepped back and made her way to the kitchen. Susan indicated she would stay.

'I know how difficult this is,' said Bryson. 'However, we must all try and eat or at least drink. We're all in shock, and it's going to be a long day.' There was little expression in his face or voice: he was clearly in shock. Victoria slid her hand into his.

He fell silent. No one else spoke, as the fire crackled in the grate. Only one sound jarred, and that was Antoine's frantic, heavy-handed typing on his laptop. He was scowling, his lips pressed tightly together, as he wrote. Susan wondered if he was already drafting his first account of Duncan's death. Did he react to everything that happened, however personal, in terms of a 'story'? Maybe he preferred always to put himself in the role of observer, but to Susan, to be frantically typing away at a moment like this seemed at the least tactless and, at worst, cold and uncaring.

Kristen, who sat alone, stared down at her hands, stroking the manicured nails on one hand with the fingertips of the other. She looked very isolated and alone and, feeling very sorry for her, Susan offered to get her something to eat or drink.

Kristen shook her head, but said, 'Maybe a glass of still water – bottled, ice and a slice of lemon—'

'Of course.'

Susan went into the Great Hall and, as she walked over to the buffet, Meera, who was just leaving the kitchen, came over to her.

'I'll go into the office if you are okay out here. I'll watch out of my office window for any arrivals, but come and get me if you need me.'

Susan agreed and went over to the buffet. She was putting ice and lemon in a glass when Lewis arrived. She noticed him pile a plate with pastries: clearly the stress was not affecting his appetite. Victoria then arrived, requested a certain kind of tea, and gingerly picked up a croissant which was carefully inspected before she placed it on a plate. Bryson joined her, but simply grabbed a piece of toast, and scraped some of the nearest spread on it. Once she had found a bottle of water, Susan returned to Kristen.

It wasn't long until there was an urgent knock at the door. Susan answered. She was surprised and impressed to see the paramedics and police had arrived quickly, despite the weather. Susan recognised one police officer, DC Kent, who she had met earlier that year after the sudden death of a headteacher in the village. The encounter had been difficult and, as their eyes met, Susan noticed a fleeting frown on the officer's face. She clearly remembered Susan and didn't look too happy to be encountering her again.

Meera introduced herself and asked Susan to take the paramedics and officers to Duncan's room. At the top of the stairs, Susan handed them over to Robert and returned downstairs.

She went back to sit with the rest of the guests in the library. The only person who seemed to be enjoying their food was Lewis. Antoine had a hot cup of black coffee next to him but was back working, the rest sat sipping hot drinks, or nibbling on food.

There was another knock on the door, and this visitor introduced himself as the pathologist. Susan escorted the visitor upstairs and was greeted there by a young officer who asked her where he could find Mrs Fern as they would now like to speak to her.

Susan took him down to the library, and the officer asked Kristen to accompany him upstairs. Susan saw the panic on Kristen's face, but the police officer was very understanding and reassured her as they went upstairs.

Looking around, Susan noticed a few of the guests had finished their drinks and offered to go and refresh them. As she went through to the Great Hall, she saw Gary coming out of the kitchen.

'How's everything going?' he called. His voice seemed to echo around the room. He cringed apologetically. Coming closer to her, he lowered his voice. 'It's such a shock, Duncan Fern dying like that.'

'The paramedics and police are here now.'

Gary ran his hand through his hair. 'I know this is awful for the family, but this throws everything into confusion for us. We have all this food in, meals planned, but now I have no idea who, if any, of the guests will be staying. I suppose no one is going anywhere today with this weather, but will they be off as soon as they can? What happens about the staff? I suppose I may get Christmas Day off—'

'Sorry. I've no idea. Hopefully, you will know more soon.'

As she was carrying the coffees back into the library, she saw Kristen returning from Duncan's room.

'You weren't gone long,' said Bryson, leading her to a chair. 'What did they ask you?'

Susan laid the drinks carefully on the small tables next to Bryson and Lewis and quietly went to sit in a chair at the side. She was anxious to hear Kristen's account.

'I needed to show the medications to the pathologist, explain when Duncan last saw a doctor, how he was when I left him, that kind of thing,' she said. 'They saw the whisky on the side and I explained it was a present but also that your dad liked a tipple in the night—'

'So, can they tell why he died?' asked Victoria, fiddling with one of her gold earrings.

'They asked a lot of questions about his heart issues. I'm guessing that's the way their minds are working. As the last person who saw Duncan they were obviously keen to know how he'd been when I left him but, as I told you, he seemed fine. I guess these things can happen without warning.'

Antoine looked up. 'Hang on, you say the last time you saw Duncan was at half eleven? But Hayley, you went in around twelve: that makes you the last person to see him.'

Hayley scowled. 'I didn't see Dad after he went to bed.'

'But you must have. Bryson told me you'd been in around twelve, and your dad didn't want to be disturbed. It was annoying. I needed to speak to him.'

Hayley stared at Bryson. 'Why did you say that? I never went in to Dad. I never spoke to him—' There was panic in her voice.

Bryson looked searchingly at his sister and then quietly conceded, 'Sorry, my mistake.'

He threw a glance at Antoine, who was clearly about to challenge her, signalling to leave the subject for now.

Kristen shivered. 'This is like some terrible nightmare, isn't it? To think I was in the room next to him the whole time, with no idea of what Duncan was going through.'

Susan frowned. Why were people being so evasive about where they had been the night before? Why was Kristen saying she was in her room the whole night when she had definitely left the house at about twenty past one, for nearly half an hour? Why was Hayley denying going into Duncan's room? And why hadn't Victoria owned up to going in there as well?

Bryson spoke gently to Hayley. 'Susan mentioned you were down here reading in the early hours. Did you hear any noises from upstairs?'

Hayley screwed her face in an effort of concentration. 'Oh, we heard some creaking floorboards. Susan, you went up to see what was happening, didn't you?'

Susan realised she'd been given an opportunity to mention Victoria's visit. 'I did. Actually, I saw you, Victoria, coming out of Duncan's room.'

Victoria went very red. She carefully and purposefully placed her cup of tea on the table. 'You're mistaken. I did not go in to see Duncan. Unlike you, Susan, I was asleep, like any sane person would be at that time in the early hours.'

Susan was surprised by the strength of Victoria's denial. Why was she so frightened to admit to going into Duncan's room?

It didn't take too long before DC Kent came down, accompanied by another officer who headed in the direction of Meera's office. DC Kent asked to speak to Kristen, and they went into the Great Hall briefly.

Kristen soon returned with DC Kent, the other officer with Meera.

DC Kent sat on a chair with the assembled guests. 'As you know, the emergency services came in response to Bryson's call and they contacted the pathologist. He has now given an approximate time of death and contacted the coroner. It has been decided that, as the circumstances are unusual, what with the weather and the holidays coming up, a preliminary post-mortem will be carried out today.'

Bryson frowned. 'But he'd been to the doctor's last week. We know his heart was in a bad way—'

'Yes, but there still needs to be a post-mortem. The fact he was seen so recently by a medical professional is the reason the pathologist is prepared to do this initial post-mortem so quickly.'

'So, they do think it was his heart?' asked Bryson.

'That is a possibility. We will know more later. I'll come to see you tomorrow to update you. Of course, if there are further issues then I'm afraid we will have to wait until after Christmas for a full post-mortem.'

'Do you have any idea what time he died?' asked Victoria.

Susan was watching her, interested that she should ask this question. Did it relate to her denial of going into Duncan's room?

'We only know, at the moment, that he died sometime in the early hours of this morning, between about midnight and four. We might know more tomorrow. Now, we would like to have a chat with each of you. Meera has said we can use her office, and my officer here will bring you through in turn. You may have seen or heard something that proves useful.'

'I hope you remember you can't trust everything you hear,' said Victoria, shooting a glare at Susan.

DC Kent looked over. 'Susan, I thought I recognised you.'

'I'm working here. I was up around the time they are suggesting Duncan died. I thought I heard noises—'

'Maybe you should come with me. You can be my first interviewee.'

12

Feeling like she was being taken to the headteacher's office, Susan followed DC Kent and they sat down on opposite sides of Meera's desk.

'So, Susan, firstly tell me how you ended up here. It's a bit of a coincidence to find you at a second death this year, one of a very well-known figure as well.'

Susan explained how she came to be working at the manor.

'I understand the family had an evening meal together. Maybe you could tell me your movements and observations after that.'

'Certainly. I went and checked the rooms, had a drink with Meera and then took my dogs out with Robert in the grounds.'

Susan observed the officer taking notes and tried to pace what she said. 'When we returned, Robert went to do some work. I read for a while. Oh, and I did overhear some people talking in the garden—'

'Oh, yes. What did you hear?'

Susan took a breath. 'Um, I heard two people talking about

Duncan. One of them said, "If only he could die." I have no idea who was talking but I know what they said.'

DC Kent's eyebrows shot up. 'Are you really sure you heard those exact words?' The scepticism coating her words was thicker than the snow in the courtyard.

'I am. I was shocked at first, but I did wonder if it was simply someone speculating about their inheritance.'

'But you don't know who it was?'

'No, nor who they were speaking to.'

'Hmm, well, I'll take a note of it. Of course, our imaginations can work overtime when we witness a shocking event.'

'I didn't imagine it.'

'Right, and what happened next?'

Susan explained about locking up, meeting Bryson at the door, then Victoria and Antoine arriving back at the house, and finally Lewis.

'I'm surprised so many of the guests went out.'

'I think some of them wanted to stretch their legs after a lot of travelling and a big meal, and Victoria clearly felt there is something quite magical about snow at night. Antoine and Lewis had gone out to use their phones.'

'So, you saw the three of them return, and we know that Bryson was already in the house. What about the others?'

'Hayley was upstairs, and possibly she spoke to Bryson—'

'What do you mean possibly?'

'Bryson says they spoke around twelve, that she told him not to disturb Duncan, but she says she didn't go in to see him.'

DC Kent screwed up her eyes. 'So, we're not too sure who the last person to see Duncan was: we have Kristen saying she went in at half past eleven, Bryson saying Hayley went in after that. I'll need to speak to them.'

Susan told the detective about seeing Kristen leaving the

house at about twenty past one. 'I have a feeling she may possibly have been going to the shack, a small shed-like building in the grounds.'

'I know the building you mean. I've visited the gardens. The shack is cosy in good weather, but hardly somewhere you'd choose to go in the middle of a snowy night. Are you sure she went there? In any case, are you positive it was her you saw? It was very dark. How could you see her face?'

'I didn't see her face,' admitted Susan. 'I only saw her hair shining in the security light.'

'So, it could have been a fox or something?'

'No. It was definitely a person.'

'And why do you think she went to the shack?'

Susan told the officer about Robert seeing the footsteps on the steps that morning.

'Okay. Well, I'll check it out. If this was Kristen, do you know what time she returned?'

'Yes, about quarter to two.'

'So, after you saw Kristen return, you slept?'

'No, I couldn't get back to sleep. I had a drink of water and then heard a noise along the corridor. I went out to see what it was.'

Susan explained how she found Hayley in the library reading. She described their conversation, going upstairs and seeing Victoria leaving Duncan's room at about two o'clock, but that Victoria denied going in.

DC Kent noted everything down and gave a half-smile. 'I'm guessing this is what she was referring to when she warned me not to believe everything some people said?'

'Yes, but I definitely saw her. After that, as I said, I went back to bed and slept through until the morning.'

DC Kent sat back. 'Well, Susan, you certainly seem to see a

lot, although of course everything you have told me may well be easily explained. I do hope you're not letting your mind run away with you over this?'

'Of course not,' said Susan, who felt her cheeks burning with anger. She tried to control her voice. 'I am doing my duty by telling you everything I saw and heard last night. There is more to add as well.' She took a deep breath. 'When I went into Duncan's room this morning, I saw the open window that I expect Robert has told you about. I also noticed that while last night I definitely saw two mobile phones on Duncan's bedside table, this morning there was only one.'

Susan sat back, crossed her arms, her lips pressed firmly together.

DC Kent gave what appeared to be an attempt at a conciliatory smile, spoke more carefully. 'Thank you, Susan. Of course you're right to tell us everything you know.' She coughed. 'However, you must try and leave this investigation to us now. I realise you were involved in the tragic death of the headmaster in your village earlier in the year, and I admit your instincts were right on that occasion. Maybe you fancy yourself as some kind of amateur sleuth out to beat the professionals?'

'Not at all. I just want to be sure we get to the truth about what happened.'

'And so do we, and we are trained to do so. We have experience and tools you don't, and we often know a lot more than you think. One thing I do know is that a lot of harm can be done by someone interfering. Most people die of natural causes, and the family and friends are grieving.'

'I know that—'

'Good. You're here to look after this family, not to stir up trouble. We shall be asking all the necessary questions. Duncan

Fern is a very well-known figure. There are guests here with influence. We're going to be very careful.'

'You want me to butt out?'

'I'm asking you to stick to the work you have been employed to do here, and not hinder me doing mine.' DC Kent stood up, signalling the end of the interview. 'Thank you for your help, I shall bear what you have said in mind. Now, I need to talk to the family.'

Clearly dismissed, Susan left the office fuming and stomped back to the flat.

How dare the officer treat her like that? She had done her duty. She had told her everything that she had seen and been treated like a busybody.

She paused and tried to calm down. Did DC Kent have a point? Should she step back, let the police do their job?

Opening the flat door she was greeted, as always, by Rocco and Libs.

'Is she right?' she asked them and collapsed onto the floor. Putting her arms around the dogs, she felt surrounded by that special warmth and comfort they always gave her.

'Hi, are you okay?' Susan looked up to see Robert had come in. 'You look upset. I'm not surprised. It's been a stressful morning.'

'Yes, really hard. And just now I had an awful interview with DC Kent. That didn't help. Honestly, I was trying to be helpful. She accused me of interfering. Let's face it. She doesn't like me.'

Robert screwed up his eyes. 'What did you tell her?'

Susan went through the conversation and then added, 'She made me feel hysterical, as if I was making it all up, and I wasn't.'

Robert grimaced. 'You must admit the words you overheard are pretty dramatic, and then there are the comings and goings that contradict the guests. It was a lot for her to take in.'

'I know, but I know what I saw and heard and when the things happened.'

Robert held up his hands. 'I believe you, of course I do. But not everyone is so reliable.'

'She knows me. She knows I don't make things up.'

Robert nodded. 'But she is trained not to take anything at face value. Mark my words, she will have taken on board all you told her. She will check things out. She has to.'

'I hope so. Something's not right here, Robert. I'm sure of it.'

Robert screwed his eyes up. 'Do you mean you believe there's something suspicious about the way Duncan Fern died?'

'It has to be a possibility. I have no idea how someone else could have been involved, but I know some people have lied. I know there are other things that don't add up. Also, remember Duncan Fern was a very wealthy man. There have to be people who benefit from his death.'

'I guess the family will be left substantial amounts of money. I'm sure they'll check everyone's finances.'

'I hope they do. Also, I saw for myself what a difficult man he was. He was rude, opinionated, confrontational. He put everyone on edge. Just in the space of the meal he'd had a nasty confrontation with Victoria, made digs at the others and then had a blazing row with Antoine at the end. That man knew how to make enemies.'

'I've no doubt there will be people who would not be exactly grief stricken at his death, but murder is another level. The police will be alert to it, though. They'll check everything.'

Susan stood up, looked searchingly at Robert. 'I suppose you're like DC Kent and think I should stop interfering, leave them to do their job.'

Robert put his head to one side. 'Look, I believe most police officers care about justice and are thorough in their investigations. However, I also know you have this instinct and passion for the truth which is pretty special. So, no, I'm not telling you to step back.' He broke off and grinned. 'Not that you would listen to me if I did.'

Susan smiled. 'Maybe not, but thank you.'

He glanced over at the window. 'The snow may be easing off for now, but there's a lot more to come. It's getting worse, isn't it? Even if the family wanted to leave, I can't see them getting anywhere today.'

Susan could see the weather appeared to have called a temporary truce, at least for a while. No snow was falling and a kind of calm had descended. 'I know it'll get worse later, but I want to fit in a quick visit to someone living close by. I'd really like to take them their present.'

'You won't be able to get your car out—'

'I know. I'll walk. It's not far.'

Robert gave her a knowing look. 'Am I right in assuming you're going to the nursing home?'

'I am. I need to go. I need to talk.' She spoke more firmly. 'I'm going, Robert. I'll be fine.'

He gave a faint smile. 'Well, there's no stopping you, is there? Just be careful, and try and get back before dark.'

There were times Susan was irritated when Robert tried to tell her what to do, but today she knew he had good reason to be concerned. And so, she responded with a serious nod and promised to take care.

'Okay, and I'll take the dogs out, so you don't need to worry about them when you return.'

Susan grinned. 'I could get used to you taking the dogs out all the time.'

'Good.' He smiled but she saw a look in his eyes. She knew he wanted to say more but was grateful he was holding back.

13

_____

Before leaving the manor, Susan put her head round the office door to let Meera know where she was going.

'Be careful, there are deep drifts now. Oh, by the way, Bryson came to see me. The guests are staying. They know the ferries will be all over the place tomorrow, even if the snow is easing off, and of course there won't be any on Christmas Day, and they're very restricted on Boxing Day.'

'This is going to be very strange for them and us.'

'I know. We'll just have to do what we can. We have all the food in, so I'm glad none of that is going to waste. Right, you get off. See you later.'

Susan left the manor muffled, with her cross-body bag, wanting to keep her hands free. She set off with the air of an arctic explorer, excited at taking on the elements.

It didn't take long to reach the main road, and Susan was pretty sure she could keep to pavements even though the snow was very thick in parts. No traffic was going past and the place was eerily deserted.

As she trudged on, she found herself tiring. The novelty of

the walk was quickly wearing off. Each step took so much more effort than normal. The layers of clothing – scarf, hat, her daughter's old parka with the hood up, gloves and her waterproof dog-walking trousers over her jeans – combined with the rucksack on her back restricted her. She was sweating, but her face was freezing. Her breath seemed to turn to ice.

A walk which should have taken ten minutes took twenty, and Susan was glad to arrive at the front door of the nursing home. She was greeted by surprised smiles from staff members as she entered reception.

'Goodness, Susan. How on earth did you get here? You can't have driven. One or two of us are living in for a few days as it's impossible to get back and forth.'

'That's very good of you.'

'Fortunately, this is a very rare occurrence, and we've swapped things around so that those of us who live close by are covering. A number of residents have gone back to relatives for a long weekend over Christmas, so that helps. It's rather nice in some ways, a real family atmosphere.'

'I didn't need to even think of driving. I'm up at the manor helping out, so it wasn't too far to walk. I wanted to see Alice before Christmas.'

'She'll love seeing you. Come on, I'll take you through. Our little Princess is with her, as you might have guessed.'

Alice was sitting in her usual chair, smartly dressed in black trousers and pink fluffy jumper, white hair neat, her iPad in her hands. Earlier in the year, Alice had promised Susan a surprise was on the way, and this was it: a little rescue cat, Princess, officially owned by the manager, but she had clearly made herself at home with everyone. She had taken a particular shine to Alice, and Susan usually found her sitting on Alice's lap. She was a pretty little cat: a violet tortoiseshell, her coat a variety of shades of brown.

'Susan, I didn't expect to see you today. Did you walk from the village?' asked Alice. Her voice had the shake of a ninety-three-year-old, but the clear grey eyes that shone from behind her glasses, and the half-completed crossword Susan spotted on the iPad, showed that Alice was still as bright as ever.

Susan explained how she had come to be at the manor.

'My goodness, I didn't realise you were there. I'm sure Robert is enjoying your company.' There was a glint in her eyes which Susan chose to ignore.

'My time at the manor has certainly been eventful. In fact, I need to talk to you about everything that has been happening.'

'Ah, I have a feeling I know what you're about to tell me.'

Susan's eyes widened. 'Now, how on earth could you know?'

'Gary, the chef at the manor. His dad lives here. Gary rings him every day. He told him what had happened to Duncan. Gary is having to rejig all the meals. He was saying that if they all leave tomorrow, he would be able to join his family for Christmas Day, the first time for years. He's always working.'

'I'm afraid Gary and his family will be disappointed. Meera told me just before I came here that the family are planning to stay put. The weather means travelling is impossible today and will be messed up tomorrow. Then of course there will be nothing on Christmas Day, and very few ferries on Boxing Day.'

'I was expecting to see Bryson and Hayley, the children of the poor man who died, on Boxing Day. Of course, they may well cancel now.'

'Duncan's sudden death has certainly been a shock for them.'

'I'm sure. They lost their mother when they were still young. So sad to lose their father as well.'

'Yes, it's been very hard,' said Susan. 'Now, before we talk any more about them, tell me, how are you? What are your plans for Christmas looking like?'

'I'm keeping very well, thank you. Originally Jo kindly offered to fetch me and take me to her house for Christmas day, and also invited me to stay the night. As much as I was looking forward to this, I've told her that I quite understand her not venturing out in this weather. She knows... I don't get into a state about Christmas. It's only one more day in the year. However, I know Jo will try. So, we will see.'

'I think the forecast said the snow was going to ease off slightly today, but I guess it depends if the gritters can get out to see to the roads.'

'Exactly. I know it's not far to the village, but I don't want Jo or her husband taking any risks.'

'Of course not.'

'And what about you?' asked Alice.

'I shall stay on at the manor. Meera needs help and I'm enjoying the food. Mind you, I'll need to go for lots of walks when I get back home.'

'So, who are the guests – apart from Bryson and Hayley, that is?'

'There's Bryson's wife, Victoria, the food critic. Hayley's partner, Lewis. He's very Welsh, born in Cardigan, went to university in Swansea, and is now a personal trainer. Finally, there's Antoine, an associate editor at Duncan's paper.'

'I see, and how do you find them all?'

'Bryson is very pleasant and friendly. I think you were sent a copy of one of his crime novels?'

'Oh, yes. *Buried at Sea*. Very enjoyable, excellent plot.'

'He's going to be on TV soon. His father-in-law helped him get a prime slot as a chat show host.'

Alice smiled. 'Oh, I can see him doing that. He was always quite a cheeky young man. Even as a teenager he would come in chatting. He was quite different to his sister, Hayley.'

'Yes, Hayley seems a lot more sensitive and anxious. She talks about spirits and ghosts, seems watchful somehow. One thing she did mention was how much she was looking forward to seeing you.'

'Ah, I'm glad, and I was looking forward to seeing her again. She really was an extraordinary child. She loved it in the shop and, when she got older, her mum allowed her to stay with me. She'd sit on the chair behind the counter reading or writing her stories. I loved listening to them. She used to illustrate them. She was a clever girl.'

'And yet it's Bryson who's now writing.'

'Yes, I think writing was a very private thing for Hayley. Bryson used to encourage her, which was nice. I remember he was very good at calligraphy and he would sometimes make her covers and write a beautifully scripted "The end" at the finish of the story. You will still find that at the end of his adult books.'

'I had the feeling there was something specific Hayley wanted to talk to you about.'

'You're right, Hayley had told me she wanted to ask me about her mother, Nancy.'

'She wanted to hear your memories of her mother?'

'Yes, in particular about her mother's accident.'

'Accident?' asked Susan.

'Yes, unfortunately on the first night of their final holiday, Nancy had a nasty fall.'

'Oh, Gary said something about it being a shame their last visit was spoiled. Is that what he was talking about?'

'So, Gary remembers? This village doesn't forget, does it?'

'He was pretty evasive. What happened?'

Alice stroked Princess thoughtfully. 'The story was that while Duncan and Bryson were out, Nancy fell and cut her face badly on the Longstone. When Duncan returned, he was horrified at the state of her face and took her straight to A and E where she had stitches.'

'How awful.'

'It was very upsetting. I remember Bryson brought Hayley to me the next day. She'd asked to come to the shop. Poor Hayley was like a little ghost. She'd seen her mother badly injured and then had to go to the hospital with them because, of course, she couldn't be left on her own. She wouldn't talk about what happened, but she did read me a story she'd written the night before. Stories were always an escape for her.'

Susan screwed her face up thoughtfully. 'I don't quite understand the accident. How did Nancy manage to cut her face so badly on the stones?'

'You're right. The story didn't quite add up. I mean, you could see from the stitches it had been a single deep laceration. There was no grazing. I knew there had to be more.'

'And there was?'

'Oh, yes. Not long after they left the island, we learned Nancy had been admitted to a facility for people with addiction problems.'

'Oh, no! Now I think of it, Gary mentioned something about drink.'

'Yes, I'm afraid she was struggling with addiction to alcohol. The accident had occurred because she'd been drinking heavily and cut her face on a broken bottle.'

14

'I'm so sorry Nancy was struggling in that way,' said Susan. 'Had you ever suspected it?'

Alice frowned. 'No, not a thing. Although people were starting to talk. There was the story not tying up with the injury and then, the day after they left, a cleaner up at the house discovered a load of empty bottles stashed away. It was as well the truth came out. Some of the rumours going around were not nice.'

'What were people saying?'

'Unfortunately, people became focused on Duncan. You see most people didn't like him. They found him condescending, abrupt.'

'I'm not surprised. I found him to be rude and overbearing.'

'Yes, not an easy man. Only Gary's father took to him, but I think that was the cars.'

'So, what were the rumours?'

'It hardly matters now—'

Susan sensed a hesitancy in Alice and was curious.

'What was it?'

'Well, as I said, people didn't take to Duncan and when they saw the injury and found the bottles, they initially said he'd been the one drinking and had attacked her.'

'Duncan was abusive to Nancy? Oh, my God.'

Alice held up her hand. 'This was just gossip, and they were proved wrong anyway. Nancy admitted to the addiction. I'm sorry the help she received didn't save her. You see, she died about two years after the accident from liver failure.'

'How tragic to die so young.'

'She was only in her early forties. And of course Hayley was only a child, twelve, Bryson twenty. I hear Duncan was heartbroken. In fact, Bryson wrote the obituary in the paper. It was very moving.'

'I hadn't realised what the family had been through. I overheard Duncan telling Bryson that he'd decided to set the record straight about their mother and acknowledge the part she'd played in his success in the autobiography he was writing.'

'He said that, did he? How interesting. I'm glad he was going to do that. Nancy was a devoted mother and wife. She was very aware of their changing status over the years, as Duncan's career progressed, and they became undoubtedly very well off. She told me she didn't want the children to become spoiled by it and I saw that. They always had a certain amount to spend on their holidays. They would count out their pennies when buying sweets. As they got older, she was the same, giving them an allowance they had to stick with. Even once Bryson went off to some expensive private school. I approved of that, it kept the children's feet on the ground.'

'I would say Hayley seems to have been more affected by the past than Bryson.'

'You must remember the age difference. Bryson was eighteen when the accident happened, and everything came out about

Nancy. Hayley was only ten. I think he had some degree of understanding about his mother's problems and maybe that helped. He does acknowledge it, though. I noticed in the acknowledgements of the book that a percentage of the profits are given to a rehabilitation centre that supports families who live with someone with alcohol dependency issues. I looked it up. He's mentioned as a trustee, does a lot of work for them.'

'His wife, Victoria, mentioned his charity work and him using his experiences for good,' said Susan. 'Now I think about it, I don't think he drinks alcohol. He had a non-alcoholic spirit from Kristen. I guess, as you say, he has found his own ways to cope with it all.'

At that moment, the tea trolley, which seemed to be on a continual loop in the home, came round. They both had a coffee and a mince pie.

'And now they have lost their father. What did Duncan die of, by the way?' asked Alice.

'They're talking about heart problems. He was on strong medication.'

Alice took a sip of her coffee and looked straight at Susan. 'Do I sense a hint of concern?'

Susan chose her words carefully. 'Look, I'm probably completely wrong here, but there is something that is really worrying me. It was something I overheard last night.'

'And what did you hear?'

'I had the doors to the patio open and I heard two people talking. I have no idea who was speaking, it was this hoarse kind of whisper, but I clearly heard part of a conversation about Duncan, "If only he could die."'

Alice took a sharp intake of breath. 'You heard that? And now he's dead.'

'Exactly. I told DC Kent this morning but, honestly, I think she's written me off as an interfering busybody.'

'Well, she should know better than that. You were proved right last time over the headmaster in the village.'

'I know. Maybe that makes her resentful of me. Anyway, I didn't feel she took on board any of my other worries.'

'Was there anything else?'

'I have lots of questions.'

Susan told Alice about the night before. Hearing Kristen outside, Victoria leaving Duncan's room, Hayley sitting in the library. She moved on to describe the next morning starting with going into Duncan's room, his bedside table and the open window, the contradictory reports by Hayley, Victoria and Kristen.

Alice frowned. 'So, we know that Kristen and Victoria are definitely lying. Victoria denying she even went into Duncan's room is particularly suspicious.' Alice's eyes suddenly lit up. 'Oh, the phone. You said there was one missing?'

'That's right. The one that had gone was in a black leather case.' Susan paused. 'Oh, goodness, I've just realised Victoria talked about the "black business phone". That must have been the one that went missing. I have obviously no details of what was on it, but I know it was supposedly evidence Duncan kept against people, although Victoria seemed to make a joke of it.'

'But say she was more worried about that phone than she let on? Maybe the reason she went into Duncan's room was to steal that phone. That's not something she'd want to admit to, but it has to be possible.'

'Of course. Why didn't I think of that?'

'I'm just trying to put the pieces together. You mentioned something about a copy of Duncan's newspaper being on the bedside cabinet, didn't you?'

'Yes, it was a copy of yesterday's edition. I remember because I saw a photograph of that girl Isabelle. They'd revealed she'd had an abortion when she was younger. Victoria, Bryson's wife, had been very upset and argued with Duncan about it at the meal. The row became very heated. She wasn't the only one who was annoyed by it. Interestingly, Antoine the journalist or editor who worked closely with Duncan was also pretty upset. From what I heard, they'd previously agreed the story wouldn't be printed.'

'Did you think Duncan was starting to regret running the story?'

'No, quite the opposite. He liked the fact the story was controversial. He was a man who appeared to me at least to be supremely confident in his own opinion.'

'Yes, he was always that way. I feel the paper being there is significant in some way. I must look up the story on my iPad.'

Susan sat back, exhausted but relieved to have unburdened herself.

'All these odd things happening, but have you got means or motive?' asked Alice.

Susan frowned in concentration. 'Well, for motive, it could be money. The family may be well off, but some people always want more, and we know Duncan was a very rich man. Hayley and Bryson gain financially from his death.'

'And their partners, as well as, of course, Kristen, Duncan's wife.'

'He claims she insisted that he didn't leave her anything.'

Alice's grey eyes shone through her glasses. 'Really?'

'Exactly. And then there's Hayley's partner Lewis, who wants to start his own gym.'

'Tell me about him.'

'I don't know much. He's Welsh, went to Swansea University,

and is a personal trainer. However, I'm a bit worried about their relationship. He's on the phone a lot and I wonder if Hayley suspects him of being unfaithful.'

'Oh, poor Hayley.'

'Yes, I hope it's not true. He does seem genuinely very fond of her, very caring. Victoria, I think, has plenty of money behind her, very rich parents. So, I doubt money would be a motive for her. However, she was very angry with Duncan about this story, and he was definitely threatening her as if he knew something about her.'

'Really?'

'Oh, yes,' said Susan. 'Bryson was very upset by his father's attack on her. He tried to protect her and then Duncan had a real go at him.'

'Duncan turned on his son?'

'He did, said he had the means to break him as well.'

'Goodness, and what about this other editor Duncan worked with?'

'Antoine? I don't see how he benefits financially, although he may be after Duncan's job. Duncan had the air of a man who was in no hurry to retire. Antoine and Duncan had a huge row after the meal, over the story about Isabelle. Antoine had already said he was very unhappy with it. I got the impression that Duncan had maybe got hold of some of the information about Isabelle in a slightly dodgy way, and Antoine was upset. He said something like, "If this gets out, they will ruin you this time, and I'm not getting dragged down with you."'

'Interesting. I do remember all the hacking scandals,' said Alice. 'It was shocking the lengths some journalists were going to get information about people: hacking their phones, getting hold of confidential records. A total invasion of their privacy. But I thought that had all stopped now.'

'So did I, but I've a feeling Duncan was not complying.'

'I'm not surprised Antoine was worried then. Journalists have gone on trial for behaviour like that.'

'Yes, in fact Victoria told Duncan that he and people associated with him could well end up in prison if he carried on like that. I guess that gives Antoine a strong motive—'

'Certainly. It sounds as if there was a lot of tension between them all. However, even given some of them might have wanted Duncan out of the way, how did they do it?'

Susan watched as Alice leant forward, her bright eyes glinting through her glasses. She glanced around at the other residents, reading, sleeping, drinking a cup of tea. It was not a place you expected to be discussing murder, but then Alice wasn't your average ninety-three-year-old. She had quietly been an exceptional person all her life. Maybe some people had seen it, but Susan guessed that now Alice was so much older, settled into the nursing home, people were even more likely to underestimate her. She thought about Bryson doubting whether she would even still read a book.

Susan realised Alice was waiting for an answer. 'If Duncan was killed, how it was done is a real problem,' she admitted. 'If it had been a dagger sticking out of his chest, or a bullet wound, it would obviously have been murder. But I have a feeling the police are most likely to put his death down to heart issues.'

'He'd have been on medication for that?'

'Yes, three different kinds.'

'I see. Depending on what he was taking, I guess an overdose of one of his medications could be fatal?'

Susan sat back. 'I don't know, but I'd have thought it highly likely. He could have taken an accidental overdose.'

'Or been given one.'

Susan's eyes widened. 'Yes, I suppose so... but it

wouldn't be easy. He wouldn't even let Kristen touch his medication. I suppose someone could have slipped them at the meal, I don't know how long they took to act.' She paused and then pictured the hip flask. 'Of course, everyone knew he had a drink in the night. Someone might have added it to his hip flask, cup or the bottle of whisky next to his bed.'

Alice's eyes shone. 'So, someone could have crushed up the pills and put them into the bottle or, more likely, the flask. Although that wouldn't be easy. Most pills have to be crushed up very finely to dissolve. Some residents here who have problems swallowing pills have these special little devices to crush the pills. I hope the police are testing the flask, and the cup and bottle of whisky?'

'Yes, they took them away.'

'I assume they'll be doing a post-mortem, but that will take some time what with the holidays and everything.'

'Actually, they're going to try and do at least a preliminary one today.'

Alice nodded. 'If pills were added to a hip flask of whisky, it gives the killer greater flexibility. They don't have to have been present when Duncan ingested them.'

'I suppose you're right. The pathologist is estimating time of death between twelve and four. Someone could have added drugs to his whisky in the hip flask any time, or, of course, possibly at the meal.'

'What does Robert think about all this?'

'He's inclined to think Duncan died of natural causes. He'd been unwell, seen a doctor in the past few weeks, had heart problems.'

'And, of course, he could be right,' said Alice, 'but on the other hand, he could be wrong. I'm glad all these guests are stuck here a little longer. It'll give you time to get to know them a bit better, ask a few questions.'

'I'm not getting paranoid, am I? When I was talking to DC Kent, I felt a bit, well, hysterical.'

'You're not hysterical. The things you've told me are all concrete reasons for suspicion. You have very good instincts, Susan. I would trust your gut feeling and observations any day.'

Susan smiled. 'Thank you so much. I needed to hear that.'

'Hopefully the post-mortem will tell us more,' said Alice.

'Exactly. Thank you for listening, but let's move onto happier things. I know we said we weren't going to do presents but, well, I couldn't resist.'

She took a wrapped present out of her rucksack and handed it to Alice. Princess, despite being in the way on Alice's lap, had no intention of moving and so Alice had to unwrap it with her there.

Knowing about Alice's arthritis, Susan had been careful not to use too much tape but still Alice took her time, reading the label carefully, admiring the wrapping paper, then finally carefully peeling off the tape so as not to damage it. Alice was of a generation that was careful about waste.

Alice put the paper onto the side table, and then admired her gift, a small soft cat lap blanket. 'I noticed Princess is shedding quite a lot of hair. I thought this would save your trousers. Mind you, she could refuse to sit on it. I won't be offended.'

'There's only one way to find out,' said Alice. She gently picked Princess up and put her on the chair next to her. The cat gave an affronted meow and glared at her as Alice spread the blanket over her lap and patted it to encourage her to return.

Princess walked gingerly forward as if approaching an unexploded bomb, sniffed it carefully and moved even closer. One paw at a time, she climbed onto the blanket, and finally curled around and settled down, although keeping her eyes open, not yet fully trusting it.

'I call that a success,' said Alice, smiling. 'Thank you. What a perfect gift. I was getting tired of all the hair on my trousers, although I was of course willing to put up with it for the joy of having this little one on my lap.' She paused. 'By the way, have you read Bryson's book, *Buried at Sea*?'

'I haven't read it, but Hayley gave me a copy.'

'You should read it.'

Susan stood up. 'Right, I'd better get back. I hope you get to Jo's tomorrow and have a good night away. I shall aim to pop in on Boxing Day, whether it's with the others or not I don't know.'

Alice gave her a serious look. 'You be careful now. If your instincts are right, then however picturesque the manor is, you're sharing it with a killer.'

15

As Susan left the nursing home, she realised the nature of the snowfall had changed. The snow was much heavier, and stung her face. Walking was harder. Even though it was only about half past three, the light was already going, and it seemed greyer and colder than before.

As she made her way back along the road, a bitterly cold wind rose up, causing the snow to batter against her, and form an almost impenetrable curtain, making it impossible to see. Susan was aware of losing all sense of where she was, even if she was walking in the right direction. Panic set in. Was she going to get lost out here, be found frozen to death in the morning?

Fortunately, she soon realised that she had reached the bus shelter and knew the turning into the manor was very close by. This gave her the final adrenaline rush she needed to get herself safely back to the manor.

Susan fell into the house, shook off as much of the excess snow as she could, and returned to the flat. She received a rapturous greeting from Rocco and Libs. 'I'm so sorry. I feel like I've neglected you. I'll be back very soon.'

Susan left them to go and let Meera know she had returned.

'Welcome home. The weather's getting worse again. Glad you're back,' said Meera. She spoke in a casual way, oblivious to Susan's traumatic walk. 'Now, Duncan's body has been taken away and we've been given permission to go into the room. I'll organise things there.' Meera grimaced. 'It's so sad. This Christmas holiday was going to be really special. Quite frustrating, really. We've been working on this for weeks.' She winced. 'Sorry, that sounds rather heartless—'

'I understand.'

'I've brought the evening meal forward this evening. No one has eaten properly today. Maybe you could play quietly in the background again?'

'Of course.'

'How was your visit to the nursing home? It must have been nice to go somewhere completely cut off from all this drama.'

'Actually, they knew all about Duncan's death. Gary's dad is there, so word had got around. The home is very much part of village life.'

'That's good. I'm starting to think I'd like to be part of a community sometime. I've spent my life living in hotels. I've never put down roots.'

'Have you ever thought of going back to live in Manchester?'

'I might have done when my parents were alive, but I've no links with the place now,' said Meera. She gave an easy smile and then glanced back at her computer. 'Anyway, I'd better get on with work. I'll see you later.'

Susan was glad to get back to the flat. Slumping down on the sofa, she realised how exhausted she was from the walk.

Rocco and Libs jumped up to sit either side of her and she was pleased to feel their comforting warmth next to her.

After such a bad night's sleep and a hectic day, Susan felt her eyes closing and soon she was fast asleep.

She woke an hour later, feeling rather hung over from the heavy sleep. She realised she needed to get some tea before the guests' evening meal.

It was wonderful to be served a large hot, delicious bowl of vegetable lasagne. She took it back to eat in the flat and felt a lot better for it.

She made her way to the library, where the guests were gathered in front of the great fire, although she noticed that Lewis was not with them. The chairs were arranged as they had been the night before, although the throne-like seat Duncan had used had been tactfully put to one side.

The atmosphere was naturally subdued. Kristen's concession to mourning was to a wear a darker fitted dress and fewer diamonds. The new ring from Duncan was no longer on her finger. Hayley, pale and still, wore her purple velvet maxi dress, her red hair falling over her shoulders. Susan was suddenly reminded of the painting of Ophelia from *Hamlet*, floating down the river. The comparison was unsettling and Susan quickly tried to scrub it from her mind. Susan felt Hayley was struggling with far more than grief: there was fear in her stillness. Her eyes stared, her breath shallow, as if even the act of breathing was terrifying.

Bryson coughed and began to lead the conversation, possibly subconsciously taking on his father's role. A waiter came and took their orders and soon after they were invited into the Great Hall.

This time, Bryson sat at the head of the table, in his father's place. Susan took her seat at the side and began playing quietly.

The delicious-looking first courses were brought in, and

even though she'd already had her evening meal, Susan could easily have tucked in.

'We should start with a toast to Dad,' Bryson said, his voice cracking. 'I don't suppose any of us have even started to take in what has happened but, well, all I can say is that it was a privilege to have such an inspirational father. We all owe him so much.' He lifted his glass of sparkling water, and everyone joined in the toast.

'Now, I know this is a bit awkward, but I feel I should share with you that Dad made me one of the executors of his will. I know what the will contains and feel it is only right to share the bare bones of it with you.'

He swallowed hard and shot a slightly nervous glance at Victoria. 'I'm telling you, Hayley, to reassure you. Dad has left us and Kristen substantial amounts of money. I will go through everything with you, but I thought it would be a relief, particularly to you, Hayley.'

'Bryson, you're making me sound desperate,' Hayley said, scowling.

'Sorry. I just didn't want you to worry. That's all. Of course, Kristen, I know you say you'd insisted Dad didn't leave you anything but, well, he has done the right thing by you, and I'm glad.'

Kristen frowned. 'This was very generous of Duncan, I'm sure, but, you know, I never wanted anything. I'm more than comfortably off.'

'What happens to Dad's job at the paper? Will it automatically go to you?' asked Hayley, glancing at Antoine.

Antoine blinked and wiped his mouth with his napkin. 'That's a matter for the owner of the paper. However, I have naturally been in communication, and he has asked me to take over as editor-in-chief at least for the time being. I wish I wasn't stranded here. Obviously, I would like to get into the office but, well, it's not possible.'

Susan followed as his gazed drifted to a Tudor wooden-framed window. The tiny pieces of glass were held together with lead lattice, and by day it could look attractive, romantic even. However, this evening, as she saw the darkness beyond, and pictured the deep impenetrable snow, the lattice felt like prison bars: there was no escape.

Antoine continued, 'I have had to work on your father's obituary remotely but it has now been submitted. It will appear on the front page tomorrow. I hope you will feel my words reflect the extraordinary contribution Duncan made to journalism, how deeply missed he will be and how highly he was regarded by fellow journalists and readers alike. We, of course, will be considering ways to make a fitting and permanent memorial to Duncan's life.'

Although Antoine claimed not to have been expecting to explain any of this, the words tripped off his tongue easily: he had been prepared.

Victoria tutted. 'So, you won't be mentioning the court cases, or the fact he was still allowing hacking and unprofessional practices on the paper?'

The empty plates were cleared away and Susan was pleased to note that even Kristen had eaten her scallops. More delicious plates of food were brought in, but the guests hardly seemed to notice. Susan felt sorry for Gary and the staff, who had worked so hard.

Bryson frowned and patted Victoria's hand. 'Not now.'

'Why not?' demanded Victoria. 'It's a relief to be free to speak our minds.'

'You may be feeling relieved Duncan has gone,' barked Antoine, 'but the rest of us are grieving a great man.'

Bryson coughed. 'Of course Victoria mourns my father's passing. She respected my father, despite their differences.'

Susan wondered if Bryson really believed that, but Antoine clearly wasn't going to let things lie.

'Respected him? Victoria respects the man who threatened her with his "black business phone"?'

Bryson shook his head and shrugged. 'That was nothing, simply a slight disagreement.'

Antoine gave a cold laugh. 'Nonsense. There was a lot more going on, and you know it.'

An awkward silence fell over the table.

Kristen carefully cut a single carrot into slices and began to nibble each piece, while Antoine tore into his salmon en croute, attacking it angrily, demolishing it in minutes.

Only Victoria gave her carefully prepared meal the attention it deserved. Susan had the impression that whether she was in an upmarket restaurant in London or a roadside café, Victoria never ate or drank anything mindlessly.

After turning the plate, Victoria breathed in the aroma, and only then began to prod her piece of duck with her knife and fork. Satisfied, she carefully sliced through the duck breast, placed it in her mouth, chewed the morsel thoroughly, her face creased in concentration. The food was apparently acceptable, as she repeated the process.

Antoine had finished his meal now. Susan doubted he would even be able to recall what he'd eaten. He slammed down his knife and fork, gulped down a full glass of wine, glared at Victoria and started to speak.

16

'I'm sorry,' said Antoine to Victoria, 'but you don't appear to be grieving for Duncan in any way. He was your father-in-law, and a remarkable journalist. And yet you appear, whatever Bryson says, to be relieved. Why is that? Why did you deny going into Duncan's room when Susan clearly believes you did?'

Susan, who had been playing a gentle medieval tune on the recorder, froze. Why had Antoine dragged her into this? Susan didn't feel she was in a position to defend herself. In any case, everyone's attention was on Victoria: maybe they hadn't noticed the mention of her name.

Susan licked her lips, swallowed hard and tried to go back to playing.

Victoria carefully replaced her knife and fork. 'I can see this isn't going to go away. As I said to that police officer, on reflection I remembered I had been into Duncan's room. The reason I forgot was that I'd taken strong sleeping pills. Bryson and I both had as we were finding it difficult to sleep. I was just drifting off when I had this awful, well, premonition you could call it. I was sure something was wrong with Duncan, and I knew I couldn't sleep until I'd checked on him. I went over to his room, saw he was sleeping soundly and left. That was the reason I went in but, of course, the police were interested because the fact I went in to Duncan at that time helps them ascertain a time of death.'

Antoine stroked the bridge of his nose with his finger. 'Interesting. You admit to going in. Did you notice if the window was open, by the way?'

'I'm pretty sure it must have been closed. I think I would have noticed if the room had been cold.'

'And the phones on his bedside table, was there one or two?'

The question darted out. Susan was surprised at the intensity of the questioning, interested that he was picking up the point about the phones. Victoria was glaring at Antoine now, clearly upset. Susan waited to see how she would respond.

'I have no idea,' Victoria said firmly. 'The last thing on my mind was the phones on his bedside table.'

Antoine raised a sceptical eyebrow, clearly not convinced. Susan was inclined to agree with him and the more she thought about it, the more she was convinced that Alice was right. The reason Victoria had snuck into Duncan's room was to steal that phone.

Susan assumed Antoine had finished his interrogation of Victoria, but he had more questions.

'What about the newspaper? Did you notice that?'

Susan blinked. Antoine, like Alice, was picking up on the newspaper.

'Again, I have no idea. I wasn't looking at the bedside table, I'd simply gone in to check on Duncan.'

At this point, Hayley interrupted and spoke to Victoria. 'You had a terrible feeling something was going to happen to him?'

Victoria shrugged. 'All I can say is that I had this uneasy feeling.'

The staff were clearing the plates away now, and desserts were brought in.

'I thought the newspaper by his bed was weird,' said Kristen.

From the way Victoria's eyes widened behind her enormous black glasses, Susan realised she was not the only one surprised by Kristen's interjection.

Kristen held out her arms, palms upwards in a questioning gesture. 'Don't you all think this is odd? Duncan only glanced at the front cover over breakfast at home. After he'd put it in the wastepaper basket, he moved on. I'm sure he didn't bring that copy away with him.'

'Kristen is right. Duncan would never be reading that day's paper late at night. Yesterday's news he called it,' said Antoine. 'So, how did the newspaper get there?'

'Don't ask me,' said Kristen as she picked up a tiny dessert fork, speared a small piece of her fruit salad and began to eat as if the matter had ceased to bother her.

'Lewis, you had a copy of Dad's paper,' said Hayley.

Lewis went red in confusion. 'I did. I just thought it was polite to read up on what he was working on. I handed the paper on to you, didn't I, Victoria?'

'That's right. It's the only paper I don't get regularly, but I wanted to see the headlines.'

'Because you wanted to read about Isabelle. It was obvious last night you were extremely upset about the story,' said Antoine, adding, 'You interviewed her recently, didn't you?'

Victoria fiddled again with her gold earring; a gesture Susan was getting to recognise now as Victoria giving herself time to gather her thoughts. 'I did. I liked her, but we didn't become friends.'

And then, without warning, Antoine turned on Susan. 'I expect you're taking notes on this conversation, aren't you?'

Susan lowered her recorder. She stared at Antoine. 'Sorry?'

'You're watching us all the time, aren't you? Furthermore, I believe you've been stirring things up with the police. For example, it's clear, from what I've been told, that someone has been hinting that Victoria and Kristen's statements are not to be trusted. I believe it had to be you. But why hint to the police we're all trying to hide something? If you ask me, you're the one acting suspiciously. If the police need to check anyone out in connection with Duncan's death, it should be you.'

Susan gasped at the unexpected attack, panicked. 'I'd never met Duncan before. Why would I want to kill him?'

Antoine sat back, a nasty grin on his face, and Susan realised she'd been played.

'So, you think Duncan was murdered? I assume you suspect one of us?' he said. He spoke in a menacing way. He knew he had her cornered.

Susan was aware of the others now all staring at her. She saw looks of astonishment, horror, even anger, and who could blame them? This strange woman, a member of staff whose sole role was to care for them, had been snooping around and now apparently was accusing one of them of murder.

From his smug expression, Antoine was enjoying watching her struggling to untangle herself from the web of her own making. One thing was certain: she realised Antoine could prove a ruthless and extremely frightening opponent.

Swallowing hard, her hands sweating as she clung on to her recorder, Susan tried to speak as firmly as she could. 'I didn't tell the police I believed Duncan had been murdered. DC Kent asked me questions and I answered them as best I could, that's all. It would have been wrong for me to withhold information. Yes, I told them about the security light coming on, and that I thought it might be Kristen. I also told her I thought I'd seen

Victoria coming out of Duncan's room. It was the right thing
to do.'

'But you didn't simply answer questions,' continued Antoine.
'You pointed out the missing phone, the open window, the newspaper – I know that was you. DC Kent is not subtle. The words
she used were, "A member of staff told me they noticed certain
things had changed since they checked Duncan's room the night
before." It had to be you.'

'That's true. I admit I tend to notice things.'

'You're an expert at noticing things, aren't you? Most people
would have been too overwhelmed at finding a dead body to
note changes to a bedside cabinet.' Antoine threw the words out
with a harsh laugh. 'You should be a journalist, I'd offer you a
job tomorrow.'

Susan was unsettled by the way Antoine slipped so effort-
lessly from the attack to almost flattering her and she guessed it
was all part of his technique in handling people. It was scary to
feel herself being so easily manipulated.

Fortunately, Susan was aware of the general animosity in the
room subsiding, and she breathed a sigh of relief. She wondered
if she should be saying anything more in her defence, but was
saved by an interruption from Bryson. 'That's enough, Antoine.
Stop bullying Susan. She was merely doing her job and trying to
assist the police, like we all did. This is all academic. How the
newspaper came to be on Dad's bedside table and the like
doesn't matter. He'd probably packed it without Kristen noticing
to re-read what was looking like a significant story. All that really
matters is that our poor father has passed away. I'm sure
tomorrow we will hear that Dad died tragically because of his
heart and that will be the end of it. I know you mean well,
Antoine, but you need to act over the next few days as our
friend, not as a journalist on the case.'

Antoine picked up his glass of wine, took a long sip, and nodded in a way that suggested he was prepared to let the matter rest, at least for now.

Susan took a deep breath and tried to relax, although it was not easy playing the recorder when her lips were trembling. She was sure the guests would at the very least be wary of her now and, if one of them was a killer, they would be watching her every move. As Alice said, she needed to be very careful.

Bryson managed to move the conversation on, and in a similar way to the night before, Lewis helped things along.

The guests moved on to coffee in the library; Bryson handed out drinks, and Susan went up to turn down their beds.

At the top of the stairs, finally out of sight of the guests, Susan faltered, her heart still beating fast. She took deep breaths, relaxed her shoulders, unclenched her jaw.

The encounter with Antoine had been frightening but she had come through and at least, as Robert had suggested, DC Kent seemed to have taken her more seriously than she imagined and had followed up on what she had told her.

Of course, she had to be careful now, but it didn't mean she had to stop her enquiries, and this opportunity to check the rooms could be revealing. She must stay alert.

She went into Kristen's room first. Now, on the second day of her stay, the room felt more lived in. Susan had noticed the smell of expensive perfume before but now she noticed other things, in particular a photograph of what Susan assumed were Kristen's family, with the Golden Gate Bridge in San Francisco in the background. Taking a photograph in a frame to a hotel was unusual, but maybe it was a way of including her family, so far away, in her Christmas. To Susan it suggested a gentler, more sentimental side to Kristen.

In Bryson and Victoria's room, the first thing she wanted to do was look for that phone. She pulled out drawers, rummaged in pockets, but there was no sign of it.

Susan began to wander around the room, trying to think where else the phone could be. Glancing in the bin, she saw some empty tea bag sachets. Victoria had set out her own tea-making equipment and there was a large box of teas, big enough to contain a phone. Susan checked, but again there was nothing. The bag of coffee beans had not been opened. The hand grinder was damp, but empty, and in any case why would Victoria use Bryson's things to hide a phone? Then Susan spotted, at the back of the tray, a brown vacuum-sealed container with the word 'tea' inscribed. That was far more likely. She twisted off the lid, although it was not easy to break the seal. The strong aromatic smell of tea leaves greeted her. Susan found a spoon, and dug carefully inside, but her heart sank: there was nothing apart from tea inside.

Susan was about to give up, but she caught her breath. She wouldn't accept defeat, not yet. Victoria would not hide this phone anywhere obvious.

She tried again, this time looking under the cupboards, under the bed and then under the mattress. This time she did succeed in finding something, but it wasn't the phone. Instead, what she found was a book. Susan pulled it out, and recognised the person on the cover. It was Isabelle, and this was a copy of her cookery book. Susan would like to have flicked through it, but she didn't have time and instead replaced it under the mattress, aware it was an odd place to keep a book.

There was no time to think about that now. She clearly wasn't going to find the phone today. She decided to move on to Hayley and Lewis's room.

17

Hayley and Lewis's room was even more of a mess than the night before but it was still clear which side of the bed was Hayley's, with the piece of rose quartz standing on one bedside table, alongside two copies of Bryson's crime books and some notes. Hayley also had a Kindle, and the cover of the device had been cleverly constructed to incorporate a photograph of a young child and older woman with the words 'Hayley' and 'Mum' underneath them. Susan looked more closely at the picture. Hayley must have been about eleven and the physical likeness with her mother was uncanny. This was where her red hair came from, and those tiny pixie features. Susan remembered Duncan saying to Bryson how like her mother Hayley was.

In the photograph, Nancy held Hayley close to her, her arm tight across her daughter's chest. There were the same crinkles at the corners of their eyes, which avoided the camera, directed nervously to the side.

One obvious difference was a long thick white scar on Nancy's cheek, which must be from the accident at the Longstone. Seeing it brought home to Susan the enormity of what had happened. Nancy would have had to confront that scar every time she looked in a mirror, every time she touched her face. It was an outward sign of the hidden battles she was fighting every day.

On the floor on the other side of the bed was a pile of fitness magazines which Susan guessed belonged to Lewis.

Last, she went into Antoine's room. His was the only room that felt 'unlived' in. He hadn't even emptied his case, which lay on the floor. Nothing was hung up; the dressing table and bedside tables were bare. The only item taken out, apart presumably from a washbag in the bathroom, was his laptop. Antoine was clearly still living out of his case, and it made Susan feel as if he was ready to leave as soon as he could. The starkness of the room, however, spoke of more, someone who didn't want to share anything about himself with the strangers who would enter his room. Maybe it was natural that a man who spent his life revealing the secret lives of others would be obsessively protective of his own.

Antoine had left his case open, presumably by mistake, and Susan peeked inside. In the compartment in the lid, Susan noticed a rosary, which surprised her, and a book with a French title which she guessed from the cover was about some kind of jazz.

Glancing around, she couldn't see anything else of particular interest and so left the room and went back down to the flat.

She found Robert getting ready to go out with the dogs. 'How was your visit to Alice?'

Susan didn't want to admit to her fears on the journey home but simply replied that it had been a lovely visit.

'Well, I was worried about you. It was quite a blizzard. It must have been an exhausting walk back.'

Susan shrugged. Determined to show that she hadn't been

defeated by the walk, she added, 'I was fine. Now, I think I'll come out with you. The snow has eased off and it's been quite an evening.'

He grinned. 'Okay, fine. Let's go.'

As she was putting on her damp coat and boots, Susan began to regret the act of bravado. She'd had enough of snow for one day. However, she didn't feel she could back out now.

Once they were all wrapped up, they left the flat via the patio doors and went out into the snow-covered garden. The walking wasn't easy, and her legs were still tired from earlier, but at least she didn't have blinding snow biting into her face. In fact, a kind of peace seemed to have descended over the garden.

The moon was bright, and the snow glistened beneath its light. The snow-covered skeletal branches of the trees formed beautiful patterns against the dark skies.

In the moonlight, Susan could make out two sets of footprints heading away from the manor, but none returning. The snow was telling them two people were out here. In the same way as a freshly washed beach, it was impossible not to leave a trace. Susan wondered who it was.

'Be careful, there's ice under the snow,' said Robert. 'So, tell me. What's been happening?'

Susan told him about Antoine's accusations at the meal.

'My God, Susan. He's an intimidating man—'

'And extremely manipulative. By the end, he was almost flattering me, complimenting me on my detection skills.'

'Hmm. Be careful how you go with him. In fact, it was probably a timely warning to back off.'

'But I'm learning new things all the time. This evening Victoria admitted to going into Duncan's room.'

'How did she explain it?'

'She said she had a premonition something was wrong with Duncan.'

'That sounds like a bluff.'

'Exactly. I'm sure now she went in and took that missing phone.' Susan explained the 'black business phone', and how Duncan had threatened Victoria.

'If she did take the phone, then I wonder where it is now.'

'I've searched Victoria's room but couldn't find the phone. Another problem is the newspaper that was next to Duncan's bed. Apparently, Duncan would read a copy first thing and that was it; he never read it later in the day. Kristen didn't even think he'd brought one away with him. The only person who appears to have brought a copy of the paper away with them is Lewis – well, Hayley told everyone he'd brought a copy, forcing him to admit it. He then claimed he'd given it to Victoria.'

'That's odd. I wonder how the paper came to be there then.'

'I was thinking the same. Interestingly, when the group were discussing the paper, everyone noticed the paper was folded in a way to highlight the story about the young chef Isabelle.'

'Ah, the story you said Victoria had been so upset about and Antoine had thought wouldn't be printed?'

'That's it. Maybe someone placed it there as a kind of warning to Duncan.'

Robert nodded. 'Yes, it's possible. We know Victoria was angry about the story, so maybe that is the reason she went into Duncan's room.'

'Or maybe Antoine placed the paper there as a kind of threat – although why bring the matter up in the conversation with everyone, I don't know.'

'I suppose he may have been concerned you were going to bring up the subject of the paper, and in particular that story, and decided he'd appear less guilty if he brought up the subject.'

Susan shone her torch onto Robert's face. She saw the light in his eyes.

'So, you agree that there could be a case here?'

Robert grinned. 'No, but I am recognising you have found some pretty strong motives for people wanting Duncan out of the way. That, though, does not mean any of them killed him.'

The dogs, possibly remembering their adventure that morning with Robert, dashed into the hedged area where the shack was. Dougie stood at the bottom of the steps, barking.

Susan shone her torch on the steps. Like the rest of the building, they were covered in snow, and Robert laughed. 'We're not going up there again, Dougie. Come on back into the garden.'

Back in the main part of the garden, Susan noticed more footsteps. However, there were no other clues as to anyone being here. No voices, no torchlight. They were surrounded by darkness. In fact, apart from the crunching of their boots, and the shuffling of the dogs, it was unnervingly quiet, even nocturnal. Life had decided to stay unheard, unseen tonight.

They trudged on through the garden, and were about to turn back when Susan made out a silhouette of someone standing at the gate that led out of the garden. As they approached, she recognised Lewis in the torchlight.

'Hi, Lewis. Are you okay?' she asked.

'I'm waiting for Hayley. She's gone up to the Longstone. She wouldn't let me go with her but I'm worried. She's a bit, um, unsteady on her feet. I don't like her being up there on her own. I wish she'd come back. If nothing else, it's bloody cold.' He laughed but sounded nervous.

Susan frowned. Hayley seemed vulnerable. She didn't like to think of her up there on her own. 'We could go on up there if you like, chivvy her along,' said Susan, glancing at Robert, hoping she'd managed to convey her concern with a wide-eyed glance. 'That would be okay, wouldn't it?'

'Of course,' said Robert.

'That's great. Thanks,' said Lewis. 'I worry about her, if you know what I mean.'

'We'll be as quick as we can,' said Susan.

They pushed open the gate and the dogs joined them as they entered the woodland. Susan always brought the dogs here in the spring, loving the heady sight and smell of the sea of blue-bells that grew here. It was hard to believe they were hidden under all that snow, waiting for their chance to peep through.

Once out of Lewis's earshot, Susan expressed her concern to Robert.

'I guessed that was what you were thinking. You did the right thing.'

The clamber up the snowy path was slippery and hard work. Susan was relieved when they reached the top.

The moonlight lit up the downs and they could make out the solitary house where Duncan and family used to stay and the tall, upright Longstone to the right.

Susan could make out the figure of Hayley sitting on the lower, sacrificial Longstone, where she sat as still as the stone itself.

18

'I'll go to Hayley on my own. I've got my torch,' Susan whispered to Robert.

'Good idea. I'll wait here. Don't be long, will you.'

Gem Gem and Dougie stayed with Robert, but Rocco and Libs kept close to Susan as she began to trudge over to the stones, the snow surprisingly deep in parts because of drifting.

She waited until she was very close to Hayley before she spoke. 'Are you okay?' she asked gently.

Hayley remained sitting on the smaller, flatter stone. 'I've been talking to the stones. As I said, they see everything.'

Susan noticed Hayley was slurring her words. Her clothes were wet from sitting on the snow-covered stone. 'Don't you think we should go back down now? You must be very cold. Lewis is waiting for you.'

Hayley didn't seem to hear but stared down at the ground. 'There's a bronze-age barrow under there. Did you know they used to lay the dead bodies out on the ground for the birds and foxes to ravage? They only buried the bones.' She looked up at Susan. 'Alice told me the pretty story about St Catherine throwing this huge stone, how good won control of the island, but that's just a fairytale. No, this is a place of death.'

Hayley pointed into the darkness, in the direction of the solitary house. 'The day had been so beautiful, so hot and sunny. We had fish and chips. I had just finished writing a new story about a family on their holiday, but one of them had an imaginary dragon she kept in her pocket. Anyway, I'd written that and was watching this stunning sunset when all of a sudden it happened. I was plunged into some kind of nightmare.'

Hayley had her eyes screwed up, staring into the darkness.

'Are you talking about the night your mother had the accident?'

Hayley nodded. 'It still haunts me, so much blood. I remember Dad taking us to A and E, sitting in the bright lights of the hospital, everyone so loud. My mother sat holding this blood-soaked towel to her face and people pushed past as if it was normal.'

'It was very traumatic for someone so young.'

'I was ten, not that young, but I was scared. My parents talked to me about it, but I was confused. When you're a child, you believe everything they tell you, don't you? You make things fit around what they say.'

'It was hard for you to understand everything that was happening with your mother.' Susan saw the look of bewilderment on Hayley's face. 'I've been talking to Alice, the lady from the shop. She told me about your mother's addiction.'

Hayley screwed up her eyes. 'She did? I need to go and see her. I've spent most of my life with this mess in my head, and then I spoke to my aunt. In a way it helped, but in others it made it worse. You see, truth is never singular, is it? One truth leads to another and then another. Truth tells you things but then abandons you. I don't think truth is that wonderful, in fact, I think truth is rather cruel.'

For a moment, Susan forgot the cold and the darkness. She only saw Hayley, wrapped up in her fear and her pain. Had she only now started to understand about her mother's addiction? Susan perched on the cold snow-covered stone next to Hayley, reached out slowly, as she would to an injured animal, not sure if it would turn on her in fear. However, Hayley didn't move and as Susan wrapped her arms around Hayley, she felt her melt into her embrace.

'You've been through so much,' she said gently to Hayley. 'You're still in shock from the loss of your father; you're grieving.'

Susan felt Hayley's body tighten and she pulled away. 'Grieving?' Her voice was becoming firmer, the heat in it white hot. 'How can I? I needed answers. Dad should have talked to me but now he's dead. How dare he die? I never thought I'd hate him—' She broke off, her breathing rapid, hands clenched. Suddenly she broke down and started to weep.

'I think we'd better go back now,' said Susan. 'Lewis is down by the gate.'

Hayley slowly turned her head toward Susan, held herself upright, her expression cold now. 'You think he'll look after me?'

'Even if you don't feel you can trust him, there are others in the manor you can. We have to go back.'

Hayley's eyes widened. The vulnerability returned. 'I don't trust anyone back at the house. None of them. I'm on my own.'

Susan placed her hand on Hayley's arm. 'You can talk to me anytime. Day or night. I will always be there for you.'

Hayley looked up at her, her eyes wide and childlike. The confusion on her face seemed to clear. 'Thank you.'

They walked back together to Robert and then back down the path through the woods, where they met Lewis at the gate.

Susan and Robert left them and hurried back to the manor.

'What was all that about?' Robert asked.

'I'm not sure. She's very confused and frightened.'

'She looked unsteady on her feet to me. Had she been drinking? I think that was what was worrying Lewis.'

'I couldn't smell alcohol but some of her speech was slurred. He was right to be concerned. I wonder if she is only just starting to really understand her mother's addiction. Maybe she blames her father: she sounded so angry with him, even said she hated him.'

'What about her and Lewis?'

'She obviously thinks he is having an affair. Interestingly, though, she's not playing the victim there. She's very astute, challenges him. Hayley is an interesting person, the kind it's easy to underestimate.'

They returned through the gate and their own courtyard and let themselves back into the flat where they removed their boots and coats. Once they were all warm, dry, and the dogs were well fed, the animals flopped into their beds, ready for a good night's sleep.

Robert invited Susan to join him and Meera for a drink and to watch TV, but Susan wanted some time to herself. It had been an emotional evening, the confrontation with Antoine and then the upset of seeing Hayley in such distress.

Susan remembered Bryson's book, *Buried at Sea*, and started to read the blurb on the back.

Detective John Strong is taking a well-earned break on a Mediterranean cruise. When the first passenger dies, the death is put down to natural causes... then another guest, sitting at the same dining table, dies. And then another.

Strong has to face it: there is a serial killer on board, but can he find them before they strike again?

Susan opened the book and settled down to read. She was a fast reader and was soon lost in the world of the cruise, gripped as the body count mounted, until she realised it was past midnight. She had to go and lock the front door.

Reluctantly, she put down the novel. Bryson had produced a cracking read. She hadn't expected someone amiable to be capable of plotting such clever murders, even if they were fictitious.

Unlike the previous evening, nobody was about as she went to lock the door and she was able quickly to return to the flat.

Susan noticed that Robert had still not returned but she tried to shrug it off and went to bed, taking the book with her. Eventually she switched off the light and fell asleep.

It was about two o'clock when she was woken by the security light outside. As she got out of bed and peeped through her curtains, she again saw blonde hair glistening in the lights. Kristen was out again, walking away from the manor, and Susan was determined now to go out and find out what Kristen was doing.

She threw her phone into her small bag, pulled on her trousers and a jumper over her nightie, found long socks and went into the main room. She saw Robert's door tightly closed. The dogs looked up at her. She grabbed her coat, boots, torch and keys, gave each of the dogs a treat from her pocket and left the flat. Turning left, she let herself out of the back door and went into the garden.

It was pitch black. She could feel the snow falling, cold on her head, and quickly pulled her hood up. Using her torch, she was able to follow Kristen's freshly made footprints. There were some larger footprints, made earlier Susan presumed, as they'd been made less distinguishable by fresh snowfall.

The footsteps led her to the small area where the little wooden shack was. To her surprise, it was not in darkness, but a light from what she guessed was a torch flickered through the windows.

Susan stood back and watched the shape of Kristen climb the steps carefully, push away new snowfall from the top step, pull open the door and disappear inside.

She tried to creep closer, but a fox started howling, and seemed to disturb the people in the shack, as the light was extinguished.

Part of Susan was desperate to go into the shack, confront Kristen and find out who she was meeting, but she remembered the looks on the faces of the guests when Antoine had accused her of snooping. This was clearly a clandestine meeting. Whoever was in there did not want to be discovered.

Maybe they would be so spooked by the sounds out here that they would decide to abandon their rendezvous and leave. She would watch, see if they came out. As she waited, the snow was still falling and she was aware of the pain in her toes as the cold ate into them. She couldn't stay out here all night.

Eventually the light in the shack turned back on. The snow on the top step was building up against the door. It wasn't going to be easy to push it open, but inside must be warm and cosy. It wasn't out here, though. Susan needed to get back inside the manor.

As she trudged through the snow back to the house, Susan thought about what she'd seen. So, Kristen had been coming out to the shack, and now she knew it was to meet someone. But who was it and why? She hadn't stayed long the night before. Maybe she had come, and he hadn't been there? It had all the appearance of an illicit rendezvous, an affair. If that was the case, then Kristen could have wanted to kill Duncan, not only for money but also to get out of an unhappy marriage. And, of course, if she did have a lover, it gave them a possible motive too. It was one thing to be in love with someone like Kristen but quite another to incur the wrath of her husband when he was a man like Duncan. Susan had seen Duncan threaten Victoria. He was a vindictive man, someone who knew how to ruin people. It might be that someone considered the risk of killing Duncan a better bet than taking him on as a rival who could break and destroy him.

But who could it be? It had been someone coming from the manor, the footsteps showed that, but there were so few men among the guests. The only viable candidates she could think of were Bryson, Lewis or Antoine, but none of them seemed an obvious choice.

Susan was glad to get back to the flat, take off her cold wet clothes and get into bed. However, the cold had crept into her, and she had to get out again to add some layers of socks and a cardigan. Slowly, she drifted off to sleep. She was in a deep sleep when she was disturbed by the security light coming back on. At first, she wasn't even sure where she was. It took a moment to remember that she was staying at the manor. She reached over to her phone. It was half past three.

Slowly it dawned on her that it must be Kristen returning with whoever she'd been meeting. She leapt out of bed, grabbed her dressing gown and went into the living room. In her haste, she fell over a chair. 'Shit,' she shouted. Rocco and Libs were out of their beds and rushed over to her, wagging their tails.

'It's okay,' she assured them, 'back to bed.' Fortunately, Robert did not appear but by the time she'd got back on her feet and made her way to the door, she was sure she was too late to catch Kristen. As she stepped into the deserted hallway, she knew she was right. The floor was wet on her cold feet. At least she knew she hadn't imagined it.

Exhausted, Susan flopped back into bed and eventually she drifted off to sleep. She was woken a few hours later by a thumping sound in the hallway. Groaning, she looked at her watch. It was just gone six o'clock. As much as she wanted to stay tucked up in bed, she forced herself to get up. Maybe it was Kristen returning with the mystery person from the shack? She threw on her dressing gown, opened the door to the flat, and looked out.

What she saw was a complete surprise.

19

SATURDAY, 24 DECEMBER – CHRISTMAS EVE

Susan was surprised to see Lewis leaving by the back door, carrying his sports bag. It seemed very early and dark to be going out for a run.

She watched him close the door behind him and disappear into the darkness. It struck her that Lewis seemed to spend a lot of time creeping around. Hayley could wake up and find he had gone off again. Susan wasn't surprised. She had her suspicions about him. He was always taking calls or sitting out in the car park on his phone. For someone who appeared superficially at least to be a pretty straightforward person, Lewis was surprisingly secretive.

Susan returned to bed and snuggled down to try to catch an extra hour under the duvet but eventually got up when she heard Robert talking to the dogs.

'Happy Christmas Eve,' said Robert. On looking at her more closely, he added, 'You look rough.'

'Thanks! Actually, I had a busy night.'

'Oh, really? What's been going on?'

'It would be better to explain outside,' she said, adding, with a smile, 'Good job it's still dark so no one can see how rough I look!'

They dressed quickly and went out into the garden, taking torches and, of course, the dogs.

Before she could explain anything, Robert coughed nervously. She wondered what he was going to tell her.

'Um, about last night. You know I went up to Meera's?'

Her heart started to race – had they decided to make a go of it together? Susan thought about that kiss on the beach between her and Robert, months ago now – the fluttering in her stomach, the burning of her cheeks, but as she had made it clear, she wasn't ready for commitment. Robert was a free man.

'I know you were up there very late,' she replied, steadying her voice, 'but that's okay. You don't have to explain anything to me.' She was almost pleading. She didn't want details.

'I know, but it must seem a bit odd that I'm up there so late most evenings, especially as you're staying with me. It's difficult. Meera has been pretty stressed with everything that has happened with Duncan. She's needed company. But, well, that's all it is. There's nothing else going on.'

Susan bit her lip and mumbled a thank you. They both knew why he was explaining himself: to let her know he was still waiting for her.

It was so difficult to explain all the reasons she had for not wanting to commit to a new relationship. She wasn't even totally sure herself. It was complicated.

'Are you okay?' Robert asked. 'You've gone very quiet.'

'I'm sorry. Just thinking.' She held her head up and a flurry of snow fell on her cheek. The cold brought her back to the present. 'Come on, we're going this way.' She led Robert to the shack.

'I'd really like to go inside,' she told Robert.

'It's not locked. Let's clear the snow off the steps. We'll be able to get the door open.'

With some effort, they managed to open the door and get inside. It was years since Susan had been in there and she had forgotten how well the space was used to make several rooms in one. Two torches lit up the whole space. There were wooden desks, comfy armchairs, a fireplace, bookshelves, a sink with running water, toilet and shower and, above all this, two bunk beds. Susan read a card that explained:

This shack was used by architects John Seely and Paul Paget as their office and living space when working on the restoration of the manor.

'The reason I wanted to come in here was because I followed Kristen out here in the early hours of the morning.'

'Hang on. You were out here in the dark on your own?'

'I had to know where she was going. There's more. Tell me you don't want to know what I saw?'

He grinned. 'Okay, you win. What did you see?'

'Kristen was meeting someone. I saw the torchlight in here as she approached and there was someone else here. I don't know who, but think about that, Robert. Kristen is having an affair.' She looked around the shack. 'It could be quite romantic, don't you think?'

Robert looked up at the two single bunk beds and grinned. 'Bit of a squash, but you're right: it's cosy in here. It was well known that the architects John and Paul were not just professional partners but were partners in life. Paget said they were a marriage of two minds, practically the same person. It makes this a special place.'

'You're right: it's unique. I would love to know who Kristen was meeting here.'

'You couldn't see?'

'No, it was all very frustrating. I waited for a while to see if they were going to come out together, but it was so cold, I gave up. I figure it had to be Bryson, Lewis or Antoine. It's hard to imagine it being any of them, but they're the only men in the manor.'

Robert pretended to be affronted. 'Apart from me.'

Susan blinked. 'You are joking, aren't you?'

'Ha! Of course I am. Now, as to the others, the only single man is Antoine.'

'He and Kristen don't seem to get on, but I suppose they could be acting. Mind you, I've seen her flirting with Bryson, although I have to say he looked more embarrassed than flattered. He'd be taking a huge risk as well. He could lose his wife and also his new job, which seems pretty dependent on her and her family.'

'What about this young man Lewis?'

'She's quite a bit older but, of course, that may not matter. Duncan mentioned that Lewis is Kristen's personal trainer. There could be something in that. Hayley has her suspicions, and I can see why. He's acting oddly, coming and going all the time, spending hours out in his car on his phone—'

Robert walked around the tiny shack, picking books off shelves, and then opened a drawer that was full of old architectural instruments. He closed it carefully, looked over at Susan. 'I grant it's not unbelievable that Kristen was having an affair with someone, but I'm not sure it gives her a motive. Most people just get divorced. She's a wealthy woman. She didn't need anything from Duncan.'

'I realise that, but Duncan was a powerful, vindictive man. I saw how he threatened Victoria when she accused him over Isabelle's medical records. It wasn't so much his words, but the threat underlying them. You knew his revenge would be cold, calculating and merciless.'

'He was known to be a ruthless businessman—'

'Exactly. And imagine how he would react to his wife calmly asking for a divorce. I can't see him quietly signing divorce papers, can you? He'd want to destroy her or the man she went off with, or even both, and I don't just mean financially. Killing Duncan may be preferable to facing reprisals from him.'

'You have a point. Maybe there's a motive there. How Kristen or this lover killed Duncan, though, is a mystery.'

'Alice suggested it might be something to do with his medication. We'll have to wait and see what the police come back with.'

'I'm getting ready for my breakfast,' said Robert, and they left the shack.

The darkness of the night sky was being replaced by the icy light blue of the day, sprawling white clouds matching the snow below. Susan was also aware that the biting cold had receded.

Although it was still early, Susan remembered that message from Steve. What was this important 'personal matter' he needed to discuss? Maybe she should phone him, find out, and get it over with. She decided now was as good or bad a time as ever and so, when they arrived at the courtyard, Susan took Rocco and Libs, and parted ways with Robert and his dogs. Susan led her slightly confused dogs away from the house and their breakfast, through the archway and up to the car park.

As she crunched over the snow to her car, she passed Lewis's car and, to her surprise, realised he was inside. He appeared to be engrossed in working on his laptop. She wondered why he was working out here, when there was Wi-Fi in the manor.

At her own car, she let the dogs off their leads, and took out her phone.

Her former husband, Steve, answered immediately. 'Susan. It's early, what's happened? Are Zoe and family okay?'

'It's not as early as when you sent me a text at four in the morning,' she replied, trying to steady her voice. 'Everyone is fine.'

'You sound as if you're outside.'

Reluctantly, Susan explained as briefly as she could about staying at the manor.

'Hang on. Didn't I hear Duncan Fern died there?'

'You did. Look, I don't need to talk about that. What was it you wanted to talk to me about?'

20

Standing in the car park, Susan heard the frantic warning call of a blackbird, which she saw was angrily shouting at Rocco for daring to snoop around under the bush. She was waiting for Steve to tell her what important matter he had to discuss. The line had gone quiet, so she urged him to get on with it and tell her what was up.

'Okay. Well, you know the house next door to yours is up for sale? I've been thinking of putting an offer on it.'

Susan suddenly felt an icy coldness spread though her body that was nothing to do with the snow. The shock of what he said stunned her.

'Are you all right, Susan?'

Susan was still catching her breath. The idea of Steve and Hester in 'her' village was horrific.

'You want to live next door to me with Hester?' she stammered.

'No, not live. You know I still have the flat over on the island? Well, I'm not coming over that often, so I'm thinking of buying somewhere to let. The idea was that I would buy the house, let it out, maybe do a kind of Airbnb and then come and stay there when for example Zoe and the family were over.'

'What does Hester think?'

'Well, she has mixed feelings.'

'I'm not surprised. I, well, I don't know what to say.'

'I understand it's a bit of a novel idea, but it's not as crazy as it sounds. I want to do all those things with Jamari that we did with Zoe and the other children when they were little: going down to Brook, picnics on the downs. Wouldn't it be lovely to do them all together?'

Pictures of them all on the beach, sitting on picnic blankets, *her* handing out strawberries from a plastic Tupperware box, Steve creating one of his magical castles out of sand, Jamari in a little white sunhat and striped bathing suit, laughing, flashed through Susan's mind.

She quickly blinked the images away. They were too close to the dreams she'd had before Steve left her. Now, the hurt and resentment would make the strawberries taste bitter. The castle would be nothing more than a heap of sand.

'No, Steve. It's not a good idea.'

'I know you need time to think about it. I've an appointment with the estate agent next week. Of course, you can't actually stop me buying it—'

Susan panicked: he was right. The village didn't belong to her. Anyone could move in, including him. But the thought was devastating. Her new world, her fresh start, would be completely ruined.

'I have to go now,' she said and ended the call, her hand shaking. There were too many emotions to handle. All she knew was that she felt like bursting into tears.

She walked back to the manor in a daze, pushed open the door, noticing the guests were having breakfast.

Meera came out of the office and saw Susan. 'Hi. Can we have a chat about this afternoon?'

'This afternoon?' Susan blinked. Her mind was still replaying that conversation with Steve.

'Are you okay?'

'Um, sorry. I've been speaking to my ex-husband. I'm a bit confused.'

'Look, go and get the dogs dry, and then come to the office. I've a tray of toast and pastries, and some very good coffee. Come and share them and we can chat.'

Once the dogs were sorted and fed, Susan returned to the office, where Meera was sitting in a comfy armchair with the breakfast laid in front of her.

'I allowed myself the luxury of eating in here today. Help yourself. Could you pour the coffee?'

When Susan had poured the coffee, and helped herself to a pain au chocolat, Meera asked, 'Come on. Tell me what happened.'

Susan told her about Steve's proposal.

'Do you want him being next door to you?'

Susan shook her head. 'Of course not, but I suppose he has the right to live where he wants.'

'So, what is this man, your ex, like?'

'He was a brilliant family doctor, a good father to my daughter Zoe and all the foster children who lived with us.' Susan could feel her bottom lip tremble.

Meera looked at her searchingly. 'And that's a good thing. It's much better for Zoe, and all those children that he was kind, and took care of them.'

'You're right. Yes, of course.'

'Can you tell me why your marriage broke up?'

Susan began to describe what had happened.

'So how did you feel the night he told you he was leaving?'

Susan looked down, felt her stomach muscles clench. 'It hurt, um, I felt betrayed.'

Meera didn't reply, but there was an empathy in her eyes that led Susan to talk about her feelings the night Steve left in a way she hadn't done before. She talked about how little she'd said, how she hadn't even cried. But it wasn't because she didn't care. It was because she was in shock and in pain. She hid away a lot of the hurt, felt almost ashamed to tell anyone about it.

'Betrayal by someone you love is terrible. You turn it on yourself, feel it's your fault,' said Meera. 'You see, you can only be betrayed by someone you trusted and, when they do that to you, you feel you should have known, you should have seen it coming.'

'Yes, that's exactly it.'

Susan took a breath, tried to steady herself. 'The split has caused me to lose confidence in my judgement of people. How did I miss that everything was going wrong in my marriage?'

'But why would you? Steve was lying to you. You'd trusted him to tell you the truth, and you were right to. Truth is the basis of trust, and without those things a relationship falls apart.'

Susan nodded. 'I know, and I keep telling myself all that but it's like it's stuck in my head and I don't really believe it down here, in my heart.'

'That takes time, and you'll get your confidence back. You're a strong woman, Susan, I can see that. Meanwhile, you will be vulnerable at times and when you are, you need to take extra care of yourself. I can't help but wonder why, if he's left you and gone off to live his best life, he wants to come back and live next door to you. It's a bit odd, isn't it?'

'I don't think it's been the dream life he'd hoped for. He has some problems with Hester. She's quite extravagant and much more sociable than him. She has some health problems now.'

'For a doctor, he seems to have shown very little foresight. I'd have assumed a job like that would keep his feet on the ground.'

'Maybe he was tired of being sensible, doing the right thing.'

Meera gave a quick nod, conceding Susan's point. 'That may have been the case, but don't fall into the trap of making excuses for him. Women do it all the time for men. He behaved disgracefully to you. He made bad choices, which sounds as if he's starting to regret. But it's not your job to pick up the pieces, to be some kind of security blanket for him. You don't have to let him come and live next door to you because you feel sorry for him. You began this conversation by saying you didn't want him to come and live next door. Why is that?'

'The village is my safe space, my fresh start. But, as he said, I can't actually stop him—'

Meera stared. 'Ah, so he said that. My God, that's awful. What a cruel, mean-spirited thing to say. You hold onto that. Remember he resorted to threats. Be firm with him.'

Susan breathed a sigh of relief, feeling she'd taken off a backpack that had been weighing her down. 'Thank you. It's been really helpful to talk.' She took a sip of her coffee. 'I can see you understand. You said your marriage had broken down?'

'It did, and some time I shall tell you all about it, but not now.'

'I understand. And thank you again for listening to me. I feel a lot better. Now, tell me. What are the plans for today?'

'Well, we have the police coming to give everyone an update later this morning, but I don't think that should take too long. Antoine showed me, online, the obituary he'd written for Duncan in today's *Morning Flame*. It's on the front page, all about his colourful career, charity work and a photo of him at Buckingham Palace. The family should be happy with it.'

'Did it say how he died?'

'Antoine used the line, "Police are saying there are no suspicious circumstances," which seems fair enough.'

'A bit presumptuous.'

'Antoine did get the okay to say that, so I'm not expecting any surprises. Now, I was wondering about getting everyone out this afternoon. Two of the staff have Land Rovers and have offered to give the guests lifts down to the beach.'

'You think we will be able to drive?'

'Yes, I know the gritters have been out. There's been no more snowfall and the temperature has improved. It would be really good if we can get the guests out. Would you be happy to go along? I'd really like to go, but obviously that's off the cards.'

'Of course. Did you have a beach in mind? Have you checked the tides?'

'I understand the tide will be out this afternoon. Which beach would you suggest?'

'I would probably go for Compton. A long sandy beach, and hopefully the steps down are undamaged by the weather.'

'Excellent, and this evening we can hopefully make things a little more festive. It is Christmas Eve, after all.'

* * *

The first Susan knew about the arrival of the police was when she heard voices in the hallway and saw DC Kent and another officer leaving the office with Meera and Robert. They were heading to the library, but Robert hung back to speak to Susan.

'They're going to talk to everyone in the library. You should come and listen. I'm sure it would be okay.'

Susan followed them and the guests came downstairs. They all took comfortable seats and Susan stood at the back, alone.

DC Kent coughed, opened her notebook and started to explain what had been happening. She began by saying that the initial post-mortem had been completed and they had concluded a time of death between about half past two and three o'clock, based on a number of factors: there were only early signs of lividity, rigor mortis had not begun in the face and, although the stomach was empty, the digestion process was not complete.

Once she had explained the time of death, she moved on.

'Now, the cause of death. The post-mortem could find no signs of trauma or violence. Mr Fern had slightly raised alcohol levels, but we knew he'd been drinking at the meal and in the night. The pathologist's initial conclusion is therefore that the cause of death was myocardial infarction. He had a number of heart conditions. He was not a well man. This could have happened at any time and none of you have any cause to think you missed anything or could have done any more than you already had. I can get you a copy of the initial report if anyone would like to see it.'

'So, we definitely know Dad died of a heart issue?' asked Bryson.

'Yes. That's correct.'

'So, can we start to think about Dad's funeral?' asked Hayley.

'There are one or two more tests to be done before the coroner can release the body.'

'What are they? What's wrong?' demanded Antoine.

'Initial toxicology showed nothing out of the ordinary, apart from slightly raised levels of Mr Fern's medications. These just need to be followed up.'

'They think his heart attack was caused by an overdose?' asked Victoria, pouncing on the words.

'Nobody is suggesting that. We just have to check everything out. Mrs Fern was able to give a very full account of how Mr Fern took his medication.'

She glanced over at Kristen, who explained, 'Yes, he took his tablets at about quarter past eleven. He wouldn't let me help but I could see he was very careful. He'd never been one to take medication unless he really had to, and he was scared of taking too many. I heard him count them out before taking them. He didn't need water. He was able to swallow them whole.'

'I can confirm that,' interrupted Hayley. 'I'd seen him take pills like that as well. He hated having to take anything. He'd have been careful to take the right amount at the right time.'

'Yes, and I'm sure he did on Thursday,' said Kristen.

'But what if he'd taken some, say, with his meal earlier, for example, and then later, that would have been an overdose?' asked Antoine.

Kristen scowled. 'He didn't take any at the meal, and I know he took the right amount at bedtime.'

DC Kent spoke firmly. 'We have all the details of the pills Duncan was taking. If he'd taken an overdose of any of them, the reaction would have been very quick. He'd have taken ill, or died, within minutes. We know he died after twelve, and so he couldn't have taken an overdose of anything before that time.'

'But after?' asked Antoine.

DC Kent shook her head. 'We have no evidence for that. Everyone says how careful Duncan was with his medication and certainly no indication whatsoever that he might have wanted to take his own life.' She looked around, giving a reassuring smile. 'I don't want you to worry about the medication. I simply want you to be fully informed. If pathologists have an inconclusive result, they need to follow it up. That's all. Duncan Fern was elderly and unwell. A heart attack, although unfortunate, is not something to be considered out of the ordinary. Now, I would expect the coroner to release Mr Fern's body very soon and then you will be able to organise the funeral.' She sat back. 'I'm very sorry for your loss, and I want you to know you can contact us at any time if you have any concerns.'

'So that's it?' The words shot out of Susan's mouth before she could stop them.

DC Kent closed her notebook, quickly scanned the room, but Susan noticed she avoided eye contact with her. Apparently satisfied that everyone had asked all they wanted, DC Kent and the other officer made their way to the front door, ignoring Susan's question.

Susan could feel the sense of relief in the library. It was as if they had been given permission to breathe again. However, she couldn't say she felt relieved.

Meera stepped forward to tell the guests about the planned trip to the beach that afternoon. Everyone, apart from Kristen, seemed enthusiastic. Meera had been right: they needed to get out. Meera indicated to Susan she would like a word.

Susan followed her to the hallway. 'Just to say, the police have told me we can use Duncan's room now. We don't need it, but I'd like it changed and made to look like a proper room again. Kristen said she'd like to go in as soon as possible to pack up Duncan's things before the cleaners. Take a break. It'll be busy this afternoon.'

Susan went back to the flat, found Robert and told him what had happened.

'Well, that's it. That's the end of the story,' he said.

21

The way Robert seemed to parrot DC Kent's words that the investigation was over irritated Susan. She sat down on the edge of the sofa. 'I don't know why you say that. They didn't explain anything: the window, the newspaper, nothing.'

'I know she didn't explain anything to you personally, but I did get to speak to her with Meera before. They did follow up on your questions and admit there aren't answers to everything. For example, why that window was open. But in view of the results of the post-mortem, they have decided they can remain unanswered.'

'So, they're happy to just let things slide so they can bugger off on their Christmas holiday?'

'That's not fair. It was a miracle the way they got that post-mortem done yesterday, and they really are very sure he died as a result of his heart issues.'

'There's this toxicology report to come.'

'From what I understand, the raised levels detected were small and could be caused by all kinds of variables. Duncan was a very ill man, more unwell than he was letting on to his family.

Honestly, Susan, you have to stand outside this, look at the fuller picture. Here was an older man with significant heart problems who had visited his doctor a week ago with worrying symptoms. The post-mortem showed a long list of things I can't pronounce wrong with his heart, and it was conclusive that a massive heart attack had been the cause of death. There was no evidence, no hint of foul play. That's all the police needed to know. His death was sad, but these things happen all the time.'

'Did they bother to check on anyone's alibis?'

'They asked a lot of questions yesterday, but at three o'clock in the morning everyone was in bed so it was impossible to check alibis. They asked Kristen questions, but what she said was confirmed by someone else.'

'I know you say they're happy now, but they must have at least done a basic check of people's financial positions. Duncan was a wealthy man.'

'None of the family were desperate. Nothing else was suspicious, like Kristen persuading Duncan to take out new life insurance. Everything appears to be above board.'

Susan sighed. Robert was sounding very reasonable, she had to admit.

'I think you're going to have to accept this is finished now,' said Robert. 'Even if you were to find more motives, I can't see how anyone could have done it.'

Susan shook her head and conceded, 'Neither can I. I'd thought maybe it was the hip flask, but they said they were all clear.' Susan sighed. 'But about the lies. Why tell them?' she pleaded. 'Hayley saying she hadn't been in to see Duncan when she had. Victoria insisting she went in because of some ridiculous premonition when I'm sure she went in for that phone.'

'But you haven't found the phone. You can't be sure about it. People lie for all sorts of reasons, some of them quite innocent. We've discovered why Kristen lied about going out, and that probably had nothing to do with Duncan's death. I know what you said about her and this lover wanting to avoid clashing with Duncan, but I'm not sure about it. He was an old man. He might have just as easily accepted a quiet divorce. It certainly wouldn't have been about money. Kristen has plenty of money of her own, Bryson likewise, and Hayley has a lot of savings.'

'Say they are okay for money; it doesn't preclude other motives. Duncan threatened Victoria and Bryson at that meal, as well as Antoine. They didn't seem idle threats to me.'

'They may well have felt threatened by Duncan, but a lot gets exaggerated in arguments. When they all cooled down, I doubt if anyone wanted to actually kill him. Most people die of natural causes.'

She sighed. 'Oh, I don't know, it's all very frustrating. Maybe you're right.'

Even as she said it, though, she knew in her heart that she was not ready to let things lie yet.

'I'll be glad to get down on the beach this afternoon with the guests. Seeing the sea always seems to sort me out. I'm taking Rocco and Libs. Shall I take yours?' she asked.

'Four would be a handful on the beach. Don't worry. I've a few jobs to finish then I fancy a good walk at lunchtime. I'll take them out.'

'Fair enough. I was thinking I ought to go and check on my car: clear it, check it still starts.'

'You're not going to drive this afternoon, are you?'

'No. I guess I'll have to go in the Land Rovers with the rest, but I'd like to check it all the same. These two can come with me.'

Susan put coats on Rocco and Libs, and then kitted herself

out. She left the house by the front door, past the library where all the guests were still seated.

Susan was startled by a noise from above and saw one of the cleaners shutting the window in Duncan's room. As they did, they disturbed the snow on the ledge, and it fell in a clump onto the bush below.

She thought of that first morning, seeing all the snow disturbed down here, and wondering about the fox. Despite the dogs pulling on their leads, she looked back up at the window, closed now. Why had it been open?

She walked through the archway, and carefully climbed the steep steps to the car park where she noticed for the first time the Land Rovers. She guessed they were the ones they were travelling in that afternoon.

Susan walked over to her car and let Rocco and Libs off their leads. They were soon totally engrossed sniffing around the bottom of a hedge close to her car.

She had not been in her car since she arrived, and it was thickly covered with snow. To clear it she needed the scraper, which she knew to be on the floor. Susan roughly brushed off the snow around the door handle and opened it with the key.

Climbing in, she pulled the door behind her, and sat in the driver's seat. It was silent: no birdsong, no rustling of leaves. There was an eerie light inside, any light from outside being filtered through the thick layers of snow. Initially she found it quite thrilling to sit there, hiding away from everyone. Then she heard a crunch in the snow outside, just by the passenger's door. She peered out and could see a shadow. There was someone out there, but she couldn't see who. She felt vaguely unsettled, told herself not to be stupid, to get out and say hello. But something stopped her. She sat listening to the steps, watching the shadow walk around the front of the car, turn. They were approaching the driver's door. Her heart was racing now, and she was very aware of being alone. She needed to get out, escape, and yet she was too scared to move. She watched the shadow stop at her door, and then, without warning, it moved away and disappeared.

She took a deep breath: the dogs were out there; she had to go and check on them. Her hand shook as she opened the door, and she nervously stepped out of the car.

Rocco and Libs were busily sniffing under the bushes. Seeing them engrossed in something so mundane was comforting.

However, Susan then noticed the disturbed snow, the footprints alongside the car. Nausea gripped her stomach. It hadn't been her imagination: someone was here. She glanced around, but couldn't see anyone. The snow was deep, and she realised she was able to track the footprints. There were fresh indentations that had followed hers up the steps, then wandered around the car park, came close to her car and most recently approached a gap in the hedge. Who had made those footprints?

She looked more carefully at them. On television crime programmes they seemed to be able to deduce so much from a footprint, but that was usually in mud, a clear outline of the shoe or boot. These prints were not even foot shaped, but rather deep indentations of varying sizes. The size must depend on how the person had placed their feet and whether disturbed snow had fallen into the hole, further obscuring the print. It was impossible certainly for an amateur like her to deduce much from them. She looked around. Who was this person? Were they watching her at this moment? She started to imagine a huddled figure, wrapped in a hooded coat, the only visible feature red, menacing eyes. She shook her head. No, this wasn't some monster from a horror film. This was a real person who had been watching and following her.

The fear that had threatened to consume Susan was replaced with a rush of anger. How dare someone scare her like this? She would go after them and confront them.

Determinedly, she started to make her way to the gap in the hedge. The footprints continued through the gap, along a short path and then out onto the main footpath.

A nudge against her leg startled her, but she realised Rocco and Libs had come to join her. Taking their leads from her pockets, she attached them to their collars and crept through the gap to the footpath.

On a summer's day, this place would be buzzing with families and dogs, but today it was deserted, the trees leaning over the path, shutting out the light. Before she lost her nerve, Susan began to follow the footprints that went in the direction of the downs.

However, it wasn't long until they came to an abrupt end. It was at a place where the path divided, but there was only undamaged snow either way. Her heart was racing. This person couldn't have just disappeared. Were they behind one of the trees watching her? Was that a breath she could hear?

The long cold branches of fear wrapped themselves around her. She felt trapped.

Rocco started to bark. What had he seen? A frantic rustle in the bush revealed a blackbird.

'Come on, we're going back,' Susan said to the dogs and they hurried back to the car park.

Part of her was desperate to return to the safety of the manor but she had come out to clear the car and if she didn't do it, it would be as if this spectre, imaginary or not, had defeated her.

She let the dogs return to the hedge while she found the

scraper from the car and started to clear the windows. Fortunately the snow came off easily, and she worked her way around the car quickly. All the time, though, she was on edge, looking around, checking she was still alone.

Susan was relieved to finish, lock up the car and call the dogs ready to get away.

As she was leaning over, clipping on the leads, she heard a crunching of snow behind her. She swung round, but there was no one to be seen. But it wasn't reassuring. The feeling it gave her reminded Susan of hiding in those childhood games of hide and seek, waiting for the seeker to come, waiting for them to grab her, declare her found. In the same way she would sometimes give herself away just to get the agony of the wait over, Susan shouted, 'I know you're there. You don't frighten me. Come out. Show yourself.'

Her words were suffocated by the snow. There was no response.

Susan pulled the dogs towards the steps, stumbling in the snow, close to tears. At the top of the steps, she pulled the dogs closer and tried to steady herself. She had to be careful now. She held the dogs' leads in one hand and clutched the snow-covered handrail with the other.

Not long now, just get down the steps and she'd be in sight of the archway leading to the manor.

Gingerly she started to descend. With each step she felt closer to safety, and she'd even started to relax her shoulder when the attack came. Everything happened so quickly. The breathtaking pain from the agonising blow between her shoulder blades, the panic as she found herself falling forwards.

Fortunately, she tumbled onto the concrete platform which broke up the flight of steps, saving her from a much longer fall.

She sat up. Every part of her felt bruised. Somehow, she'd kept hold of the leads and Rocco and Libs licked her face.

Susan glanced up the steps. All that remained of her attacker were footprints in the snow. Her assailant had gone. She covered her face with her hands, started to sob, overwhelmed by so many emotions, relief the spectre had gone, pain from the bruising, anger that someone had done this to her.

Eventually the storm subsided, she pulled herself up and staggered back to the manor. At the front door, she tried to compose herself, took a tissue out of her pocket and attempted to wipe her face.

She was relieved not to meet anyone and went straight to the flat. Her coat and trousers were soaking from melted snow. She hung them up and laid newspaper on the floor beneath them. After giving the dogs their lunch, she went to run herself a hot bath.

As she undressed and examined the red bruise marks on her arms and legs, the horror of what had happened started to sink in. She had been attacked; someone had wanted to cause her harm.

Susan carefully climbed into the bath, tears falling now. Why would anyone do that?

She could still feel that push on her back. This had been no senseless attack by a stranger. This person had targeted her.

Susan cupped warm water in her hands, washed her face and then lay back. She needed to cut through all this emotion, try and think straight.

She remembered when she first looked around the car and tracked the footprints of this person. They had come up from the steps, and logically that was most likely from the manor.

It strongly suggested that the attacker was someone staying at the manor.

The next question had to be why. Why did someone attack her? Of course, it could be simply spite. Someone may have taken a strong dislike to her. But it felt more calculated than that. Not only would this person have caused her pain with that fall, but she could also easily have broken a limb, or been even more seriously hurt. She would have been sent to hospital or sent home: either way she would be out of the way.

Susan sank deeper in the bath. Why did someone want her out of the manor? That attack had happened after the visit from the police. They had assured everyone that Duncan's death appeared to be the result of natural causes. However, she had then blurted out in response, 'So that's it?'

Susan sat up. Of course, she had made it clear that she wasn't happy the case was closing. Now, if there had been no suspicious circumstances around Duncan's death there would be no one to be alarmed by that. However, the fact someone felt threatened by her showed there was someone with something to hide. But who was it?

They had all been in the library when she'd left the manor earlier. They all knew she'd gone out. Any of them could have followed her, so that was no help.

Surely she'd noticed something when she was out there in the car park? It was so hard. All she remembered were footprints made by boots in the snow, which told her nothing.

Then Susan remembered reading that a criminal unconsciously always gave away something about themselves when they committed a crime. Had her attacker showed her anything about themselves in the way they attacked her?

Well, there had been a calculation in their movements. They had been following her, watching her. They'd hadn't simply rushed up behind her. This was someone who planned, thought ahead.

Also, there had been no weapon involved, so no proof of another person's involvement. If Susan had been hurt, the fall might well have been put down to an accident. The outcome was less easy to predict, but it gave maximum protection to the assailant.

So she had learned her attacker was someone who planned, thought ahead, was willing to take a chance on the level of hurt they inflicted. It also showed someone who saw violence as an acceptable way of resolving their problems.

Realising the bath water was no longer warm, Susan climbed out, carefully patted herself dry. She could feel her muscles tightening up all the time and she walked stiffly back to her bedroom.

She felt she'd come a long way in her thinking. Most importantly she'd learned that there was a case here, someone was hiding something and she was convinced that secret was the killing of Duncan Fern. That killing had been by someone who planned but also took calculated risks, someone who believed violence was acceptable. She had no idea which of the guests it was, or how they'd done it, but she was sure now one of them had killed Duncan Fern.

She remembered Alice's words about being careful: she might be sharing this beautiful old manor with a killer.

Susan shivered as the true horror of her situation started to sink in. This person would soon discover that their attempt to get rid of her had failed. She was under no illusion that this would be the end. No, they would try again. Next time they might be less subtle, more daring. Susan had no idea what they might try next time: the only thing she could be sure of was that they were definitely going to try again.

22

After lunch, Susan found herself reluctant to join the guests she could hear gathering in the library. How was she meant to smile at them all, believing that one of them had attacked her earlier that day?

Of course, she could pack her bags and leave. If she told Robert what had happened, he would want her to go home. But Susan knew she couldn't just walk away. Firstly, she felt an obligation to Meera. Also, she knew that if she left and there was a killer here, it was highly likely they would get away with it. She couldn't allow that. Finally, there was something inside her that refused to be frightened off by an anonymous stranger. No, she would stay, but she had to be careful.

As they split into groups to travel in the Land Rovers, Susan realised Kristen wasn't with them, apparently having preferred a quiet afternoon. There was an excited air; Meera was right: everyone needed to get out.

The car park at Compton Bay was empty apart from a few surfers' vans.

Even on a freezing cold day, Susan loved the view over to the cliffs of Tennyson Down. Snow coated the clifftops, and the wind was sharp and cold in her face. The Tennyson Monument was a smudge at the top of the cliff.

'We need to be careful going down the steps,' she said. 'They could be slippery.'

Susan approached the wooden steps nervously, looking over her shoulder to see who was behind her. She let Rocco and Libs off their leads so that they didn't unbalance her. As she climbed down, she was aware of how stiff and bruised she felt from the fall that morning.

However, it was good to be down on the beach. It was a relief to leave behind the claustrophobia of the manor, to breathe in fresh salty air, to feel that sense of freedom that came with the sight of the sea and miles of sandy beach.

Rocco and Libs ran ahead but she knew they would keep away from the cold sea. Susan spotted Victoria walking on her own and went to join her. She was aware she had some bridges to build between them. She started to ask her about her work as a restaurant critic. Victoria spoke about some of the restaurants, some with measured enthusiasm but, more interestingly to Susan, vividly describing the more disastrous experiences. What really intrigued Susan, though, was when Victoria started describing the disguises she sometimes wore.

'I take measures to prevent people recognising me. I have a range of wigs and glasses. Sometimes I even put on accents. I'm good at them.' She grinned. She clearly enjoyed it. This was another side to Victoria; one Susan hadn't expected to see.

'That sounds exciting. I've also read some of your interviews. I feel I get to see a different side of people.'

Victoria turned her smile softer now. 'Thank you. That's what I'm hoping to achieve. People unwind and talk in a way they wouldn't if you were just sitting in a room opposite each other. Eating together is very important. Our parents insisted on us all sitting together for the evening meal.'

'I met Hayley up at the Longstone,' said Susan. 'She has some difficult memories of her time staying up by there.'

'Yes, she's told me about them, and so has Bryson.'

'I hear their mother had addiction problems.'

Victoria looked at her sideways, picked up a pebble and rolled it between her fingers. 'It was so sad. She sounds like she was a very good mother, very kind, very devoted. Bryson says she taught them to be respectful of everyone, never wanted them to get spoiled. He remembers not going on some trip. Hayley wasn't allowed a car until she was twenty-one. But Duncan wanted to help them both buy their first homes. When Bryson dropped out of university, Duncan set him up with a flat, and gave him work at the paper until, well, his books took off.'

'It's all working out well for Bryson now, though. It must be exciting for him to be on TV. I shall be watching.'

Victoria smiled. 'He'll be very good on a chat show. He has a way of making people feel relaxed.'

'I'm sure he will be very good. So, how did you and Bryson meet?'

Victoria breathed in the sea air. 'It was quite romantic. We met on one of those arty chat shows. He was talking about his books. I was there talking about writing my column. We got chatting in the green room after. He asked me out and on the first date confided in me. He was so frank and open. It was love at first sight. Anyway, my dad had seen him on that programme, thought he was a natural and started giving him odd spots on other programmes. It went very well. Now my dad thinks he is ready for his big break. It's going to be the making of him.'

At that moment, Bryson caught them up and put his arm around Victoria. 'This fresh air is good for us. We used to come here when I was little. It's brilliant here in the summer, half empty if you walk along a bit.'

Bryson looked ahead at Hayley and Lewis walking hand in hand. 'I was so glad to give Hayley the news about the money. Of course, the circumstances are terrible, but it will solve a lot of problems for her.'

'I was surprised when you said last night she was having financial problems,' said Victoria. 'I didn't realise. I thought she had a lot of savings. Your father has been putting money into an account for her. I know that much.'

Bryson lowered his voice, came closer to Victoria, and Susan moved slightly away, sensing this was a confidential matter.

'It's not that straightforward. The money Dad gave her as a deposit for the flat: she actually gave it to Lewis to put down a deposit on gym premises.'

Susan's ears pricked up. Although she had moved, she could still clearly hear what Bryson was saying. He seemed to have totally forgotten she was there.

'Why on earth did she do that?' asked Victoria. 'She hasn't known Lewis for long. She shouldn't be throwing money at him.'

'I agree. She knows it was reckless and she was scared of what Dad would say. She's been trying to cover it up by raising the deposit herself, taking loans from some pretty dodgy people, huge rate of interest and far more than her savings will cover. They're demanding the money back now.'

'Oh my God. How do you know all this?'

'Hayley was very drunk one night, told me a lot of it, showed me her account. The rest I found out.'

'Why didn't you tell me? We must help her.'

'I know. I was going to speak to you this weekend and then, well, Dad died, and now I know she's okay.'

'But we could still support her.'

'Of course, but don't mention this to her. I don't want to embarrass her but we must keep an eye on her.'

Susan was looking out at the grey churning sea, the white foam dancing on the waves. However, she was also paying close attention to what Bryson was saying. So, Hayley needed money, was in a fix and it was something the police had not picked up on. Furthermore, she didn't like what she was hearing about Lewis. Not only was he being unfaithful to Hayley, but he had also accepted a lot of money from her. No wonder Hayley was getting so upset.

They had reached the end of the beach, where the cliffs met the sea with nothing in between. Those ahead waited for them. 'Let's go back now,' Susan suggested.

The walk back was more challenging as the wind which had brought the snow was from the east, but the party made it back to the steps and the car park without incident and the Land Rovers took them back to the manor.

Most of the guests changed their damp, cold clothes, and gathered in the library for fresh mince pies, baked biscuits, crumpets, and hot drinks. Meera came out to tell them when the evening meal would be. Bryson suggested they all bring down their hip flasks of whisky as it was Christmas Eve, and it was what Duncan would have wanted. Hayley came through the front door carrying a large log.

'This is our Yule log,' she announced. She spoke like a priest going through a kind of ritual, her voice measured and steady. 'Yule is the name for the winter solstice festivals. This log is meant to be lit on Christmas Eve and, although ours may not burn for twelve nights, it is symbolic of hope, renewal, and the turning of the seasons.'

She took it over to the fire and placed it on the coal and

smaller logs. They watched as the flames reached around it. Satisfied, Hayley sat down.

Antoine suddenly arose. 'Well, I think we'll add another tradition to this.' He left them and disappeared upstairs, soon returning with a rectangular box.

'This is one of my family's nativity sets. We would always put them out on Christmas Eve. I shall arrange it on this table not too far from the fire.'

'Oh, a crèche,' said Lewis.

'Yes, that's right,' said Antoine, smiling.

'Wait. I'll bring down the wreath I made,' said Hayley. She returned with a small intricately woven wreath and placed it by the nativity set.

'I'd like to go to mass this evening,' said Antoine.

'Meera has left details in the folders in our rooms. They hold a Midnight Mass in the Anglican church over the road,' said Hayley.

'Good,' said Antoine. 'I'm Catholic, but that's okay by me.'

Meera took Susan to one side. 'Could you pop to the kitchen, ask them to make up a tray for Kristen? I haven't seen her, and she must at least need a cup of tea or something.'

'More like vegetable smoothie. I'll check with Gary, see what smoothies she liked and if he has any other ideas of what to take up.'

Gary reluctantly made up a smoothie and added some cake, sandwiches and tea which Susan took up to Kristen's room. She knocked gently on the door and Kristen summoned her in.

Kristen was sitting in an armchair reading her tablet. As always, the smell of expensive perfume enveloped her. She was wearing a white mohair fitted dress, diamond jewellery, and animal-print boots. Her hair was stiff blonde curls. Susan was

reminded of a character she had once seen in a series of
Dynasty.

Kristen's look was eighties power-dressing, designed to shout
wealth, status. But it was as if she was a child grabbing all the
shiny clothes from the dressing-up rack, trying to play the part
of someone rich and famous.

Kristen looked surprised when she saw the tray. 'Oh, thank
you, but I didn't order that.'

'Meera was wondering if you would like a drink, something
to eat.'

'That's kind. I never eat that much. I'm even less hungry
today.'

'You've had a terrible shock.'

Susan placed the tray on the table next to Kristen, who leant
over, picked up a piece of shortbread, but held it over the plate,
crumbling it between her thumb and forefinger.

'Yes, I suppose I have. He was older than me, of course, and
not that well, but Duncan had that energy that made me feel he
might go on forever. It's hard to imagine *The Morning Flame*
without him.'

'Do you think Antoine will make big changes?'

'Maybe. He's more cautious, but I don't think he would have
misjudged the Isabelle story the way Duncan did.'

Susan blinked. Somehow, she didn't expect Kristen to have
any interest in the paper or Duncan's work. She had put Kristen
in a box and labelled it: not bright, only interested in money and
pleasure. Married an older rich man, prepared to have other
men on the side. It was all too easy, and yet as Kristen spoke now,
Susan saw a deeper understanding in her eyes. She was more in
control than Susan had given her credit for.

'In what way do you think he misjudged it?'

'Duncan should have left Isabelle alone. He looked like a bully. Also, this business about the abortion. Victoria isn't the only one to be asking questions about how he got hold of that information. Duncan used to sound off about their great circulation numbers and everything, but I know he was worried. Everything is changing; the clamour for news is frantic now. He was getting desperate for the old-style scoop and that clouded his judgement.' Kristen paused, then added, 'I'm sorry if this sounds disloyal. I loved Duncan more than anyone knew, but I wasn't blind to his faults. I also knew that he would never love me the way I loved him. He would never love anyone as much as his first wife Nancy. He wore that signet ring she gave him even on our wedding day. We didn't exchange rings. He never wore one for me. He was straight, honest with me, generous, kind, but there would always be a limit to how much he loved me. I understood.'

Kristen spoke in a very pragmatic way, but even the fact she was talking about it made Susan wonder if she had been secretly hurt.

'I had noticed Duncan's signet ring.'

'It has Nancy's and his initials engraved on it.' She laughed coldly. 'Nancy was lucky. I've never been loved like that.'

Kristen, for all her outward glamour, suddenly looked very sad and neglected. Susan felt sorry for her.

'It was good of him to leave me that money. I hadn't expected it,' continued Kristen. She gave an awkward laugh. 'It looks a bit suspect, doesn't it? Me losing two rich husbands in a row. Good job the police are so sure he died naturally. Anyway, I was able to explain what I was doing at the time Duncan died, and that is that.'

She looked hard at Susan. There was a warning in her eyes to back off. Susan decided to ignore it and continued, 'Why do you think that window was open, by the way? It was odd, wasn't it?'

Kristen put her head to one side. 'If the police aren't worried, neither am I, and,' she added with emphasis, 'neither should you be, Susan.'

Susan blinked. 'Sorry?'

Kristen's voice had changed. There was no wistfulness there now, no softness. 'You know what I'm talking about. All the snooping around you did. Watching out your window, sneaking around our landing at night, passing on messages to the police about us all. I'm surprised at how much you've noticed, thought about it all. After all, you're just staff.'

Susan's eyes widened. 'Just staff? Maybe you have a habit of underestimating people you see as "just staff". It doesn't mean they're not as bright or capable as someone who, through the roll of a dice or wealthy family, has ended up flying around in private jets.'

Kristen raised her eyebrows. 'Goodness. I hadn't expected some Marxist rant.'

She got up from her chair, stepped closer to Susan. 'Look, I'm trying to help you. I heard you question that police officer. You're still not satisfied, are you? What you're doing is threatening us all, and some of the guests here know how to fight dirty. People like Antoine are experts at digging up guilty secrets. They can even take something fairly innocent from a person's past, blow it up and, by the time they've refuted the insinuations, the mud has stuck. Their reputation is in tatters.'

Susan caught her breath. This was clearly aimed at her, but what could a journalist like Antoine ever dig up on her? She mentally flicked through the album of her own past, frantically searching for anything she would want to keep hidden.

Flashes of that time she smoked pot at a festival, those

vindictive parents of children she taught who for some reason stirred up a vendetta against her: they'd say anything for the right price. And there must be other examples. At the end of the day, the press could build something out of nothing and it would be there, online forever. One day Jamari could find it, and Zoe would have to explain the pack of lies that had been written about her nanna.

Susan looked up. Kristen was watching her.

'You see. It's scary, isn't it?' said Kristen. 'It could happen to anyone. It could happen to you. So, stop stirring up trouble, Susan. Get on with your job and leave us alone.'

23

Back in the flat, once Susan had calmed her mind, she realised that the last thing Kristen had achieved was to put her off the investigation. On the contrary, it had a similar effect to the push down the steps in the car park. Why make all these threats if there was nothing to hide?

Susan was reminded of the larks up on the downs, trilling in the sky in the hope of distracting predators from their nests. Maybe it worked in nature, but for Susan, the singing actually alerted her to the fact there was a nest nearby.

The conversation with Kristen had been illuminating. There had to be a reason Kristen had told Susan that her last husband who had also died suddenly had been a rich man. Maybe Kristen was worried Susan would find out another way and assume she had been hiding it. Kristen had also been quick to refer to her alibi. She was clearly threatened by Susan, and all that must mean she had something to hide. Susan made herself a drink, sank into the sofa, and tried to relax. However, as she was closing her eyes, her mind took her rushing back to the exact moment of that morning's attack. She felt the freezing air biting into her face, was staring down at the snow-covered steps, when she felt that sharp, violent push between her shoulder blades and saw the steps rushing towards her.

The experience was so vivid she gasped in pain and when she opened her eyes, she felt her heart thumping.

Weary of closing her eyes again, Susan decided distraction might be a better way of unwinding and picked up Bryson's book, *Buried at Sea*. She had been close to the end when she'd had to abandon it the night before. It might be a good idea to see how the mystery was resolved.

Reading proved to be exactly the escape she needed and she was soon lost in the fictional world of murder and intrigue. The plot was gripping; there were twists and turns that kept her guessing. The final revelations laid out by Detective John Strong were complete and satisfying.

Susan laid the book down. It had been a good read. She must congratulate Bryson. She particularly liked the method which had stayed a mystery right through the book. Each victim had died at the dining table. The first victim was assumed to have died from an overdose of drugs they were taking recreationally. However, the next person had no history of drug taking and their sudden death was harder to explain.

One thing all the victims had in common was that they all ate at the same dining table. No traces of poison were found in any of the food or drink. It was up to the detective to spot the crucial point that they all drank wine from the set of identical crystal glasses. He worked out that the killer had put poison in the victim's glass, but once they'd drunk out of it, she swapped the glass for an unadulterated one, made an excuse to leave the table, then threw the glass with traces of poison into the sea.

It was a clever plot, and Susan was pleased to be caught out by it. However, the coincidence of reading about an unexplained apparently accidental death while trying to answer questions about Duncan's was not lost on her. It did cross her mind that possibly the book itself, written by Bryson but apparently read by most of the guests, had given someone ideas.

Looking at her watch, Susan realised it was time for the evening meal. Grabbing her recorder and music, she made her way to the Great Hall where the guests were already seated, ready for the first course. She slipped into her seat and began to play.

Bryson sat at the head of the table, with Victoria on one side and Hayley on the other, next to Lewis. Bryson was being particularly attentive to Hayley, passing her breadsticks and olives, filling her glass. Next to Victoria sat Antoine, then Kristen, who wore a very sparkly dress, although it was black, possibly in a slight concession to mourning.

There was a quiet atmosphere this evening. Each of the guests had brought down their silver hip flasks as suggested by Bryson. The first courses were brought in and Bryson gave a toast to Duncan as they charged their flasks. The table was set with candles and the intricate Celtic design on the hip flasks caught the light. The guests each took a sip from their hip flasks and were about to start their meals when Antoine surprised them by making a further toast to Duncan, talking of his accomplishments at the paper. Susan noticed that Lewis and Hayley were sharing a hip flask, although of course she didn't know whose they had brought down. The flasks were all the same.

The thought was shouting in her head: all the same. Remember the book, remember *Buried at Sea*. The killer had added the drug to his victim's wine in one of the ship's beautifully cut wine glasses. After the fatal sip, the killer swapped the victim's glass for his own, a clever sleight of hand. No one noticed – all the glasses were the same.

Was it significant that everyone had an identical hip flask to Duncan? Had that given someone an idea, possibly someone who had read *Buried at Sea*?

As Susan continued to play the recorder, and the guests ate, her mind kept working. In the book, the glasses had been switched. The glass used by each victim was found to be uncontaminated. Had the killer added drugs to Duncan's hip flask, knowing he drank at night? Then somehow, had they returned and swapped Duncan's flask for their own clean one?

Susan closed her eyes. The recorder piece was easy: she could play it automatically. She needed to try to get inside the mind of the killer.

Tonight, I will kill Duncan. I don't want anyone to suspect he was killed. An overdose of his medication – that's it. Not too much: enough to kill, but not to show up as unusual on a post-mortem. I've nothing to lose as long as I don't get caught. I need him to take these meds when I'm not around. Of course, he has a slug of whisky in the night. Ideally, the meds would be in that. But how? If I can get them in that hip flask, if I'm lucky, he'll drink it.

First, I will sneak in and pinch some of his pills. He'll never notice a few missing. Next, I need to get into his room and add crushed pills to his flask. But the mouth of the hip flask is so tiny. I can't afford any of the mixture to spill. It would be found.

All the hip flasks are the same. I could add the crushed pills to some whisky in my own flask. It will be so much easier to creep in and swap the flasks once Duncan is asleep. If he was to wake... I'll make an excuse, but I should be okay.

Susan stopped to think. Yes, so far, so plausible. But what next?

After twelve, any time before half past two or even three, I creep out of my room carrying my flask with the drugs in. The hallway is deserted. Enter Duncan's room, which will be in darkness. I can hear him breathing. Keeping the flashlight on my phone facing down by my feet, I creep over to the bedside table, pick up Duncan's flask and cup, replace them with mine.

Susan thought about the layout of the bedside table.

With the flask I place the newspaper.

And then Susan remembered the phone. She believed Victoria took that. The killer could even be Victoria, swapping the flasks and taking the phone at the same time.

I go back to my room, it's done. But I mustn't sleep. If I don't go back to take the contaminated flask, everyone will know. I wait a few hours. It's a guessing game but I daren't leave it any longer. This is no longer the middle of the night. It's still dark but people will stir at noises now.

I get out of bed, pick up the flask I took from Duncan's room, go back into his room. I can't use the light on the phone but somehow I find my way to the bedside table. All is quiet, too quiet. Is it possible he's dead? Hands shaking, I turn on the phone light, and inch the beam towards Duncan, look at the unseeing eyes staring at the ceiling. The enormity of what I've done starts to sink in. I've killed a man. Duncan is dead.

Quickly, I swap the flasks. I replace the silver tot cup from the flask next to the bed, carefully arranging it, pour a little whisky in. I have the flask with the drugs in… I need to get out…

Susan paused, what next? What would the killer do next?

24

A clatter of dishes brought Susan back to the present. She was surprised to see the guests were finishing their main course, and she was sitting holding her recorder. She had stopped playing.

She quickly started again. She would need to carry on thinking later, but she was excited, convinced she had finally found a way someone could have killed Duncan. If this was the way things had happened, the time frame of the murder was much longer than she'd first thought. Anyone could have gone into Duncan's room once he was asleep and swapped the flasks, returned later and swapped them back.

After the meal, the guests sat around having a drink by the fire while Susan went up to turn down the beds. She needed to check the rooms again.

Susan went to Bryson and Victoria's room first, and started with the wardrobes where their cases were stored. The cases were empty.

She stood, staring at Victoria's neat array of teas, well used compared to Bryson's coffee beans, which were still unopened.

She repeated the search she had undertaken the day before,

pulling open drawers, looking under the bed, the pillows, even going through the sponge bags in the bathroom, searching among the stack of towels. She found nothing.

She sat on the edge of the bath, frustrated. Where was that damn phone?

Susan decided there was no point in going over the room again. In any case, the guests could come up any moment. She needed to get on, so moved on to Hayley's and Lewis's room. This seemed even more of a mess than before, but a quick search revealed nothing new.

She was about to cross over to Antoine's room but looked up the hallway. She was curious to return to Duncan's room. Kristen had been in to remove his belongings. The cleaners had changed the bedding. But she still wanted to revisit the room. Maybe it would jog her memory, remind her of some detail she'd forgotten.

Susan let herself in, turned on the light, and walked over to the bed. It felt so strange, almost sterile, as if someone had worked hard to remove any hint of death from it. The message was that nothing untoward had happened in there. And yet Susan knew better. Maybe one day there would be stories of the ghost of an old man being seen in there.

Susan sat on the edge of the bed, tried again to get inside the mind of the killer. Her mind went back to *Buried at Sea*. What had the killer done after swapping those glasses back? That was it: she had wandered up on deck, pretending she needed a cigarette and, in the darkness, thrown the glass overboard. The evidence was buried at sea.

Susan wandered over to the window, opened it, looked down. From her pocket she took a pen and dropped it, holding her torch to see where it landed. It went straight down, disappeared behind the bush. Was it possible the flask was still down there? She had to look.

Susan felt her heart race with excitement, a broad smile spread across her face. Had she really discovered the way the killer had murdered Duncan?

Before she went back downstairs, she went through Kristen's and then Antoine's rooms. As she pulled Antoine's door behind her, she nearly collided with Antoine, who was coming out of Hayley's and Lewis's room. He looked startled, guilty even.

'Can I help you?' Susan asked.

'No, no. It's okay. I went in the wrong room. Too much to drink.' He retreated into his own.

Susan didn't believe him, but why would he be in Hayley's room? There was no time to think about that now. She went back downstairs and was relieved to see that there was nobody about. She nevertheless crept quietly to the front door, and went outside, pulling the door behind her. The cold bit through her dress. She should have put a coat on, but it was too late to fuss with that now.

She shone the light from her phone at the base of the bush. There was less snow there now and she could see specks of mud, but her arm got wet as she pushed back the branches to examine the ground behind the bush. Her heart sank. There was nothing to be seen, apart from the pen which she had dropped, and which she picked up. However, her torchlight caught a gleam of something on the wall. She leant forward, and saw it was a scraping of silver. Looking up, this was directly below Duncan's window. If the killer had wanted to be sure the flask landed behind the bush, they needed to drop it straight down, and that would have meant there was a danger of the flask scraping the wall.

Susan examined the scrape more closely; she was sure it was

silver. She knew how soft silver was as a metal. She had watched a friend etching on a silver ring, seen the silver peel away. Her friend had said that because of its purity, fine silver could be a nightmare to work with but its beauty and lustre made all the hard work worth it.

But where was the flask? Unlike the killer in the book, this one couldn't simply throw it into the sea. Would they have taken it back to their room, washed it out, and have been using it that evening? She had not been looking carefully to see whether one had a scratch on it.

Susan returned to the flat and changed into dry clothes. There was nothing more she could do this evening. Everyone had their flasks with them. But she was determined to look the next day.

Susan decided to go to Midnight Mass with the guests and a number of staff. She gave the dogs a quick walk and then joined everyone to walk to the church at twenty past eleven.

The group were still quite subdued. Hayley was clinging on to Lewis's arm and he was glancing down at her, looking concerned.

They left the manor and crunched through the snow. As they approached the church, the bells rang out for the first service after sunset, the start of Christmas.

There was something strange but reassuring about joining the locals, people divorced from the drama of the manor, smiling, wishing each other a happy Christmas. Susan was pleased she had come. It was the first time this year she'd really felt any of the Christmas spirit, and she recognised a few people from the village. Although Bishopstone had its own church, St Jude's, they took it in turns with this much smaller church to host Christmas Eve mass.

Tracy came over and gave her a hug. 'Lovely to see you. I was so sorry about the tragedy at the manor.'

'Thank you. Yes, it's been difficult for the family.'

'Not what Meera needed, was it?' Susan could see Tracy was fishing for more, but fortunately they were being hustled into the church. It was lit with candles, and pleasingly full. The vicar was new, a young woman. She gave them all a warm welcome.

It was good to sing Christmas carols, to listen to the familiar Christmas readings, to hear a message of peace and hope. At the end, everyone hugged, wishing each other a very happy Christmas. It was a perfect start to the celebrations.

For a moment, Susan wished she could forget all the qualms about Duncan's death, simply enjoy Christmas and that exciting call tomorrow with Zoe, sharing her granddaughter's first Christmas. But she couldn't do that. The conviction that the truth mattered was part of her DNA, and she wanted her granddaughter to grow up in a world where people were prepared to fight for it.

The party crossed the road, walked back toward the manor and made their way back to the library. Everyone, staff, guests, Meera and Robert, were there, standing in front of the fire drinking port, nibbling chocolates. Susan's only concern was Hayley, who seemed very unsteady on her feet now and was helped into a chair by Lewis. Susan caught Bryson looking over at Hayley, noting the concern on his face. However, he stayed with Victoria and the atmosphere remained cordial.

Eventually the gathering broke up and people started to retire to bed. Robert said he was going to watch a film with Meera. He invited Susan along, but she was exhausted and said she was ready for bed.

The dogs greeted her, and she opened the patio door to let

them run. Finally, she was able to settle them for the night and get ready for bed.

As she did, she was aware of footsteps outside and of the security light coming on. Was this Kristen going out to meet someone again? She was desperate to know, so pulled on her coat and wellies, rushed out of the flat and out through the back door. However, she stopped quickly as she realised that whoever had left had not gone far. She heard someone talking, she guessed on their phone.

'If only he could come,' they were saying. It must have been the smell of cigarette smoke that jogged her memory, because suddenly she was transported back to the night Duncan died. The voice was louder but held the same urgency and she knew for sure this was the voice which spoke those words, 'If only he could die.'

She crept closer to the edge of the wall and peeped around the corner.

Susan came almost face to face with Victoria who, startled, dropped her cigarette and ended the call.

'You've discovered my guilty secret,' she said. 'Bryson would be horrified if he thought I'd started smoking again. Also, it's a bit of a no-no in the world of restaurant critics. Our taste is the most important of our senses. Doing anything to damage it is anathema, and what could be worse than smoking?'

Susan wasn't really listening. All she was thinking was that this was the person she heard the night Duncan died. Before she could stop herself, the words came flooding out. 'It was you. You were speaking that night.'

'Sorry, what are you talking about?'

'The night Duncan died. It was after dinner but before I'd locked up, not long before twelve. I was cleaning my boots and I heard voices on the other side of this wall. One said something about Duncan, then the other, and I'm sure it was you, said, "If only he could die."'

'No way—'

'Yes. I know it was you. I smelled the smoke. It was you speaking.'

Susan watched Victoria pause, clearly deciding how she was going to respond. When she did, she spoke slowly, choosing her words with care. 'You did hear me. I'll concede that, but there was a context for those words. I'm not prepared to say who the conversation was with and that's all I am going to say on the matter.'

Susan knew she had to accept this and changed tack. 'Duncan died later that night. You must know how this looks.'

'I'm not discussing it.'

'You've admitted to going into Duncan's room.'

'I've explained that: it was a premonition. I wasn't looking for anything.'

'Really? That's a lie, and you know it.'

'Enough,' said Victoria. Her voice shook with anger. She was clearly rattled. 'I'm not justifying myself to you any more. I've told you why I went into Duncan's room. I wasn't looking for anything. You need to stop messing about. This is dangerous, Susan. Just stop.'

Victoria pushed her out of the way so roughly that Susan stumbled back, fell against the wall, and banged the side of her head. For a moment she felt dizzy, shocked not just by the pain but what felt like an assault.

Stunned, Susan made her way back into the house, and to the flat. She was relieved to close the door behind her. Her head hurt so she checked it in the mirror. It wasn't bleeding, just sore to touch.

Susan went into her bedroom, peeled off her clothes. Her

head thumped as she leaned forward. Her back hurt. The bruises on her legs were dark and ugly. As she touched them gently, she started to shiver, and not simply from the cold. As much as the bang to her head upset her, it was the attack that morning that still shocked. She could feel the fear starting to wrap itself around her again. Those injuries had been caused intentionally. The person who pushed her didn't care how much pain they inflicted. She fought her mind that seemed to want to drag her back to the moment of that violent push. Quickly she grabbed her nightie, a cardigan and socks, climbed into bed and curled up like a cat in her duvet, trying to get warm.

Tomorrow would be Christmas Day. Susan could only hope that the peace and goodwill that had been lacking over the past few days might finally be part of the season's celebrations at the manor.

25

SUNDAY, 25 DECEMBER – CHRISTMAS DAY

When Susan awoke on Christmas morning, she was relieved that, despite everything that had happened the day before, she felt that familiar thrill which took her back to her childhood. Christmas had been the one day her busy parents set aside for family. They weren't great present givers, but she still found a stocking of good books, beautiful sketchbooks and, the best thing of all, a chocolate Father Christmas. Not forgetting her one aunt who would always send her a doll or, as she grew older, jewellery or make-up.

Glancing at her phone, she saw that it had managed to download a text sent in the early hours from Zoe wishing her a happy Christmas. It warmed her heart and she resolved to make a determined effort to take time off the investigation and celebrate this special day. She tried to reply to Zoe but the text didn't send because the signal had dropped.

Although she guessed Zoe might well have gone back to sleep, she decided she wanted her to see a reply first thing. It wouldn't take Susan long to go up to the car park. She could also suggest a time for them to arrange a Zoom call that morning.

Susan got out of bed as quietly as she could, hoping not to disturb Robert in the next room, and dressed without showering. She whispered to the dogs that she would be back soon to take them for a walk.

She popped on her coat, left the flat and approached the front door. Unlocking it, she hung the key back up and went outside.

It was still dark, but that freezing edge of the past few days was missing. The snow was still thick on the ground but there was less of a crunch to it and, as she walked through the archway, she felt an icy cold drop of water fall on her face. She shone her torch up and could see icicles above starting to melt and drip. With a sense of relief, she realised that the end of the snow days was in sight.

Up in the car park, it was all still snow-bound, and she crunched over to her car. After her previous experience, she was slightly nervous about getting in the car, but she made herself do it, and sat in there composing the text to Zoe, pressed send, and saw it go.

With a sense of accomplishment, she got out and started making her way back to the steps. However, as she did, she spotted a light in Lewis's car. Curiosity drove her to go over and knock on the window.

He jumped, startled to see her. She could see he had his laptop open. He turned to put it on the passenger seat, then opened the car door.

'Morning, Susan,' he said, his voice sharp and alert.

'Um, happy Christmas, sorry to surprise you. You're up early.'

She glanced over at his laptop. She wasn't sure what she expected to see on the screen but what she did was still a surprise.

'Oh, I hadn't realised—' she stammered.

Lewis smiled. 'It's okay.'

'I didn't realise you were religious,' she said, looking at the service displayed on the laptop.

'I was brought up Catholic. It's why I've been coming out early in the mornings. We were always encouraged to attend daily services in the week up to Christmas Day. I would obviously prefer to attend mass at a Catholic church but, well, the weather has stopped that. I come out here to the car for the privacy.'

He leant over and turned off the laptop screen.

'Oh, please don't do that because of me,' said Susan.

'It's fine. It was nearly finished. There'll be a lot more today, but I wanted to start the day properly.'

He got out of the car and looked around. 'It's a bit milder today, isn't it?'

'Yes. I noticed signs of a thaw. It's a relief, isn't it?'

'It would be nice if we could see a bit of the island before we leave.'

Lewis locked his car and then looked sideways at her. 'What are you doing out here at this time?'

'Just texting my daughter. She's up in Scotland. There was no signal in the house again.'

'Long way away.'

It was only as Susan began to descend the steps with Lewis close behind her that she realised the vulnerable position she'd put herself in. Just suppose Lewis was the attacker from the day before? Suddenly, she felt his hand on her shoulder. She turned and screamed, 'Don't you dare—'

'Sorry,' he replied quickly. 'I was worried you might slip.'

Susan shook her head, too shaken to reply, and continued down the steps. They walked across the courtyard in silence.

'I unlocked the front door. We can go in that way,' she mumbled to Lewis.

As they entered the house, Susan could hear sounds coming from the kitchen. 'The kitchen staff are about early,' Lewis commented. 'I'm very impressed with the food.'

Susan tried to compose herself. If Lewis's action had been as innocent as he claimed, he must have found her reaction very odd.

'I'm glad you have at least enjoyed the food,' she replied.

Lewis didn't seem to be in a rush to get back upstairs and lingered in the hallway.

'Um, I haven't told Hayley about my faith. If you get to talk to her, I'd be grateful if you didn't mention anything about it,' he said, anxiously.

'Of course. But I wouldn't have thought she'd mind.'

'She's into her pagan thing, and she may think the whole Catholic stuff is a bit heavy. I'd rather she got to know me better first.'

Susan found his reasoning a bit odd. She couldn't see why Hayley would object to his faith. But she didn't comment. Instead, she leant over to add some new logs to the fire which she noticed was going down. The warmth from the flames felt like burning on her face and she stepped back.

'Hayley's Yule log is ash now,' Lewis said quietly. To her surprise, he began to confide in her. 'I've been worried about Hayley. I know she's bound to be distressed at losing her father, but I've never seen her drinking like this. I was surprised when I heard she'd had bouts like this before.'

'I'm sure a lot of it must be stress.'

'Of course, and I will try to look after her. You know, she's so clever. Not many people realise.'

'Alice, the lady from the village who knew Hayley when she was a young child and who Hayley's going to visit tomorrow, told me how she always had her nose in a book.'

'She's still like that. She did an English degree.'

'I'm surprised she doesn't write novels like her brother.'

Lewis paused, observing Susan as if weighing her up.

'What are you thinking?' she asked.

'I was wondering whether to share this very close family secret with you,' he said. His smile seemed suddenly so warm that, for the first time, Susan really understood why Hayley had been attracted to him.

'Go on,' she said, smiling back.

He looked around, lowered his voice. 'The truth of the matter is, it's Hayley who writes Bryson's crime novels, not him.'

Susan gasped. 'You're kidding!'

'It's true. Bryson dropped out of university and went to work at *The Flame*, but his dream was to write novels. He found he was brilliant at coming up with ideas and plots, but he never had the patience to get the words down. Hayley loved that side of it and she started doing more and more of the writing for him.'

'So, she's his ghost writer?'

'Yes. He suggested they publish under both their names, a brother and sister team, but she preferred the idea of ghost writing. He's great at all the social and marketing side. She hates it. So they decided to split the money fifty-fifty. They hadn't really expected the books to take off, but of course with their dad behind them, well, they had a lot of doors open to them.'

'But surely once the books became popular, Hayley must have wanted recognition for her work.'

'Nope, never. Honestly, she loves this ghost-writing thing. She's done different genres, even some erotica.'

'She really is full of surprises, isn't she?'

'That's Hayley.' He gave a slightly ingratiating, smug grin: a child informing a teacher on another pupil. She wondered for a moment why he'd told her something that was clearly a closely guarded secret. Had he been playing a high-ranking card to win Susan's favour, to get her on his side?

Lewis looked down at his wet feet. 'I think I ought to go and change. It's good to talk, but don't mention the secret. Only Duncan, Hayley, Bryson and myself know about it. Right, hope it's breakfast soon. I'm starving.' He left her and Susan watched him run up the stairs, two at a time.

Susan made her way back to the flat. She had already learned a lot that morning. It surprised her that Lewis was a devout Catholic, but she couldn't quite understand why he was keeping it a secret from Hayley.

As to Hayley writing Bryson's books, that was quite the revelation. Whatever Lewis's motive had been for telling her, it was a valuable piece of information. It was hard to imagine innocent, vulnerable Hayley immersed in writing complex murder scenarios dreamt up by Bryson. Fictitious, of course, but all the same: it showed a different side to her.

The title of ghost writer seemed particularly appropriate for Hayley, who seemed to spend a lot of her time in the shadows. Did it connect her in any way to Duncan's death? Susan wasn't sure it did.

However, there might be more implications for Bryson. Keeping this a secret from Victoria was huge. Integrity meant everything to her. That evening of the meal, Duncan had threatened Bryson. What had he said? 'I made you and your writing career. I can just as easily break you.' That must have been a threat to tell Victoria. Duncan knew that Victoria, and her influential family, would have been devastated to learn Bryson was lying. It might well have ended the marriage and Bryson's bright future career. Yes, that had to be a motive. Bryson could well have imagined his future was a lot safer with his father out of the way.

26

'Happy Christmas,' Robert said, his arms outstretched. He gave her a huge hug. Seeing the snow on her boots, he said, 'Now where have you been? I was about to take the dogs out for a run before breakfast.'

'I just went to open the front door. It would be good to go for a walk with the dogs. If we're quick, we'll catch the sunrise.'

They walked briskly up through the garden where the snow was becoming slushier on the surface, and occasionally Susan could hear a sudden whoosh as a clump fell off a tree branch. In the woods, Susan began to see patches of mud. 'We'll have muddy as well as snowy paws to contend with now,' commented Robert.

They went up onto the downs and towards the Longstone. They let the dogs off and walked past the stones, along the path that led to wonderful views over the sea. The sun was just creeping over the horizon, and spread a warm, yellow-orange glow over the snow-covered downs.

Susan realised Robert was looking down at her, his smile reflecting the warmth of the sunrise. Her heart leapt a little, but in a comforting way, and he put his arm around her. She stood very still. Neither of them spoke. Neither wanted to break the spell of the moment.

Susan didn't know how long they would have stayed like that but out of the corner of her eye she noticed that Dougie was carrying a huge take-away box in his mouth. Robert laughed but went quickly to retrieve it. 'It's okay,' he called. 'No food in it.'

They called the dogs together and began to walk back to the manor.

It was nearly light now, and Susan could see the garden beginning to emerge from the snow. Heads of snowdrops were peeping through, bringing the promise of warmer times, of spring. She knelt down and examined one of these precious plants, the white flowers arching over whisper-thin stems. The flower was perfect, not shouting for attention, just quietly being beautiful.

They followed the dogs, who had now incorporated a frantic check of the area where the shack was into their walk. The steps and the hut were showing fewer signs of the thaw, with a thick layer of snow still leading to the shack.

Robert called Gem Gem. 'These dogs are obsessed since we came here on Friday. I wonder if they can smell the remains of food from when the café was open last summer?'

Susan paused. 'Didn't you say you went in the shack that morning?'

Robert nodded. 'That's right. I'd seen footsteps leading up to the shack and was curious as to who would be in there at that time in the morning.'

Susan grabbed his arm. 'Exactly, and didn't you say the top step was clear, that there had been melting snow inside?'

'Yup, the door to the shack was easy to open.'

In her excitement, Susan stood on tiptoe and kissed him on

the cheek. 'You're a genius. I'd assumed the footsteps and the cleared snow were from Kristen's visit in the night. But that was a huge mistake. Kristen had left here before two in the morning. There had been heavy snow all night. By the time you came out, those footprints should have been pretty much covered. The top step would have also been re-covered with fresh snow. Any remains inside from somebody's boots or shoes in the night would have completely melted. Don't you see? Someone had been in there since Kristen and not long before you came out with the dogs.'

Robert blinked. 'I suppose they had, but what's the big deal?'

'Because I'm sure they had a very special reason for coming out here this early. Come on, we need to look in the shack, see if we can find it.'

'Find what?'

Susan didn't reply but ran up the steps. She needed to calm down now, do this methodically. Slowly she worked her way around the shack looking in cupboards, under the cushions and the mattresses, and in the shower. She was starting to think the whole thing was a waste of time when she checked another cupboard. Instead of just glancing inside, she felt right to the back of it, into corners she couldn't see. Then she found it.

Her hand shook as she pulled out the flask, with the cup still attached, and she was close to tears of relief as she saw a scratch on the outside. She had been right all along: she wasn't imagining things.

Her hand started to shake. Everything was now horribly real. It wasn't a game: someone really had killed Duncan.

Robert stood open-mouthed. 'What's that doing out here?'

Susan explained what she'd worked out.

'That's incredible, Susan. Well done. We must give this to the police.'

Robert began to rummage in his pockets. Since he'd been on a foraging course with Susan a while ago, he always kept a spare plastic bag in his pocket, and he dug it out now. He held it open and Susan slipped the flask into it.

'That's the best we can do. It needs to be tested, although I'm not hopeful for fingerprints. It may even have been washed out. This person is clever – but not that clever. After all, they made the mistake of leaving the window open.'

'We can't do anything today, can we? It's Christmas Day.'

'Hang on. I wonder if there's signal in here?'

Robert took out his phone. His eyebrows shot up. 'Who'd have thought it? I've got three bars. Right, let's see what I can do.'

He made a few calls. 'I'm impressed. They're out gritting even on Christmas morning. With the thaw, they're hoping to get all the roads open again. I was thinking I'd like to get this flask into the station. Someone will be there, but I wasn't sure if it would be possible through the snow.'

'It can wait until tomorrow. No one is going to be doing anything today, are they?'

'That's true.'

He smiled at Susan. 'Well done again. I'm impressed.'

'Thanks,' said Susan, but she was preoccupied. 'Did you see anyone out here on your walk on Friday morning?'

Robert shook his head. 'No. It was very early.'

'It was. I went over to the car park to make that call to Steve. I left the house with Bryson. I remember seeing you, and we met Lewis. And there was someone else. Oh, yes: Antoine came in later. He said he'd been for a long walk and then moaned about the phone signal. Of course, any of the others could have sneaked out earlier, though.'

Robert frowned. 'You do realise that finding this flask means there could be a killer in the manor, and they may well be aware you're still digging around? You have to be careful. I don't want anyone having a go at you.'

Susan cringed. 'It's a bit late for that.'

She regretted her words as soon as she saw the look of consternation on Robert's face. 'Sorry, it was nothing,' she added hastily.

'What was nothing? Come on, Susan. Tell me what happened.'

Susan began to tell him about the push on the steps, and why she thought it had been someone from the manor. As she told Robert, she felt her breathing quicken, her voice shaking.

Robert leant forward, laid his hands on hers. 'Susan, this is serious. Why didn't you tell me about it?'

'I don't know. We were so busy the rest of the day and I didn't want to think about it, I guess.'

'But you can't just ignore what happened. You should report this.'

'There's no point. We both know that. I didn't see anyone. I have no proof. They will assume I fell and am dramatising a straightforward accident.'

'You shouldn't underestimate the police like this. However, given it's Christmas and there will be few people on, maybe you're right to leave it, at least for the time being. Have you thought about leaving, going back home?'

'I'm not going anywhere,' Susan said firmly. 'I'm going to see this through. I promise to be careful, but you can't make me go anywhere.'

Robert sighed. 'No, I realise that but, well, make sure you keep alert. And if you have any worries, you must tell me.'

'Okay,' Susan replied, then looked down at the bag. 'You have to admit, I am starting to make some progress. This is an important clue. If I'm right, the police took away Duncan's flask. The one we found in here must have belonged to the killer. Last night, when they did the toast at the meal, someone must have been missing a flask... who was it? I should be able to remember.'

She closed her eyes, picturing the guests sitting around. Her face lit up. 'Hayley and Lewis were sharing a flask.'

'I suppose one of them may have forgotten to bring theirs down.'

'I guess so, but I've more to tell you about Lewis.'

Susan told Robert about her conversation with Lewis that morning, about him being a Catholic and Hayley writing Bryson's books.

'It seems odd to me that he kept his Catholicism a secret,' said Robert.

'I agree. I don't think Hayley would be that upset about it. Do you? She came to Midnight Mass with everyone last night.'

'And so Hayley is writing the crime books. She doesn't look the sort, does she?'

'I know. It shows a different side to her but, of course, Bryson comes up with the ideas.'

They returned to the flat and gave the dogs their breakfast.

Robert tucked the bag with the flask away. 'I'll deal with that tomorrow. Now, we need to go and eat. And, by the way, I am officially giving you a day off investigating. It's Christmas.'

They went to the kitchen. The smell of turkey roasting might not be everything Susan would like as a vegetarian, but it still resonated with those early memories of Christmas.

'Ah, Susan,' called Gary. 'Happy Christmas.'

'And a very happy Christmas to you. What on earth time did you start?'

'God, I hardly went to bed, but I love my job so I'm not complaining. Now, for you I have made my very special pancakes with fruit and maple syrup. I have also made my own pastries this morning.'

'That's incredible. Thank you so much.'

Susan sat down with Robert to her wonderful breakfast, and Meera joined them. Susan noticed she was walking more confidently with just a stick now and she was using her bandaged hand.

They all wished each other a happy Christmas before Meera turned to Susan. 'I'm sure you'd like to talk to your family today.'

'I had been planning a Zoom call, but my laptop is back home.'

'Oh, like I said before, please feel free to use the computer in the office.'

Susan smiled. 'That would be brilliant. Thank you.'

'Good. Well, we should be able to leave the guests to their own devices for the morning. They're planning breakfast, gift giving and possibly a quiet walk in the grounds. They'll be given an early light brunch and then the full works at three. I will be doing a staff Christmas dinner after that. Susan, have a break until the meal and let's hope we can have a day without drama.'

As they finished their own breakfast, Susan saw the guests arrive in the Great Hall for theirs. After wishing them all a happy Christmas, Susan left Meera chatting to them as they helped themselves to the sumptuous buffet which Gary had prepared and ordered cooked food.

Back in the flat, Rocco and Libs looked at her expectantly despite the long walk they had had not long ago.

'You're not getting another walk yet but you can come and join the phone call. Zoe will want to see you two.'

27

Susan managed to send a text to Zoe, who replied that it was a good time to chat, and so they set up a Zoom call from Meera's office.

Susan was greeted by Zoe, her wife Fay and baby Jamari, now sitting up, smiling. Jamari had changed again and was growing more like Zoe every day, with her little pixie face and blonde hair. She had been conceived by sperm donation. Although she was not genetically linked to Fay, Susan could see she miraculously had Fay's smile, and the looks passing between the two showed an incredibly strong bond.

They wished each other a happy Christmas, with Jamari babbling and giggling the whole time. Susan was surprised and pleased they had saved the presents she had sent for Jamari to open during the call. Zoe and Fay helped her open a book of signed nursery rhymes, which Zoe was very enthusiastic about. 'I've heard about signing even with hearing babies. It's good for their language development.'

'Yes, I was reading about it. I thought it would be fun.' The next present was a stripy cuddly diplodocus which made Jamari squeal with glee and the adults all laugh.

Susan opened her presents from them, which she had brought from home. The first was a cookery book, *One is Fun*, which she guessed correctly Zoe had chosen and was an unsubtle hint from her daughter to stop living off ready meals. Susan thanked her enthusiastically and accepted it in the same spirit she had received the *Yoga for Seniors* DVD the year before. The other present was a pair of white cashmere gloves. Fay grinned. 'Totally impractical, but gorgeous, don't you think?'

Susan thanked Fay. She and Zoe opened their presents from Susan: perfume for Zoe, beautiful silver earrings for Fay.

They continued to chat until Jamari started getting restless, so they ended the call. It was harder than Susan had expected to say goodbye. It was so lovely to share their warmth and see her granddaughter, and now they seemed a long way away.

She looked down at the computer: maybe she could check a few things while she was here to take her mind off missing her family.

She started with doing a search on Victoria. There were a lot of entries under her name. Susan found a number of the interviews Victoria had done, sharing meals with famous people. She was particularly pleased to spot the one with Isabelle, who had featured on the front page of *The Morning Flame* a few days ago. Victoria's interview was more recent than Susan expected, only taking place in mid-November. Susan guessed it was just the time the tabloids were really starting to take an interest in her.

Susan read the brief description of Isabelle.

Isabelle Dumont rose to fame when she became the first winner of the BBC vegan cookery competition. She grew up in a small village in southern France. Her family are Catholic, a faith Isabelle renounced for a time but is devoted to now. She became vegan in her teens, not easy in an area where dairy farming and meat production were central to the way of life of most people. When she was eighteen, Isabelle moved to England and worked in well-known vegan restaurants in London. Her family were not supportive of the move, and she felt very alone. She stepped away from her faith, and these early years were difficult. Isabelle spoke little English and was barely paid a living wage. Isabelle admits she made some bad choices at this time, and this led to her parents in France disowning her.

Despite all this, she never gave up on her dream of owning her own vegan restaurant and winning the competition enabled her to do just that. Her first book, *Kind to the Planet, Kind to Yourself*, stayed in the *Sunday Times* bestseller list for six months. Fame has not always been easy. Isabelle is shy, quietly spoken, self-effacing and shuns the limelight. However, she has strong convictions and I admire her speaking out on matters such as the effect of meat production and consumption on the individual and the planet, as well as supporting curbing sales of alcohol. Isabelle has an innocence, a naivety about her I find refreshing, and her cooking is just sublime.

It is my great pleasure to share a meal with her today in one of Isabelle's own restaurants in the heart of Bethnal Green in London. I could feel my stress levels drop as soon as I entered. It is an oasis of calm and the smells from the kitchen are divine.

Susan read on, as the conversation meandered through

Isabelle's upbringing in France, her passion for vegan cookery, her concerns about climate change and animal rights. As she so often did, Victoria managed to bring out a side of her guest not always seen. Isabelle talked about how she had entered the competition simply to meet like-minded people and to spread the word about vegan cookery. She was not prepared for the celebrity which winning would bring. At first, she had been pleased that she had been able, in a quiet way, to share her passions and convictions. However, she was shocked to find she was now attracting particularly vicious trolls online. The press seemed obsessed with following her around and commenting on every aspect of her private life, including printing articles about a difficult time in her life. She was worried these would get back to her parents. She had not had an easy relationship with them in her teens but now she was desperate to rebuild the love and trust they used to have. They knew she was attending mass again, which meant the world to them as they were very devout Catholics.

Susan sat back. The interview gave her a new insight into Isabelle. The shyness, the naivety rang out. It made what Duncan and the paper had done to her feel all the worse.

She went back to the webpages relating to Victoria, and spotted a name that rang a bell. Zac Ledger. She screwed up her eyes: where had she heard that name?

Susan clicked on the entry. The article was titled 'Recipe for a Scandal'.

In the article, Victoria began by reminding her readers of a scathing review she had written about Zac Ledger's new restaurant, where she described his food as the worst she had had the misfortune to experience in all her years as a food critic, even worse than the undercooked seafood she had consumed eight years before which had landed her in hospital.

She went on to describe how confounded she had been after her visit to see the restaurant featured in a Sunday supplement, given huge credence by their own well-respected food critic. Victoria explained how she started talking to other critics, none of whom were prepared to question this very influential man.

Victoria had not been prepared to walk away. She had kept digging and finally discovered a financial arrangement between Zac's very wealthy sister and the restaurant critic.

Susan was gripped by the drama of the article. Who'd have thought such scandals could happen in the refined world of gastronomy?

The article clearly had been a major exposé, and there were several other articles in different papers and news outlets where the story was retold or expanded upon. It had been a huge scoop for Victoria and devastating, Susan guessed, for the reputation of both the chef, Zac Ledger, and the critic.

Susan looked down at Rocco, who was close by her side, his eyes bright. 'I know where I've heard that name. Zac Ledger was the name Duncan referred to when threatening Victoria. He said he knew where that story came from.' Susan re-read the story. Victoria talked about 'further digging' to find out how Zac had come by that excellent review, but she didn't name a source who had told her about the scandal. Duncan had called her a hypocrite so presumably he knew that she had used dubious means to ascertain what had happened and could prove it. Was this the evidence that was on Duncan's black business phone?

Susan decided she had spent enough time on her research, closed the browser, and took the dogs back to the flat.

Once the dogs were settled, she went in search of a decent cup of coffee. She was walking through the library en route to the kitchen when she spotted Victoria sitting alone by the fire, reading. Victoria looked up and, catching sight of her, put her book down and walked over to her. After the encounter of the night before, Susan was initially nervous but then she saw a softer look on Victoria's face.

'Susan, I should apologise for last night. I reacted badly and really shouldn't have pushed you the way I did. I hope I didn't hurt you?'

'I'm okay, thank you. I realise I wasn't very tactful, and I'm sorry for that.' She paused, summoning up her courage to ask about the interview.

'I was looking up your interview with Isabelle online. It was very interesting. It feels as if you got to know her very well.'

'Quite well, yes.' Victoria looked away.

'I noticed you had a copy of Isabelle's vegan cookery book in your room—' As soon as she said the words, Susan regretted them with good reason. Susan saw Victoria's quick, defensive glance. 'Why were you looking under my mattress?'

Susan felt her heart race. 'Um, I was just tidying your bed in the evening. I put my hand under there as I tucked in the sheet.'

She waited. Victoria's face relaxed. She seemed to accept the rather tenuous explanation.

'I see. Well, yes, I did admire Isabelle. She put up with a lot from some sections of the press, particularly the journalists from *The Flame*. I saw it first-hand the day we did the interview.'

'What happened?'

'We were eating and I recognised two *Flame* journalists at a nearby table. I realised they were taking photographs and recording us. I went over and asked them to stop. To be fair they did, and they left. Now we had rearranged this venue as a place to meet literally five minutes before we met. I'd gone to the restaurant we were meant to be at, found it closed, so I texted Isabelle and we arranged to meet at her new place. It made me wonder how the journalists knew we were there. Isabelle said it happened a lot. Even when she changed plans with friends at the last moment, journalists from *The Flame* would be waiting. She'd fallen out with friends thinking that they were selling stories, blamed men she met on dates when again journalists from *The Flame* would turn up. Eventually she realised that somehow *The Flame* must be hacking her phone and getting her messages.'

'But I thought that had all stopped.'

'It should have, but Duncan allowed it to carry on. In the same way, I'm convinced they used some kind of illegal methods to get hold of Isabelle's private medical records to run that story about her abortion.'

'That's terrible. No wonder you got so upset with Duncan.'

'Yes. I was very angry about it all.'

'At least she knows you stood up for her.'

'I tried. Thank goodness this should be the end of all the intrusion into her life. Antoine knows what Duncan was up to. He could have landed the paper in a lot of trouble. In many ways, Duncan's death was quite fortuitous for him.' Victoria looked over at the nativity set. 'I'm glad things are sorted between us. It's Christmas, after all. I hope you have a good day, and aren't working all the time. Right, I'd better go and see how Bryson is.'

Susan watched her go back up the stairs, and went to find her coffee before returning to the flat. As she did, she mulled over the conversation. She hadn't missed that passing shot of Victoria's about Antoine. Had she been hinting she suspected him of involvement in Duncan's death or was she simply trying to distract Susan away from herself?

Back at the flat, Susan was greeted by Robert, clearly waiting for her to return.

He held out a glass of port. 'I thought you might enjoy a Christmas tipple. Did you get to speak to Zoe?'

'I did, and I saw Jamari and Fay. It was lovely, but not easy knowing how far away they all are.'

'I know. I felt the same with mine. I just went out to the car park and phoned and texted them.'

He blushed and then said awkwardly, 'Actually, I have a Christmas present for you.'

'And I have one for you,' she replied, smiling.

Robert looked unusually shy as he handed her the wrapped present. Opening the package, Susan found a set of pencils and a sketch pad. 'I thought it could be a new hobby. If you don't like it, well, nothing lost.'

'That's so lovely. Thank you. And this is for you.'

Suddenly Susan felt shy too. A knitted jumper was so personal: would he hate it?

Robert held it up and grinned. 'Wow. I haven't had a hand-knitted jumper since I was, what, about eight! It's really lovely. It must have taken you ages. Thank you. I'll try it on.'

It fitted perfectly and Susan was thrilled.

The rest of the day passed peacefully. The guests seemed content to amuse themselves until late afternoon when they were served a magnificent Christmas feast.

The women had all dressed up and Kristen had outdone herself, wearing a white sequinned dress. Victoria wore a black wrap dress, her hair in a slightly more severe and formal bun. Hayley wore a long red silk dress. It clung to her, hip bones and ribs pushing through the cloth. She also wore a long red silk scarf tied around her head, like a streak of blood. Susan paused: what on earth put that picture in her head? She tried to push it away, but it didn't seem to want to disappear.

The men were in formal evening wear. Bryson had added a

red silk cummerbund to his dinner suit while Antoine's was well worn, with a slight green tinge from age, but strangely that added a touch of class. Lewis, on the other hand, had obviously grabbed the one suit he'd had for years, not having tried it on before today. If he had, he would have seen that it was now at least a size too small. He reminded Susan of those sportsmen she saw on award shows, all looking awkward, poured into suits their muscles had outgrown.

Susan sat playing the jolliest medieval tunes she could find, noting the guests seemed to be ready for a break from the tensions and threw themselves into cracker pulling, sharing the lame jokes. Even Kristen wore her unflattering paper hat. Gary and the staff had done an amazing job. The main course was of three meats: goose, duck and turkey, all with extravagant side dishes.

This was followed by sorbet. Then the Christmas pudding was brought, held high, the brandy set alight. Other dishes of trifles and tortes came next, followed by island cheeses, chocolate, and more drinks.

It had been a feast, and the guests all staggered away from the table, making their way into the library to sink into comfortable chairs, while staff quickly cleared up, with an urgency that showed they were eager to get this done so their own celebrations could begin.

The guests looked relaxed apart from Antoine, who Susan noticed was anxiously checking his phone. He hastily excused himself, found his coat and went outside.

Susan showed the guests the table nearby with a range of drinks, chocolates laid out, while Bryson started a game of charades.

He was busy acting out an over-enthusiastic rendition of what was clearly, to Susan anyway, the film *Jaws*, when Antoine came rushing back in. He was deadly white and Susan thought he might faint.

'Oh my God,' he exclaimed.

'Is something wrong?' asked Kristen.

'Wrong? It couldn't be worse news.'

28

'It's Isabelle,' Antoine stammered as he slumped into a chair. 'She's dead. She took an overdose.'

'Oh my God,' gasped Victoria, looking very pale. She grasped hold of the arms of the chair. 'Are you sure? Who told you?'

'A neighbour of Isabelle's called one of our journalists. She told him that a friend had called to see Isabelle and found her dead. They think it was an overdose.'

Victoria shook her head. 'A neighbour called one of your journalists? You had someone spying for you?'

'Everyone has contacts. Oh, God,' said Antoine, desperation in his voice. He ran his hands through his hair and shouted a loud expletive.

'Was the overdose intentional? Did Isabelle take her own life?' asked Hayley.

Antoine shook his head. 'I'm waiting to hear more.'

Victoria shook her head at Antoine. 'I knew you wouldn't be satisfied until she was dead and now it's happened. Your paper has to take some responsibility here. You've literally hounded Isabelle to death.'

'We merely reported. Isabelle made choices.' Antoine's words stumbled out, but they lacked conviction.

'No, you and Duncan as good as killed her.'

'Stop,' interrupted Bryson. 'That's enough, Victoria. My father was a good man, he never wanted this to happen. Hayley doesn't need this.'

Susan glanced over at Hayley, who sat very still, tears streaming down her face. Bryson looked over at her. 'Don't cry, this wasn't Dad's doing, he never meant anyone any harm.'

Lewis put his arm around her and she slumped into him. Lewis kissed her head, comforting her. 'Shush now. I know, it's awful and no one should die alone on Christmas morning. But don't take it so much to heart,' he said gently.

Susan quietly got up and went to find Meera to update her.

She knocked on the office door and, without waiting for a reply, walked in. Before she spoke, though, all thought of the news went from her head as she caught sight of Meera.

'Wow, you look stunning,' she said, and she wasn't exaggerating. Meera was dressed in a beautiful green and gold sari. Her black hair shone against the colours of the fabric, and she wore gold jewellery that accentuated the beauty of the garment.

Meera smiled slightly self-consciously. 'This was my mother's Banarasi silk sari. It was part of her wedding trousseau. I have only recently started wearing her saris. This is one of my favourites.'

'I can see why. It's gorgeous.'

'For a long time, I was very shy about wearing a sari, particularly in business settings over here. I didn't want to look different to everyone else in the boardrooms so I stuck to safe black suits.' Meera grimaced. 'It goes back to my childhood. In our little village outside Manchester, we were the only Indian family, and I was desperate to fit in. I hate to admit it now, but I was ashamed of my mother wearing a sari, and if I ever wore one for a family party, I'd hide it under my coat when we went to the car, so my friends didn't see.'

'You were scared of what they would all think of you?'

'I was, although we were very fortunate where we lived. I had lovely friends, and my parents were well-liked. However, learning to be proud of my heritage has been a longer process. I'm glad I started before my parents died. I have all Mum's saris now and am determined to wear them.'

Susan looked down at the same old jersey dress she'd been wearing for the past few days. 'You put me to shame, Meera, me in this old dress.'

Meera's face creased with concern. 'Don't ever feel shame like that. Be proud of yourself. Now, when you came in, you looked worried. What's up?'

Susan told Meera about Isabelle's death and the upset of the guests.

'Oh, no. Just when they were all looking more settled. Sorry, I know it's very sad about this girl but, speaking as someone trying to give her guests a wonderful experience, I can't help feeling that the universe is against me.' She rubbed her forehead. 'I guess I'd better go and see them, not that there's anything I can do.'

Susan followed Meera into the library to check on the guests and after a few words she explained she would be going to the staff dinner, but of course, they could ask for anything they needed.

Meera indicated to Susan to follow her, and they walked through the Great Hall on their way to the kitchen.

As they did, Susan glanced over at the guests' table, which was now cleared, but she saw Victoria's large handbag resting against the chair where she'd been sitting. Victoria must have forgotten it. She always kept it so close to her.

'I'll just take Victoria's bag through to her,' Susan explained to Meera. 'You go on.'

Susan leant down and picked up the bag but, as she did, an idea came to her. She had looked everywhere for that black phone, but this bag could be a perfect hiding place. A handbag was a kind of private space for a woman and few people, even their partners, went into a person's handbag without asking. Unless Bryson was suspicious about something, he wouldn't be rummaging in his wife's handbag.

Glancing around, Susan could see she was alone. She couldn't resist having a quick peek. She opened the bag and began working her way through all the pockets, and it reminded Susan why she hated bags like this.

In one was a mirror, in another Victoria's purse. One had a blank envelope, containing a single piece of paper, with black writing on it: 'Certified...' Susan heard a noise from the library but she kept going through yet more pockets until finally she unzipped a pocket that at first seemed full of bundles of tissues but then further down she felt something hard. Trembling, she pulled it out, unwrapped the tissues and then she saw the black leather case with its gold edging. Duncan's missing phone!

She was right: Victoria had been in Duncan's room stealing this phone.

Susan slipped the phone into the pocket of her dress, zipped up all the pockets of Victoria's bag and took it into the library.

Victoria hadn't realised she had left the bag behind and was very grateful to Susan for returning it. Susan quickly went to the flat, where she couldn't resist trying to turn the phone on, but found the battery was flat. Fortunately, her own charger was compatible, so she left it on to charge and rushed back to join the others for the staff dinner.

The dinner was to be held in the kitchen, which had been decorated with a long table with a Christmas runner, candles and crackers with their names on. The smells of roast meats, garlic, rich gravy filled the air.

Susan sat down beside Robert, opposite Meera. Christmas music was playing in the background.

Meera thanked everyone for their hard work, and they clinked glasses of prosecco.

'Are you okay? You look upset,' Robert asked Susan.

She told him the news about Isabelle.

'That's terrible. You're right,' he replied. 'Somehow these things are worse at Christmas.'

'Yes. That's what Lewis said.'

'Have a sip of wine. Try to relax now.'

Susan gave a brief smile and sipped her wine as the first course of sharing platters of vegetable fritters, bruschetta, seafood, and cannelloni stuffed with pheasant was served.

It was an amazing spread, and she could see Gary watching them all, eager for a reaction. 'This is fantastic,' she said and plastered on an enthusiastic smile.

She selected some slices of bruschetta and began to eat. Despite all the drama she was hungry, and this was good food.

The first course was cleared away, and main course brought in. There was a plate of sliced roast turkey and all the trimmings, but also ham and a nut roast. Finally, there was a steaming bowl of Pav Bhaji, the vegetable curry with hot bread rolls in a basket which was placed in front of Meera.

'Gary has done us proud,' said Meera to Susan. 'Do tuck in. Just the smell takes me back to the street vendors back home.'

Susan took a spoonful of the spicy vegetables and a roll and tasted it. Meera was right: it was heavenly. 'This may be my new regular Christmas dinner,' Susan said. 'It's gorgeous.'

'I'm so glad you like it. Food was so central to our family life. Mum was always cooking. It was intrinsic to being a Hindu.'

Meera raised her glass, saying, 'Let's raise a toast to great food.' They clinked glasses.

The rest of the meal was a success. The desserts included Christmas pudding, but there was also pavlova with winter berries and panna cotta.

After the meal, Meera stood up and gave a toast to Gary and the kitchen staff, gave them gifts and they were duly applauded for all their hard work. After everyone had helped clear up, they all moved to a side room with comfy chairs and shared drinks of brandy, port and coffee.

It was lovely to sit in the warm glow of candlelight, chatting and relaxing.

Susan thanked Gary again for the wonderful meal.

'I'm glad you enjoyed it. Meera taught me how to make the Pav Bhaji. I shall be making that again.'

'It was delicious.'

'I hope the guests enjoyed their meals as much. Have you had any feedback from Victoria? She's been clearing her plate, which is a relief, but I've been caught out before. You never know with restaurant critics.'

'I guess not, although Victoria always seems fair. Mind you, I read her exposé of Zac Ledger. That was brutal – although that wasn't really about his food, was it?'

'No, but it ruined him all the same. I'm not excusing Zac's behaviour but, the trouble is, chefs get desperate. The statistics of how many restaurants go under each day is frightening. These critics wield huge power and there are so many chefs fighting for survival. One bad review, next day numbers are down, and so it goes on. Anyway, fingers crossed for a decent review of our food.'

Susan smiled. 'Well, I can't imagine she has any complaints about you. The food has been outstanding.'

Gary thanked her and went to get a drink.

Susan was feeling very sleepy now and was just thinking of leaving when Meera came to sit next to her. She lowered her voice. 'It's been a good evening, hasn't it? I'm obviously very frustrated about this accident, but I am very pleased to have met you through it.'

'Thank you, it's been lovely to meet you as well. It really helped me talking to you about my ex.'

'Good, and I was thinking, I would like to tell you about what happened with mine.'

Susan didn't know whether it was the wine, or simply that Meera was more relaxed this evening, but she sat back, ready to listen.

'My husband didn't go off with anyone. I didn't meet someone else. We came to a point where our business was struggling. That was hard enough, but then I discovered he'd been lying to the shareholders. I was horrified. I'd never have sanctioned that, whatever hole we were in. He, however, seemed to think I was making a fuss about nothing. I talked to staff and discovered he'd also lied to them, promising them pay rises and bonuses I knew we couldn't afford. Finally, I talked to a close friend and I discovered he'd been fabricating all kinds of stories about our so-called successful business. I think he was aiming to get some kind of loan out of her. I was devastated. When I confronted him, I was shocked at the way he so easily admitted to the lying. He really believed it didn't matter. How could I trust him after that? I didn't see how our marriage could continue. He couldn't believe this was grounds for me wanting to end it, which in itself proved I was doing the right thing.'

Susan nodded. She understood exactly what Meera was saying. She felt the conversation was coming to an end but then Meera turned and spoke in a slightly more businesslike way, 'Now, there is someone else we need to talk about and that is Robert.'

Susan could see Robert sitting in another corner, with Gary, laughing, telling stories. Facing Meera, she wondered if she was about to hear her confess some feelings for him.

'I really like him,' said Meera, 'and he has been so kind, sitting up with me, playing Monopoly, watching TV, when I know he'd rather go to bed.'

'I don't think he stays through a sense of responsibility,' replied Susan. 'He enjoys your company. He told me that.'

'Thank you, and yes, I know there is an element of mutual support. The thing is, Susan, I've learned something about myself since coming here.'

Susan waited.

'What I've realised, Susan, is that I am tired of being on my own. I thought I was the kind of woman who was happy to go it alone, but it's not true. I'm shocked to have discovered that about myself. You know how hard it is to trust after betrayal, but I think I am ready to take the risk.'

'And you have found Robert.'

'Well, I have found him but, no, I haven't found the new love of my life. Any more, may I add, than he has in me. Business-wise, I'm fine. In fact, in many ways I prefer running things on my own. If it hadn't been for this accident, this would have been a pretty straightforward set-up. However, I have come to realise that outside of work I long for company, but not Robert. I didn't want you to worry—'

Susan screwed up her eyes. 'I appreciate you telling me all this, but you should realise that Robert and I aren't an item. We never have been.'

'I know. He told me, but he does have feelings for you.' Meera grinned. 'If you don't mind me saying, he seems a better man than your ex.' She added with another smile, 'He's better than my ex for sure.'

Susan nodded. 'I think you're probably right, but I'm not ready for that kind of commitment.'

'I understand. Maybe in time you will feel like me and be ready to take the risk again.'

'Maybe. I can't imagine it yet but, well, we shall see.'

After a few more drinks, Susan decided it was time to leave. She thanked Meera for a fabulous evening and then went over to Robert.

'I'm off now. I'll give my dogs a quick walk. Shall I take yours out as well?'

She could see he was about to resist but could also see he was very content where he was.

'Go on,' she urged him. 'I can manage. We'll stay in the gardens. You have another drink.'

With the slightly hazy look of a man who'd enjoyed a few drinks already, he agreed, and Susan left.

The dogs were ready for company and a walk by the time she returned to the flat. She found all their coats and leads and left through the patio doors and back gate.

It was definitely wellies rather than boots weather now. The ground was slushy and muddy, but it was colder again now that night had fallen.

Instead of going into the main garden, she turned left out into the courtyard and then took the dogs down into the much smaller sunken garden below. There she let them off the leads, although they all stayed close to her. There was a full moon which lit up the garden and she could keep them all in her sight. In daylight she knew she would be able to see the sea in the distance and although it was impossible now, she could sense its presence. The air felt different when you were closer to the sea. She loved that. It was one of the very special things about growing up on an island. The sea was never far away. It was part of her.

She became aware of the shape of a figure sitting on a bench in the corner. It seemed extraordinary on such a cold night, and she walked over.

29

'Are you okay?' she called. Close up now, she realised it was Hayley.

Hayley didn't reply, but took a long swig out of the water bottle she was holding.

'Are you all right?' Susan repeated. 'It's very cold to be sitting out here.'

'This is keeping me warm. It's warming my body and soul,' said Hayley, lifting up her bottle. 'Don't you understand the relief of not being able to feel anything? I'm so tired of feeling angry, sad, hurt, confused.' Tears were falling down her cheeks, her words slurred. Susan sat next to her on the wet wooden seat and put her arm around her. She felt something cold and wet on her leg, and realised Hayley was spilling her bottle. Taking it gently from her hand, Susan sniffed it: there was definitely alcohol in there.

'That is miracle water: it takes all your worries away,' said Hayley. 'My poor mother. I wouldn't have blamed her for turning to drink.'

Susan was very concerned. She had to get Hayley back into the house, but she also had four dogs to manage.

The dogs, clearly sensing something was wrong, came over. Susan was able to lean down and put their leads on.

'Come back to the house with me,' she pleaded with Hayley.

'No. I'm not going back in there.'

'I'll get Lewis.'

'No. Not him.'

'Look, I'll be back as soon as I can,' Susan replied, and she walked quickly back to the house.

She rushed down to the flat with the dogs, left them there, and returned to the library, where she had seen Bryson with Victoria and Antoine. She told them about Hayley.

'I'll get Lewis,' said Victoria.

Susan cringed. 'Hayley said she didn't want him.'

Victoria shot Bryson a look. He nodded. 'I'll go. Where did you say she was?'

'I'll take you there,' said Susan.

Bryson ran up the stairs and was soon back wearing his coat and boots.

As they left the house, Bryson was talking rapidly. 'This can't happen again. I can't see Hayley go the same way as Mum. When we're back, she'll get the best help there is. Losing Dad has sent her over the edge.'

They reached Hayley and he ran over to her. 'Hayley, love. I'm here now. Come on, let's go back. It's so cold out here.'

'No. I'm not coming.'

'Come on. I'm going to look after you.'

Hayley pulled away, but Bryson nodded to Susan to go around to the other side. Hayley went limp. Together, they helped Hayley out of the seat. She was totally compliant now, but very unsteady on her feet. It was hard work getting Hayley back to the house as she leaned heavily on them both.

Inside, Bryson thanked Susan for her help. He said he would take Hayley up and when she was settled, he would fetch Lewis.

Susan went into the library to explain what was happening.

'I'll go up in a minute and check on them,' said Victoria. 'Bryson will know how to handle Hayley. It's not a happy end to Christmas Day, is it?'

Susan returned to the flat. Now she had time to dry the dogs properly and settle them down. Robert returned looking happy and mellow and he grinned at her.

'Thanks for taking the dogs out.'

'It turned out to be more eventful than I expected.'

He saw her sober look and asked, 'What happened?'

She told him about finding Hayley.

'That poor girl. She really has a lot of issues, doesn't she? I'm glad she has family to look after her.' He sighed. 'Fancy a bit of TV before bed? How about *Love Actually*?'

'Is Meera okay? She can join us.'

'She's fine. Gary and a few of the staff have gone up to her flat. They look set in for a few hours yet.'

They made decaffeinated coffee and sat together to watch the film. Rocco and Libs sat on one side of Susan, Dougie and Gem Gem on the right of Robert. It was quite a squash on the sofa and Robert and Susan were very close. Susan started to feel relaxed, and Robert slipped his arm around her shoulder. It was lovely to feel warm and safe. Slowly her eyes closed. She was woken by the closing music.

'Enjoy the film?' asked Robert, grinning.

'Brilliant,' she said, laughing. 'I'm so tired, sorry.'

'It's fine. I had a doze as well. Time for bed, I think.'

They caught each other's eyes. Robert had a slight questioning look in his. Susan bit her lip. She wanted to stay here, close to Robert. A cold empty bed wasn't inviting. However, her head said no, not yet, and Robert read that in her eyes. He smiled back, silently understanding.

Glancing at her watch, she saw it was nearly two o'clock in the morning: no wonder she was tired. As Susan made her way into her room, she saw the security light come on outside. As soon as she made out the blonde hair shining, she ran back to Robert.

'That's Kristen again. I wish I knew who she was meeting.'

Before she had finished the sentence, Robert was out of the room. She heard him run along the corridor and the back door open.

Part of her longed to know what was going on out there, but the idea of going back out in the cold was not appealing. She decided to leave this to Robert and sat waiting.

It wasn't long before he returned, hardly out of breath.

'I saw them. They turned their torches on as they went into the shack.'

'And who was it?'

'It was definitely Kristen and I saw who she went in with—'

'You're kidding. Who was it?'

Robert grinned smugly. 'I saw his face. He was holding his torch. It was Antoine.'

Susan gasped: Antoine. 'Kristen is having an affair with Antoine? She really was pretending to hate him. I can't say I think much of her choice in men.'

'Just because they're having an affair, it doesn't necessarily give them motive to kill, though,' said Robert. 'People can get divorced, and they're both wealthy in their own right.'

'Like I said, Duncan would be a scary opponent. He could have ruined them.'

'Possibly, but I'm just saying, don't jump to conclusions.'

'Thank you. At least I can go to bed with one question answered.'

Susan returned to her bedroom, but then remembered Duncan's mobile phone. It had been charging for a few hours, so hopefully she would be able to look at it now.

She unplugged the charger, opened the black wallet-like cover and turned the phone on. Her heart sank: of course, it would ask for a password. It was naïve for her to think she was just going to open the phone and access it. She wondered whether Victoria had been able to get into it. This was valuable. Duncan wouldn't have used any old password, nothing obvious like his date of birth or the name of a pet, although Susan had no idea even of those.

Frustrated, Susan put the phone back on to charge. She would think about it in the morning.

She climbed into bed, closed her eyes and started to drift off to sleep. As she did, she remembered watching them at that first meal. Duncan sat at the head of the table: one minute the charming host, the next a threatening bully. His harshest words were for Victoria. He had been so angry when she had accused him of using 'dark arts' to get hold of Isabelle's medical records. She could still see the venom in the way he looked at her, threatening her with the evidence on the phone, his eyes cold as ice, and his hands... Yes, his hands: what had he done with his hands? Something strange. Yes, he had patted the enormous gold watch. Susan opened her eyes, suddenly very alert. Was there some clue there? Had he subconsciously tapped the watch when he talked about the phone because there was a link? Maybe the password was the make of the watch, of something inscribed on the back.

The only way she would know would be to find that watch.

Kristen had all Duncan's possessions in her room. Somehow, tomorrow Susan had to get into Kristen's room and find the watch.

She realised that she only had everyone here for two more days. After that they would leave: no more investigating. The killer would get away with murder. She had to get on tomorrow, dig deep. She had to get answers.

30

MONDAY, 26 DECEMBER – BOXING DAY

Susan was woken the next morning by Robert knocking on the bedroom door. She shouted for him to come in and he said, 'I've taken the dogs out, sleeping beauty. It's half past seven.'

'Oh my God. I'm so late.'

'Don't worry. Everybody's behind this morning. It's a beautiful day. The sun is shining. The snow is thawing. Mind you, it was very slushy and muddy everywhere. Now, I think I'll just have coffee and a piece of toast, shall I pick you up the same while you go and shower?'

Susan thanked him and went into the bathroom. After a quick breakfast, Robert said he was going to clear his car and take the flask into the police station in Newport.

'That's brilliant. Listen, could you do me a favour? I was thinking I'd like to go in for the swim at Ventnor. I've always wanted to do a Boxing Day swim but Steve always talked me out of it. I've no bathers with me so if I give you my keys, could you pick mine up from the house? I've no idea what the close will be like. You might need to park by the shop.'

'Of course, I'll try. Give me your keys and I'll be off.'

After he had left, Susan went into the library and saw the guests were all making their way into the Great Hall for breakfast. This was her chance to go and search Kristen's room.

She went quickly upstairs and into Kristen's room, which was still filled with the aroma of expensive perfume; a beautiful silk nightdress and robe were strewn across the bed. She looked around for a box or case that might contain Duncan's belongings, suddenly panicking that Kristen might well have asked Meera to store them all somewhere.

Susan looked under the bed, then in the wardrobe: there they were, Duncan's cases. Susan sat on the floor, unzipped the main suitcase, then hesitated as she had a slightly uncomfortable feeling that she shouldn't really be rummaging amongst a dead man's belongings. But she had to know the truth, so she started digging among the clothes until she came upon a hard leather case, and pulled it out. Opening it, the gold of the watch strap caught the light and she took the watch out of the case.

She turned it over, looking to see if there was anything etched on the back, but there was nothing. Suddenly, she heard somebody outside the door. Her heart raced. She pushed the watch into her small bag, and flung the case back into the wardrobe, just as the door flew open and Kristen came in.

'Susan, can I help you?' Kristen was clearly annoyed.

Susan leapt up. 'I was just checking the rooms, I wanted to see if your fridge needed refreshing.'

'And yet you are over by the wardrobe.'

'Um, yes. I saw the door hanging open. Just checking it was in full working order.' Even as she spoke, she cringed, knowing she was talking nonsense. 'Anyway, I'll leave you in peace. Are you coming to the swim at Ventnor?'

'I'll come and watch. I will not be going in. I'm not an idiot.'

Susan left the room and retreated to the flat. Back in her

room, she caught her breath, just glad to be out of there. With a hot flush of panic, she remembered she had left the suitcase unzipped. She just had to hope Kristen didn't notice. Taking the watch from her bag, she examined it.

Susan picked up the mobile phone and tried typing in various combinations of the letters that made up the make of the watch. Nothing worked. The only outstanding feature about the watch that she noticed was that it was very thick. Was that significant? She found her own phone, was relieved to see she had a whisper of Wi-Fi, and was able to look up the watch online. She found the details. It was described as an exclusive 'stash watch' and a photograph showed how to open the back, where the owner could secrete small valuable items or even medication.

Following the instructions, she discovered the back did indeed reveal a tiny compartment, and in this she found a piece of paper. On this was written a jumble of letters and numbers: 1BRS5%L#a+@. Susan picked up the phone, typed them in and, to her huge relief, she was in.

There were a number of file icons. She clicked on one file, nothing recognisable there, but when she clicked on the next, she struck gold. Here was a photograph of Victoria talking to a man in a café. It had to be significant, but Susan had no idea who the man was or the significance of Victoria meeting him. She sent a copy of the photograph to her own phone, then closed down Duncan's. Maybe someone could tell her who the man in the photograph was?

She reassembled Duncan's watch, planning to return it that evening when she went to turn down the beds. She realised that she had not made a lot of effort to hide Duncan's phone before, and decided that she had better try now. She went into the kitchen. She remembered seeing a film where somebody emptied a box of fruit juice and hid things inside the carton. She spotted the bag of dogs' kibble. She wrapped the phone in a bag and buried it deep inside the sack. That would have to do for now.

Half an hour later, Robert returned. 'All went well. The flask is now at the station. Someone should be able to look at it in a day or two.'

Susan frowned. 'That'll be after everyone has left. It's not ideal.'

'No, but it's all they can do. Found your bathers – here they are, exactly where you told me they were. Are you sure you want to swim? It's freezing.'

She screwed up her eyes, looked straight at him. 'I want to try.'

He beamed. 'Fair enough. The For Sale sign is still up next door to you, then?'

'Yup.' Susan hesitated. She wondered whether to tell him about Steve's proposal, but decided against it. She knew now she definitely didn't want Steve buying the house and was planning to try to explain that to him. At one time she would have been certain Steve would see her point of view, but now she wasn't so sure. When he said that she couldn't stop him, it had been a real wake-up call as to how much their relationship had changed.

'Shall I give you a lift over to Ventnor?' asked Robert. 'I want to go home and check over my house. I can drop you at the beach, take all the dogs home with me, pick you up later?'

'Oh, thanks. They'll love playing in your garden. Right, we'd better go and join the others.'

Everyone was standing around close to the entrance. Hayley was with them, but slightly apart. She was pale with a very serious look on her face, and avoided eye contact. Susan wondered if she was not only feeling hungover but embarrassed about the night before.

In the car park, there was a vestige of snow on the cars, and shady areas clung onto the freeze, but it was melting fast.

The guests travelled in the Land Rovers but Susan got into Robert's car, and they secured the dogs in the back. The route they were going to take was through Susan's village, Bishopstone, then along the coast and as they approached the village, Susan felt a growing excitement. It felt like she had been away for ages, even though it had only been four days. Robert pointed out of the window: 'That business is still up for sale too. I wonder who will move in there.'

'There's been all kinds of rumours, as you can imagine. Oh, look, there's Tracy and Lottie.' Susan waved through the window and Tracy waved back.

'It'll be good to see my house again,' said Robert. 'A neighbour has been going in to keep an eye on things so there shouldn't be any nasty surprises.'

They drove south along the military road which hugged the coast and had stunning views over the sea, which twinkled in the morning sun.

The fields now looked scruffy, with patches of melting snow. They passed the country's oldest theme park, Blackgang Chine, turned inland, made their way to the village of Whitwell, then through St Lawrence until they finally arrived at the road that led down to Ventnor beach.

Without thinking, Robert turned into Susan's old road. Her heart raced. Although she had visited Ventnor once since moving, she hadn't seen her old house.

'Oh, sorry,' said Robert, realising what he'd done.

'It's okay. Can you pull in opposite? I'd like to see how the house is doing.'

Susan looked over at the tall Victorian house, expecting a wave of familiarity. She had lived there for forty years, but now it felt very strange. The new family had taken possession of it and were starting to make it their own. There were new curtains and blinds. The front door was a different colour. There was scaffolding at one side of the house. She wondered what they were having done, and felt inexplicably hurt. Wasn't her house good enough for them? But, of course, it wasn't her house any more.

She felt Robert's hand on hers, and suddenly realised how tightly her hands were clasped together in her lap.

'Okay?'

'It feels odd,' she admitted. 'It's the same, but different. I feel like the house has betrayed me, letting them make all those changes. Is that stupid?'

'Of course not. You gave the house forty years of your life. You trusted it in a way. But there's a new family there now. It's looking after them, but it doesn't mean it's forgotten you, or Steve, or Zoe, or all the foster children you cared for.'

Susan felt tears prick her eyes. Her lips were trembling, and she didn't speak.

'Come on. What you need is a quick dip in some freezing water,' joked Robert as he drove on and headed down to the beach.

Susan could see the Land Rovers from the manor parked up, and a small crowd of locals gathering on the beach. Close to, the sea didn't seem quite so inviting: definitely greyer and colder-looking than from up on the main road.

'You sure about this?' asked Robert.

'No, but I'm going in. I'm starting to wish I had a wetsuit. Maybe I'll become a proper sea swimmer: you know, like those older people you see going in the sea in all winds and weathers every morning.'

'I can't quite see you doing that. You hate being cold. Anyway, have a good time today. I'll be back in an hour.'

He dropped her off and Susan saw Libs and Rocco looking through the window at her, wondering where she was going without them.

She joined the excited guests, and they went together down onto the beach. Kristen was wrapped up in her fur coat and leather boots, which Susan could see getting ruined by the wet sand. Most of them had worn swimsuits under their clothes, and Susan wished she had thought of doing the same thing.

Victoria and Bryson had wetsuits which they were pulling on, while Susan was left with the embarrassing struggle of trying to get undressed and then into her bathers under an inadequate bath towel.

Finally, they were all ready to go in. The air was freezing and Susan was already regretting doing this. She was sorely tempted to simply get dressed again and stand and watch. But that felt a bit weak, so she joined with the others to make their way down the beach.

There was a great atmosphere, lots of cheering and shouting. It was very different to the quiet walks Susan used to have down here in the winter with only her dogs and a few fellow dog walkers for company.

All too soon they were at the water's edge, and it was then the panic set in. The water really was icy cold, and Susan heard the screams, saw people retreat and then return.

'Come on,' shouted Bryson. 'We can't chicken out now.'

'It's okay for you,' shouted Antoine. 'Wetsuits are for wimps!'

Hayley, looking very pale and thin, was holding hands with Lewis. He didn't appear to feel the cold and was full of enthusiasm.

Susan was trying to go in slowly. There was no way she was running in like some of the bathers. However, the waves mocked her, sending cold spray at her, and she decided that if she didn't get her shoulders under soon, she would back out altogether.

They were in a close huddle as they waded in. Susan being short, was soon up to her waist and then her elbows when Bryson declared that on the count of three they should all dive in. Lewis began to swim while the others just jumped around and suddenly Susan felt something knock against her leg. She fell forward, her face striking the water, the sea water stinging her eyes. She tried to get back upright but a hand grabbed her right shoulder and pushed her under. She tried to push against it but couldn't get up. Her mouth was full of water; she couldn't breathe. Susan had never known fear or panic like it: she was fighting for her life.

31

Susan couldn't hear anything apart from the panic in her head. She couldn't scream or shout. She couldn't breathe.

Suddenly the hand moved, the pressure released. She clawed her way to the surface, coughing and spluttering, desperate to breathe. Somehow, she found the strength to pull herself through the water until she reached the shallows. She stood, shivering and crying. No one noticed her. To her horror, she realised that no one, apart from whoever had pushed her under, had any idea of what she had been through. She could have died out there and no one would have known until it was too late. Her death would have happened under the surface, unseen.

Cold air penetrated her lungs. She walked quickly to the beach to where the pile of clothes lay. Kristen stood next to them.

'You don't look like you've had much fun,' she said, an unkind smirk on her lips.

Susan felt very sick. The taste of the salt was overwhelming. It stung the back of her throat. She grabbed a bottle from her bag, swilled her mouth around, and spat the water on to the sand. She repeated this several times.

She was desperate to get out of her swimming costume, so roughly dried herself and got dressed quickly, not really caring about decency.

The others were coming up the beach and she stared at them. Had one of those people actually tried to kill her? But who?

'How did you find it?' Victoria asked. 'You didn't stay in long.'

'No, I had to get out,' replied Susan.

Victoria began peeling off her wetsuit and seemed unaware of Susan's distress. The only person who appeared to notice was Antoine, who asked, 'Are you okay?'

She pulled her coat around her, scared to speak. Was he the one who'd just tried to pull her under the waves?

'You look petrified. Did something happen out there?'

There must have been something in his voice that made the others pay attention because they were all looking at her now: she had to say something, but she knew she wasn't going to stand there and accuse someone of trying to drown her. Apart from sounding crazy, it would be confronting the person who did this, and she was too frightened to do that.

'I thought I was going to drown. I lost my balance.' Susan started to tremble and she couldn't control her voice or the tears that fell.

Hayley swung around, alarm on her face, and grabbed her hand. 'Why did you lose your balance? Were you on your own?'

Susan flinched at the pain of Hayley's fingers digging into her hand. She pulled it away, saw red marks on the back of her hand.

Hayley grimaced. 'Sorry, are you okay?'

Susan stared back at Hayley and was shocked by the look of terror.

At that moment Kristen produced a large flask of coffee and poured her a drink. Susan gratefully took the cup, cuddled it as the heat warmed her hands. She lifted it to her face, felt the steam warm her cheeks and sipped the hot liquid, feeling the warmth seep into her body.

The others joined in with expressions of concern. They sounded so genuine but Susan knew that one of them had just attacked her in the sea, maybe even tried to kill her.

She was relieved when she saw Robert approaching them. 'I seem to have missed all the fun,' he shouted to her. 'I came early, hoping to catch you still in.' He came closer, saw Susan's face. 'Oh, something happened?'

'She nearly drowned,' said Hayley. Her voice was sharp, too loud, verging on hysteria.

Lewis quietly walked forward, and put his arm around Hayley.

Robert frowned. 'You look all shook up. Shall we go back to my place, get you warmed up before driving back?'

Susan nodded. They walked up to the car where the four dogs were waiting patiently. As they pulled away, Susan could see them looking out at the beach, clearly disappointed to be missing out.

At his home, Robert put the heating back on and made coffee. The dogs went out into the garden while Susan sat huddled in an armchair. On the wooden dresser she saw a photograph of Robert standing proudly with his arm around a pretty fair-haired woman of a similar age. This was Carol, his wife, who had tragically died six years before. Robert didn't talk about it, but Susan knew how much he missed her.

Robert gave her the drink and a biscuit and sat down opposite. 'Tell me everything.'

Susan told him exactly what had happened. Robert listened without comment, although his face grew increasingly grave.

When she had finished, he took a breath. 'I'm not surprised you were so upset. Now, tell me. Can you remember anything that could help identify who did this?'

Susan shook her head, but then remembered the feeling of something hard digging into her back, maybe a ring on someone's finger.

Robert nodded. 'Look, I know this sounds weird, but can I have a look at your back? There may be some kind of indentation, something to give us a clue.'

Susan lifted up her jumper. She could remember exactly where the hand had been pushing.

'It's red in one part of your back and there's a scratch. It could have been a ring, but I can't be sure. No, it's not going to be much help.'

'It shows I didn't imagine it, though,' she said.

'I'm afraid it does.'

'You're going to tell me this is my fault, aren't you?'

Robert shook his head, his face red with anger. 'No, Susan, this is not your fault. Someone tried to cause you significant harm, maybe even kill you and this isn't their first attack, is it?'

'You think it's the same person who assaulted me in the car park?'

'I think it's highly likely. Someone is very serious about getting you out of the way. You know what I'm going to tell you, don't you?'

'That I should go to the police?'

'Exactly. And you have to leave the manor and go home. The

guests have only got today and tomorrow left. Meera can manage without you. It's not safe for you there now.'

'I can't let Meera down.'

He said firmly, 'These rich bastards can look after themselves. I've had enough of them all. They've been spoiled rotten, and if they don't like it, they can fly off in their bloody private planes back to the mainland.'

Susan stood up and leant against the radiator, which was wonderfully warm. 'It's tempting, I admit. But if I go to the police and leave the manor, it will be the end of my investigation. I'm so close to solving this, I'm certain of it. These attacks prove I'm getting close.'

'You're rattling the cage of a very dangerous person, I'll give you that. You're not equipped for this. Hand it back to the police and get the hell out of there.'

Susan shook her head. 'I can't go. I say I'm close but apart from the flask, I have no solid proof to hand over. I know that if I leave now the case will go unsolved. The person who attacked me and, I believe, killed Duncan will go free.'

Robert groaned, shook his head. 'I can't make you do anything you don't want to, I admit that. I even acknowledge there is probably some truth in your words. If there is a killer among the guests, they will most likely get away with it. But you mean more to me than any of that. I can't bear to think of you in such danger.' She heard in his voice, saw in his eyes such a deep, loving concern that she almost relented.

'I don't deserve you,' she said with a slight smile. 'Please understand. I have to see this through. I can't be frightened off by this person.'

Robert nodded. 'I understand, of course I do. Thank God we only have two more days to get through. Like I said after the attack in the car park, you must get me as soon as you get so much as a hint anything of something not right.'

'I promise.'

'Okay. Well, I guess we ought to be getting back to that damn house.'

They got the dogs together and drove back to the manor. As they parked, Susan saw Antoine in his car, looking serious, talking on his mobile. She wondered if he had any more news about Isabelle's death.

Susan tried to swallow the fear that seemed to grip her every time she approached the steps now. She was also aware of a growing feeling of dread about returning to the manor. Her words of bravado to Robert earlier began to sound hollow. She was fighting a desperate urge to grab Robert's arm and plead for him to take her home. She knew he would do it in a heartbeat, but the quieter but persistent voice telling her to keep fighting made her to go in.

She was thinking of heading straight down to the flat, but the guests all looked over at her, obviously expecting her to join them. However, she needed to take the dogs and her bags back to the flat.

Once back, she asked Robert if he could sort out the dogs while she went back to join the guests.

'Are you sure you want to go back out there?'

'Of course. I have a job to do.'

'Okay, but I'll come and join you when everything is sorted here.'

Back in the library, Susan found that the heat from the roaring fire and the sumptuous smells from the kitchen created a cosy atmosphere. One of the staff brought them out large glasses of port, brandy, and snacks. They all sat down, sipping their drinks, most seemingly in good spirits with the smug air of people who'd been out and conquered the elements. Hayley sat slightly apart, staring into the fire, but then turned to stare towards Susan.

Susan wanted speak to her but at that moment Antoine returned, sat down and spoke quietly. 'I've heard some more about Isabelle. They're sure now that Isabelle took an overdose of pills and alcohol early in the morning while she was alone. The police have issued a statement saying that there are no suspicious circumstances, so I'm afraid we can conclude she took her own life. It is tragic. I have decided we need to make a statement. I plan to put a public apology for printing the story about her abortion on the front page of *The Flame*. In the end, I know she made the choices, but that story shouldn't have gone out.'

Slowly Antoine reached inside his jacket pocket and took out a framed photograph. 'This is a very special photograph of Isabelle when she was younger, before the world destroyed her.' He handed it to Hayley, who stared at it, her hands shaking. 'Where is this from?' she asked, her voice barely louder than a whisper.

'I found it in one of the rooms, here in the manor—' Antoine replied. He glanced around, as if waiting for someone to challenge him, but no one spoke.

Hayley sat transfixed until Lewis gently released it from her hand, and the photo was passed around until it finally arrived with Susan. Isabelle looked so much younger, more innocent than those smudged, seedy photos in the paper. A young girl smiling shyly, sitting on a wooden bench in a garden on a summer's day, her long brown hair shining.

Susan was about to hand it back to Antoine when she saw him bow his head, and so she held on to the photograph. The frame it was in was made of leather and folded like a book. After Antoine bowed his head, the others joined him.

Susan continued to look at the photograph and noticed that it had become dislodged. It was a tight fit, and to straighten it she needed to take it out and reinsert it.

Carefully she slipped it out as Antoine prayed.

'Eternal rest grant unto her, O Lord, and let perpetual light shine upon her. May her soul and the souls of all the faithful departed, through the mercy of God, rest in peace. Amen.'

But Susan was not listening to the prayer. Her attention was caught by the words written on the back of the photograph.

32

The inscription said simply: *My 'sister'*.

Susan blinked, noted briefly that the word 'sister' was in inverted commas, and quickly refitted the photograph back in its frame.

Antoine genuflected and sat back so Susan handed back the photo and Antoine returned it to his pocket.

Her mind was churning. Where had Antoine found that photo? Surely the wording suggested that one of the guests had to be related to Isabelle. If they were, they were keeping very quiet about it, and with good reason. This person would have a very strong motive for killing Duncan, even before Isabelle's tragic death.

No one spoke. Susan felt it was time she left, and returned to the flat.

The dogs were all snoozing after their busy morning. Robert was standing with a cup of coffee. He looked up, relieved, as she entered.

'Good, you're back. I was about to come and join you.'

'It's very kind, Robert, but you can't just follow me around all the time. Look, I'll make sure my phone is on me all the time.'

'I know, but I'm worried—'

'Hang on.' Susan fetched her small cross-body dog-walking bag from the bedroom. 'I didn't want to take this to the beach, but I will keep it on at all times now. It means I will always have my radio with me.'

Robert seemed to be weighing this up and replied, 'Okay, but you know you don't even have to speak to me. If you can press the side button, I will know you are trying to contact me.'

'Thank you. That actually makes me feel a lot better. Now I need to go and have a hot shower.'

'Okay, but one more thing. I want us to start locking the flat door. Hang on, there are spare keys in here.' He found two keys in a small drawer. 'Put that with your car keys and from now on we keep that door locked, even when you're in here, okay?'

She smiled, but she could see it made sense. 'Of course. It's a good idea.'

'Then I guess I could go and do some work, but remember, just call, okay, and lock the door behind me.'

Robert left the room, the dogs watching him as he left. Susan was surprised how nervous she felt in the flat without him. She was aware of how far away from everyone the flat was, how thick the walls. No one would hear her scream. She took out her key and locked the door. Trying to put away such nightmare thoughts, she took the radio out of her bag, and checked the battery. She put it in the charger on the side table.

As she stood under the hot water of the shower, her mind went back to the attack that morning. She'd been right before: the person who had assaulted her in the car park had tried again. This time had been even worse. The idea of drowning had always terrified her. She could never watch such scenes being played out on TV dramas.

Looking down at her legs, she could see numerous bruises from the fall. The only mark from the attempt on her life that morning was that scratch on her back and that would heal quickly. It had been more serious, though: no element of chance here. This time the person had wanted her dead.

She wrapped herself in a towel, and went to get dressed. To try and take her mind off the nightmare in the sea, she made herself concentrate on the photograph of Isabelle and the words on the back.

Who could it have belonged to? Susan guessed it had to be Victoria, Lewis or even Antoine himself. He could have been bluffing when he said he'd found it. But it seemed absurd to think that Antoine was Isabelle's brother. How could an associate editor work at a newspaper which published such scurrilous articles about his own sister? Why not stop it? Protect her?

Of course, Isabelle had fallen out with her family. They disapproved particularly of the choices she made when she was a young adult. Antoine was still following the Catholic faith like his parents. He may have let the earlier stories slide until becoming very upset about the final headline, maybe knowing she was trying to get back to her faith, and to be reconciled with her parents and family.

Susan had seen his anger towards Duncan. If Isabelle really had been his sister, this had to be a strong motive for murder. Of course, Isabelle had died after Duncan, but Antoine would have known what their stories were doing to her and that the one about her abortion would have cut deep. His anger over the story might not simply have been about the danger to his career, but it could also be the devastating effect it was going to have on his sister. Maybe he'd even been to see her the morning the story had been published, seen how badly it had affected her?

Susan's mind tracked back to the newspaper by Duncan's bed when his body was found. No one understood what it was doing there, but if Antoine had killed Duncan because of his sister, it would be particularly pertinent to place the copy of *The Flame* with the photo of Isabelle next to his bed.

Susan changed into what she thought of now as her working clothes, checked the radio which had charged quickly, put it in her bag, left the flat and decided to go and see Meera. She found her working in her office.

'Was the swim a success?' Meera asked.

Susan decided against sharing the full story. 'Um, they're all having a drink now to warm up, but Antoine has just shared further news about the young woman Isabelle who died yesterday. It's all very sad.'

'Oh dear, there's a lot for them all to cope with. I think a few of the guests are planning to visit someone in the nursing home this afternoon, aren't they?'

'Yes, and I'll go with them if that's okay. My friend Alice is there and in fact she's the person Hayley and Bryson want to see. She worked in the village shop, and they got to know her when they were little.'

'Well, that sounds a nice gentle afternoon. Good.'

Susan could see that Meera wanted to get back to work, so left her to it. As she was leaving the office, she saw Antoine looking down the corridor, and he walked towards her. Susan panicked, wondering if he'd seen her reading the back of the photograph. She wanted to turn away, run back to the flat but he called her name and she knew she had to go and see what he wanted.

'Susan, I wonder if I could have a quick word with you. I'm

sorry to disturb you but it's important. Maybe we could speak in my room.'

Susan was torn. She was desperate to know what he had to tell her, but she was also aware that going to his room alone might be placing herself in danger.

'I won't take much of your time,' Antoine urged her and turned away, clearly expecting her to follow him.

Susan suddenly remembered the radio, and checked her bag. She slipped it out and put in into her pocket. Now she knew she could contact Robert at any time. Feeling reassured, she followed Antoine.

Inside the room, Antoine indicated one of the armchairs for her to sit in. The conversation suddenly had the feel of an interview.

'I need an honest answer,' he started bluntly. Susan's heart pounded, but the question surprised her. 'Do you believe somebody attacked you in the sea today?'

Susan hesitated. She had only just discovered a very strong motive for this man to have committed murder. If he was the killer, he might have assaulted her twice: once in the car park, and more seriously in the sea.

Sensing her hesitation, Antoine added, 'I understand you have no reason to trust me. However, you must remember that I'm the only other person here who has expressed doubts about Duncan's death. We do at least have that in common.'

'Do you still have those doubts?' Susan asked.

'I was relieved when the police gave their verdict but, yes, there are still things left unanswered. I don't like untidy endings and I'm guessing neither do you.'

'It's true. I've had my doubts.'

'You're very wary of me, aren't you?' he said, observing her carefully. 'I suppose I'm as much a suspect in your eyes as everyone else here. Maybe you think I tried to drown you this morning—'

Susan felt her mouth go very dry, slipped her hand into her pocket and wrapped it around the radio.

'I didn't, by the way,' Antoine continued. 'But I do think you've got someone rattled. What I keep wondering is why you care so much. This family are nothing to you. In fact, I saw the way you looked at Duncan that night when I confronted him about Isabelle. You looked as disapproving as Victoria—'

Susan opened her mouth to respond, but Antoine held up his hand. 'Don't deny it. I'm paid to notice things. I read faces. You didn't even like the man. Why should you care about how he died?'

Susan licked her lips, coughed and tried to speak. 'Because if Duncan didn't die through natural causes, someone here is a killer, and I don't believe they should be allowed to get away with murder.'

Antoine's eyebrows shot up. 'That's very direct, but I can't argue with your logic. But how did they do it?'

'That's a problem, yes,' she answered haltingly.

It was tempting to blurt out her theory but she managed to stay impassive.

'I was watching you when you were playing at dinner last night. Your face suddenly lit up, as if you'd had some kind of revelation. It was after the toast and so I've been wondering about that flask of Duncan's. That's the only way he could have been poisoned, but nothing was found—'

Susan gasped. Antoine had noticed so much more than she realised. But then he was a journalist. It was his job to notice things, to dig under the surface. She should have remembered that.

'I don't know,' she stammered, but she could see from his face he didn't believe her.

'I don't blame you for not telling me. Kristen said she'd found you searching her room at breakfast time. You'd been in the wardrobe where she had put Duncan's belongings. The case was unzipped.'

Susan silently cursed her carelessness: so Kristen had noticed.

'I was wondering what you were after?'

Suddenly Susan remembered thinking Antoine might be able to help her solve the riddle of the photograph of Victoria with that man.

She took her own phone out of her bag, and showed him the photograph of Victoria talking to the man in a restaurant.

'How did you get hold of this?'

Susan explained that she had found Duncan's phone in Victoria's bag.

'I think you should come and work for me, although maybe not now. Your methods are a bit old school. Duncan would have approved, but I'm not Duncan. Where is the phone now?'

Susan was about to tell him, when she felt a nudge of caution. 'It's safe.'

Antoine let it go. 'You got results. Kristen told me she wondered what you'd been up to in her room. She was right to be suspicious of you. Do you suspect her?'

'She told me she has an alibi.'

'I see. Well, let's look at this photo more closely. This appears to be Victoria talking to a person we call "the master", by which I mean the master of the dark arts of hacking. At one time he did a lot of work for *The Flame*. Duncan and he were great mates. He was never officially employed but for a price he could get you any information you wanted and more. Since the hacking scandal was uncovered, we've cut off all contact with him.' Susan sensed the hesitation. She thought about Victoria's accusations that the paper had accessed Isabelle's medical records, but she left it: she had to find out about Victoria.

'So, the question has to be, why was Victoria meeting with him?' she asked. 'Didn't Duncan mention a story about Zac Ledger?'

'Exactly. Victoria maintains she got the information from anonymous sources. This photo suggests the source is not so anonymous.'

Susan shook her head. 'Victoria used someone who hacked into Zac's bank accounts?'

'That's how it appears. However, a picture can speak a single truth or a hundred lies. This photo is fabricated. I can see it, and I'm sure Victoria and her lawyers would as well.'

'How on earth can you tell that? So you think Duncan faked this?'

'I do, but not terribly well. Victoria is right. He was a dinosaur, but the problem was he still thought of himself as the king of the jungle. This photo is awful quality, but I bet he never noticed how terrible it was. He was going to get caught out very soon.' Susan saw a blast of anger fly across Antoine's face and thought again about the story of Isabelle.

'Duncan had become quite a liability at the paper, hadn't he?'

Antoine looked closely at her. 'He had, but not enough for me to consider killing him.'

It struck Susan again what a complicated man Antoine was. He went from fury to enjoying the game of it all so quickly.

He sat forward and pointed at her. 'You only have my word that I didn't kill Duncan, and that must be frustrating for you. I can see that. But, you see, somebody will swear that I was with them from the moment I returned at midnight if necessary.'

'Kristen?'

'Very good, yes. You can't prove she left the manor. On the other hand, she will swear I was in her room with her. She will do anything for me.' There was that hint of an unpleasant smile again.

'How long has the affair been going on?'

'Affair?'

'I've seen Kristen going out in the night. Last night someone identified you as well.'

'We'd become sloppy,' said Antoine, 'but it doesn't matter now. It was fun while it lasted.'

'It's not serious then?'

'God, no. Not on my part, anyway. Kristen has got a bit, well, carried away. But that's not important. Now, I saw you reading the back of that photo of Isabelle. Everyone else had their heads bowed respectfully, but not you.'

'And you weren't exactly concentrating, were you?'

'I was genuinely sorry for the girl. Now, my guess is that you're wondering if I am Isabelle's brother.'

Susan looked back at Antoine, felt herself relax. She let go of the phone in her pocket, her hands rested easily on her lap. 'I did wonder—'

'The photograph doesn't belong to me and, no, I'm not related to Isabelle. You can find out all about me online. I didn't grow up in a little village in France. I grew up in Paris. You can trace the schools I went to. My parents, both academics at the Institut Polytechnique de Paris. They're scientists. My two brothers work in Paris. I have no sisters.'

Antoine rose from his chair, and took his passport from his

case, Antoine Martin. 'I came to this country thirty years ago.'
He paused, smiled. 'It's all true. I promise you.'

Susan had to admit he appeared to be speaking the truth.
'So, where did you find the photo?'

'I don't think I can tell you that, but it was in one of the
bedrooms. I am sure it means someone here is related to
Isabelle.' He paused and added, 'I've given away a lot more to
you than I would usually. I must be getting soft. Right, I think
that will do for now, but it's been interesting to talk to you.'

He got up and walked over to the door, clearly indicating the
conversation was over. Susan walked over to join him and was
about to leave when he stepped in front of her, barring her way.

'By the way, I'd like to dispose of that phone safely. I know it's
all nonsense on there but I should just check it and then get rid
of it. Maybe you could bring up that password as well.' He
smiled, but there was a coldness. This wasn't a request.

Susan felt a wave of panic. She wasn't ready to hand over the
phone or for it to be thrown away. She only had Antoine's word
that the photograph of Victoria was fake. Maybe it could still
prove to be useful evidence.

'Um, maybe I should hand it to the police?'

Antoine shook his head and took a step towards her, his eyes
narrow now. 'No, that phone belongs to me. The police could
misconstrue all kinds of things from it. You need to go and get it
for me now.'

Susan didn't quite understand the level of desperation in his
voice, but it made her more inclined to hold onto the phone.

She slipped her hand in her pocket and clasped the radio. In
one deft move she managed to swerve past Antoine and out of
the door, shouting as she did, 'I just need to go and help Meera,
but I will find it later.' With this, she ran down the corridor and
back to the flat.

Back in the flat, she locked the door, and rushed over to the bag of kibble where the phone was hidden. She opened it, took out the phone, buried it even further down, then put the bag in the cupboard. It was the best she could do, but she must remember to keep locking the flat door.

There was no doubt about it, Antoine was an intimidating man. The way he seemed to read her mind was terrifying. It might make him very good at his job, but it was horribly unnerving.

She was relieved that she would be seeing Alice later. Not only did it get her out of the manor, but Alice had a way of calming her. Her sharp, practical mind had a way of putting life into perspective. Nothing seemed to shock her. She set about every problem in a wonderfully pragmatic and honest way.

33

The trip to the nursing home was planned for three o'clock but Susan decided to go earlier, to have a word with Alice alone.

She found Alice in her usual chair, iPad in hand. Princess was curled up on the new blanket on her lap. Alice looked up, her eyes shining. 'Susan, how lovely to see you, my dear.'

Susan sat down. 'It's lovely to see you too. Coming here is like a safe haven at the moment.' She leant forward to stroke Princess. 'And, of course, it's particularly wonderful to see you,' she said. Princess opened one eye, even gave a short purr, but clearly would rather not be disturbed.

'I guess things have not settled down at the manor,' said Alice. 'Somehow, I didn't expect them to.'

'No. I've come before the others because I need to chat to you, go over things. But first, tell me, how was your Christmas?'

Alice told Susan that she had been able to go to her daughter, Jo, and how lovely it had been to see her granddaughter and grandson. Susan told her about her call with Zoe, and they both reflected on how lucky they were to have family at Christmas.

There was a slight air, however, of getting the niceties out of the way before they got down to business.

'So,' said Alice. 'Tell me everything that has happened.'

'Oh, where to start, Alice? I'll get us a drink from the trolley. We need this.'

Susan fetched them both a cup of coffee and a mince pie. She put them on the table next to Alice and began.

'Firstly, I can see now why you were so keen for me to read Bryson's book – well, actually, I learned that Hayley ghost writes the books.'

'Now, that doesn't surprise me. I could imagine Bryson having all kinds of ideas but couldn't see him actually buckling down and getting words on the page. Whereas Hayley would have the determination to sit and work something through carefully, she'd make sure that there were no plot holes, no stray storylines. But doesn't she resent that her brother has made all the money and has had all the glory from the books?'

'It was her partner Lewis who told me. He says not, but I haven't spoken to her. Anyway, the book was very illuminating.'

Susan had just taken a huge bite of a mince pie. It was slightly dry, she guessed leftover from Christmas Day. She took a sip of a coffee to wash it down.

'Throwing the glasses overboard, the open window,' said Alice.

Susan laughed. 'You worked it out. Why didn't you tell me?'

'Because I could so easily have been wrong, and sent you off in the wrong direction.'

'It was such a relief to finally work out how it was done. And I am sure now, because I've found it: I found the missing hip flask.'

Alice sat up, beaming. 'I'm so impressed. Tell me how you did it.'

Susan went through it in detail.

'So, you've worked out how it was done. That's marvellous. But does anyone suspect how far you have come with the investigation?'

'Unfortunately, I think they do. I've had two incidents. One in the sea was particularly frightening.'

Susan told Alice about what happened and Alice frowned in consternation. 'Oh, Susan. That's very serious.'

'Robert thought so too. In fact, he wanted me to contact the police and leave the manor, but I told him I can't. I've no solid evidence of either attack for the police and if I leave the manor, the killer will have got away with murder. That attempt at drowning me shows they're more than capable of killing again.'

'But is it worth putting your own life at risk? I admire your courage, Susan, and I have to admit I enjoy it when you bring me these interesting cases. But I'm also aware it's very easy for me to sit here and speculate. You're the one on the front line, as it were.'

Susan sat forward. 'But how could I go home and rest easy knowing I was letting a killer go free? I can't do that.'

Alice nodded, stroked Princess. 'I understand. By the way, I saw the tragic news about that girl Isabelle. How awful. She must have been desperately unhappy. And her poor family—'

'It's terrible. Actually, I have something interesting to tell you about that too.'

Susan began to tell Alice about the photograph Antoine had shown everyone of Isabelle.

'The thing is, Alice, on the back of the photo were written the words *My "sister"*.'

Alice blinked through her glasses. 'That's very interesting, and Antoine insists he found the photo in someone's room?'

'He did, mind you, it crossed my mind that Antoine may be

bluffing and that the photo belonged to him. However, when I spoke to him, he was able to prove conclusively that he is not related to Isabelle. That ruled him out but of course, it still indicates that there is a relative of Isabelle's among the guests.'

'And they would have a strong motive for seeking revenge on Duncan.'

'I agree. As far as I can see, the relative of Isabelle has to be Lewis, Kristen or Victoria and thus one of them would have a good motive for murder. Of course, there are other motives too, a particularly strong one for Victoria.'

Susan told Alice the story about the photo on Duncan's phone.

'For all Antoine says,' replied Alice, 'this staged photo may have worried Victoria more than he thought it warranted. She took the risk to go in and get the phone after all.'

'And of course, Victoria also spoke those words about Duncan in the garden, "If only he could die."'

'I wonder who she was speaking to,' said Alice.

'So do I,' said Susan. 'I had an interesting chat with Hayley's partner. He's been going out to his car to watch church services online. I would never have guessed that. Apparently, he comes from quite a devout Catholic family.'

'Now, that's interesting. Isabelle's family are Catholic, of course, as well.'

'That's true. Oh, I also discovered that Antoine, the associate editor at *The Morning Flame*, has been having an affair with Kristen, Duncan's wife.'

'Goodness. How did you discover that?'

Susan explained. 'I'm pretty sure it's quite one-sided. Antoine spoke in a very disparaging way about her. He did say that she would do anything for him, even swear that they were together the night Duncan died. I really don't like him. I feel there is more to him, something darker to be found out.'

Alice sat forward. 'You must hold on to that feeling. Your instincts are very good. Be careful, though. How about the others?'

'To be honest, I find Hayley a complete mystery. One minute so vulnerable, confused and childlike and the next angry, perceptive, calculating even. She's been drinking more. Last night I found her very drunk in the garden. Today on the beach she seemed very scared about what happened to me.'

'I'll be interested to talk to her. How about her brother?'

'Ah now, I've been thinking about him. Remember that row the first night at the meal when Duncan threatened him? I've realised this business with the book and the ghost writing must be what he meant. You see, we know Victoria knows nothing about it. I think if Duncan had told her the truth, she would have been furious. The thought of Bryson lying about something so important all through their married life would be devastating. I could see it ending their marriage, actually, and probably ruining his career in TV as well.'

'Goodness, I think you're right, and I have to admit I can imagine Duncan doing this if he felt threatened.'

'I'm sure Bryson felt that as well.'

'And that would have been a very powerful motive for murder,' said Alice.

'Exactly.'

'Now, this is all very interesting,' said Alice, 'but of course we mustn't forget the one person who, let's face it, would normally be one of the prime suspects: the wife. You tell me she's having an affair and, of course, she's the person who found the body.'

Susan grinned. 'Yes, Kristen. She does stand to inherit a lot of money, by the way. She also let it slip that this is the second rich husband she has had die on her.'

'My goodness.'

'But she apparently gave the police a plausible alibi. I wish I knew what it was.'

'You said Antoine said she'd swear they were together. She could have confessed to the affair to the police as her alibi?'

'I suppose so, yes.'

'It would be very convenient for Antoine if she did, as it covers him too. Personally, I wouldn't take it on trust that they were together, and if this was Kristen's alibi, well, it's not worth anything.'

Susan nodded. 'You're dead right. I need to keep Kristen in my sights.'

'You've found out a lot in a few days.' Alice looked at the time on her iPad. 'They should be arriving any moment. Let's have another drink. Arm ourselves before they arrive.'

Alice was right. Before long, they looked up to see Hayley, Lewis, Bryson and Victoria being brought over by one of the carers.

They seemed quite a large group. It was fortunate Alice was sitting in a corner, enabling the carer to form a circle of chairs around her without disrupting other residents. Princess remained sitting on Alice's lap, although her ears were pricked up and she watched through half-closed eyes, clearly not approving of the disruption.

Bryson greeted Alice enthusiastically, although he spoke more slowly and raised his voice in the way some people do when speaking to the elderly. Seeing the wry smile that played on her lips, Susan realised Alice was well aware of what he was doing. He introduced Lewis and Victoria, but they, like Susan, sat back, leaving Bryson, Hayley and Alice as the main group involved in the conversation.

Alice naturally conveyed her condolences about the loss of their father and this led easily into them reminiscing about their holidays on the island as children.

Although Bryson seemed to lead the conversation, Susan noticed that Alice quietly guided it away from talking about herself to the times Bryson and Hayley had stayed on the island as children. Bryson tended to dominate, but Susan noticed Alice watching Hayley out of the corner of her eye. In fact, once she could get a word in, she turned and spoke directly to Hayley.

'Of course, I saw you first, Hayley, as a tiny babe in arms. You lay there with big eyes, staring around. You always were one to watch those around you. When you were older and sat in the shop with me, you would often comment on the customers after they left. Although you always seemed to have your head in a book, you didn't miss much.'

'I used to love sitting behind the counter. You gave me my own chair and a packet of sweets.'

'You loved the lemon sherbets.'

Hayley smiled in a way that Susan hadn't seen before. 'I did, they were my favourite. Terrible for my teeth but so yummy. Looking back, I was very little to be left like that—'

'Yes. I think you were about three the first time you spent a morning with me. You asked your mum. She was worried you'd be in the way. But you were as good as gold.'

Bryson interrupted, maybe feeling a little left out, 'I loved coming in as well.'

'I remember, even as a teenager you enjoyed picking out sweets. Even then you'd be working out what was the best value.'

'We always had to be careful with money.'

'Yes, I could see your mother was teaching you to budget. I approved of that.'

Hayley grinned. 'The trouble was my brother was at that fancy private school and all his friends seemed to have loads of money. He was always moaning about not having the latest trainers.'

Not only was this the first time Susan had seen Hayley smile properly, it was also the first time she'd seen Hayley tease her brother. Bryson seemed thrown by it and shrugged moodily. 'It's easy for you to mock. Those things never mattered to you.'

Alice tactfully moved the conversation on to talk about their favourite beaches and places to visit on the island.

Bryson once more did most of the talking, and was enthusiastic about his holidays. Alice sat stroking Princess, listening, but not saying much. However, Susan saw that glint appear in her eyes, and there was a firmness in her voice as she asked, 'You had lovely holidays here. I was sorry when you stopped coming. Of course, your mum had that accident on your last visit, a very nasty cut on her face. I remember you bringing Hayley into the shop the next day. She wanted to come in.'

Bryson nodded. 'Yes, poor Hayley. She really needed to come to see you, Alice.'

'And I was pleased to see her. She was so quiet. She couldn't talk about the accident but read me that beautiful story about the imaginary dragon. It was a good story and, of course, illustrated and with that fancy writing at the end. I was worried about you. You were in shock, I think.' Alice paused and looked at Hayley. Their eyes locked for a second, then Hayley looked away.

'I expect you know all about Mum's problems,' Bryson continued.

Alice nodded. 'I heard about her struggles with addiction, but I was surprised.'

Hayley, who seemed to have gone into some kind of trance, blinked and sat forward. 'Why do you say that?' she asked.

'It had never crossed my mind. That's all.'

'Unfortunately, it's not always obvious to outsiders,' said Bryson.

At that moment a member of staff asked Bryson and Victoria if they would come and meet some of the residents who were fans of Bryson's books.

Susan noticed Alice's shoulders relax slightly and, once they'd left, she turned to Hayley.

'So how are you, Hayley?' Alice asked.

Despite the earlier smiles, Hayley was now terribly pale, and was winding her hands, one around the other. However, as if making an effort to chat, Hayley sat up and said, 'I'm busy editing. I always did love books, didn't I?'

'You did, and they were your escape, which I understand,' said Alice, who continued, 'You said on the phone that you wanted to talk about your mum, about the accident.'

Hayley blinked. 'I did. I've been so confused, but I think now it's better to leave it be.'

'Are you sure about that?'

Hayley sighed. 'Thank you, Alice. But it's safer this way. I'm sorry because I used to love our chats. You were always so honest. So few people are with children. I believed then that the truth was a good thing, but now I'm not so sure. It can be dangerous.'

Alice gave a sad smile. 'But the alternative is lies. I know the truth can seem daunting, overwhelming even, but when you become reconciled to it, you can find peace. Lies will never allow that. They eat away at you like a maggot in an apple. Eventually they destroy you.'

Hayley looked deadly serious. 'You always were very straight speaking, but I have to make my own decisions now.'

Susan watched the words flashing between Hayley and Alice, but it was as if they were speaking in code. Seeing the expression on Lewis' face, Susan decided he was equally mystified by the turn in the conversation.

Hayley looked down at her hands, fiddled with her rings.

'Coming back here has been a lot for you to cope with,' said Alice.

Hayley shot a glance at Susan and then looked very directly at Alice. 'I expect you've been told about my drinking episodes?'

Susan was surprised to suddenly be dragged into the conversation.

Alice was not to be deterred, though. 'I'm worried about you.'

'You think I'm becoming an alcoholic? Who could blame me for having the occasional drink? I don't know how I got into the state I was in last night, but at least for a few hours I wasn't scared, nothing mattered. It was bliss.' Her manner changed again. She went back to fiddling with her rings. Her voice was shaky now.

'What are you really frightened of, Hayley?' Alice asked quietly.

Hayley looked sideways at Lewis and then down at her lap, mumbling. 'I'm scared because I know someone out there would be a lot happier if I was dead.'

'And who is that?' Alice's voice took on an almost hypnotic quality, and Hayley held her gaze as if under a spell. Susan held her breath, waiting for the answer.

However, before Hayley could speak, Lewis sat forward and grabbed her hand.

'This is all a bit heavy, Hayley. We'll be depressing poor Alice.'

Alice turned to Lewis. Susan thought that if he had known her better, he would have taken a note of the sharpness in her voice, and the way she sat slightly forward.

'I haven't had a chance to get to know you yet,' she said. 'I'm guessing from your accent you're from Wales?' She continued to lead the conversation into a discussion of his childhood and life.

She seemed excited when he said he'd been to Swansea University, and was able to tell him that her granddaughter had been there. To Susan's surprise, Alice started to ask Lewis very detailed questions about his time in Swansea, asking him if he'd seen the impressionist paintings in the National Museum, seen anything at the New Theatre, been to The Pen and Wig. She went on to ask even more detailed questions, and Susan was amazed that Lewis sat back and happily answered them all. He was completely off his guard. He had missed the twinkle in Alice's eye, the slightly raised eyebrow to some of his replies. It was clear to Susan that Alice was playing some kind of game with Lewis but that he was totally oblivious to it. Susan could only conclude that he assumed that because of her age, Alice was harmless and naïve. He couldn't have been more wrong.

As they talked, Susan observed that Hayley didn't touch her tea and was now holding herself so that she was almost cuddling herself. Alice occasionally shot a look to show she too had noticed.

Eventually, Bryson and Victoria returned. Hayley touched Lewis's hand and smiled at Alice. 'I think I could do with some fresh air now. It's been good to see you again, Alice.'

'Thank you for visiting. Look after yourself, Hayley. I'm serious. Take care.'

Hayley held her gaze for a moment, then, as Lewis slipped his hand into hers, they walked away.

Bryson threw himself back in the chair, legs crossed loosely, and grinned. 'It's really good to be back here, Alice. You look wonderful. I bet you still keep up with all the gossip from the village.' Alice smiled briefly and turned to Victoria. 'It's lovely to meet you as well. I've read some of your columns. I enjoy your interviews.'

Victoria's eyes widened in surprise. 'You've read my articles?'

'Oh, yes. I particularly enjoyed the one you did with that poor girl who died yesterday. I think her name was Isabelle. She was a chef.'

Victoria blinked, looked more closely at Alice. 'That's exactly right.'

'I feel you become very close to some of the people you interview. It must be particularly hard when a tragedy like this occurs.'

Victoria put her head to one side as if assessing Alice. 'You're very perceptive, Alice. I can't imagine much gets past you.'

Susan noted that Victoria was no Lewis. She was under no illusions about Alice.

Alice gave a tiny shrug. 'I do hope not.'

Bryson brushed his knees with his hands, and moved forward in his seat. 'I'm sure we've all worn you out, Alice, and we should leave you in peace now.' He stood up, and so did Victoria. 'Thank you so much for seeing us. I can't believe how well you look. In many ways, you haven't changed at all.'

'How kind of you,' replied Alice, 'and thank you so much for taking the time to visit me. I shall look out for your new programme on the TV. I'm sure you'll make a great success of it.'

'Thank you,' replied Bryson and with that he and Victoria left.

Susan moved to sit closer to Alice.

'Well, that was some visit,' she said.

Alice nodded, but seemed thoughtful. 'Yes, it was very interesting to meet them again. Hayley reminds me of her mother in a lot of ways. She's a very frightened woman. I wish she could have spoken more about that. I'm sorry Lewis interrupted so abruptly. Bryson is as chatty as ever, but evasive. We must read his book again, particularly the ending, I think. I enjoyed meeting his wife, Victoria. What an interesting life she must lead.'

'I was surprised you'd read the interview with Isabelle.'

'Yes. Isn't it wonderful how you can find everything online now? I thought I should look at her work with them possibly visiting. It seemed polite to have read it. Anyway, them aside, the person I'm really worried about is Hayley.'

'What did you make of her saying someone is trying to kill her?'

'I think if that is what she believes, then she's probably right. Whether it's because of what she knows or what she's done is the question.'

Susan frowned. 'You're talking in riddles, Alice.'

'I'm sorry, but there are things I need to think over. I can't simply go throwing accusations around.'

Susan nodded. 'What did you make of her partner, Lewis?'

'He seemed to be genuinely caring about Hayley. I wondered why he felt the need to lie the way he did.'

'He lied?'

34

'Oh, yes,' continued Alice. 'Lewis certainly lied. I set up a little test for him. You said he claimed he went to Swansea University, and so I swotted up on a few facts to do with Cardiff. Not so far away from there, but far enough. Anyway, I simply inserted a few Cardiff references, asking if he'd been to them in Swansea, and he fell for it. I'd swear he never went to Swansea University, and I have to wonder why he would lie about that.'

Susan opened her eyes wide. 'Of course, I should have realised. Even I know that the National Museum is in Cardiff, but why lie about living in Swansea?'

'I don't know, but he will have a reason for covering up his background.' Alice looked directly at Susan, adding, 'Keep an eye on him.'

'I will.'

'I think I might have a chat with Gary's father, catch up on the old days. Now, you have yourself to take care of. I know it's hard when there's so little time to investigate, but don't go taking any risks.'

'Robert has vowed to look after me, not that I need it, of course.'

They sat and chatted a while longer before Susan realised it was getting time to go.

'Um, one thing before you leave,' said Alice.

There was a hesitancy in her voice and Susan wondered why.

'Is something the matter?' she asked, concerned.

'No, not like that. I just don't want you to be offended.'

'I'll be fine. Tell me what it is.'

'There's a John Lewis bag on my bed in my room. It's from my daughter, Jo. She wondered if you would like it. Please, if it's not your thing, that's absolutely fine.'

Susan was curious now so she went to Alice's room where the bag was on the bed just as Alice had said. She picked it up, glanced inside, gasped and returned to Alice.

'This is from Jo?'

'Her husband brought it home from a work trip abroad. It doesn't fit her but he can't return it. She just wondered if you could use it but, please, don't worry about it.'

Susan smiled. 'It's lovely. I shall take it and try it on. Please thank her for me.'

Alice looked relieved and Susan leant forward and kissed her on the forehead. 'You could never offend me, Alice. Thank you so much. I'll be back to see you very soon.'

Susan was surprised at how anxious she felt as she got out of the car at the manor car park. She glanced around and walked quickly to the steps and back to the manor.

Susan showered and changed, ready to get herself something to eat before the guests' evening meal.

She was just walking through the library when she saw Lewis coming in through the front door. Alice's questions burned in her brain; she had to know some answers. There was no one around: now was a good time to ask.

She tried to start off casually.

'Did you enjoy your visit this afternoon?'

He shrugged. 'It was okay. I'm not that fond of nursing homes, to be honest, but Alice seemed very with it.'

'Oh, she is. In fact, after you'd left, she told me she was a bit confused about a conversation you had with her.'

'Really. Why was that?'

He seemed so unconcerned that she wondered for a moment if Alice had got the whole thing wrong; maybe she should just leave it. But she knew she couldn't.

'Alice said that she's sure you didn't go to Swansea University. I know it's a little thing but, well, I just wondered...' Her words trailed off. Susan wished now she hadn't said anything.

Lewis grinned, and Susan felt relieved: at least he didn't look furious.

'You know, I wondered why she was asking me all about Swansea. Actually, she's right. I didn't go there. I'm ashamed to admit I never went to university at all, but you know this family: they're all such high achievers. I thought I'd better beef up my CV for them.' His eyebrows creased. 'You won't tell Hayley, will you? I know I'm going to have to admit to it at some point, but we're only just getting to know each other and, well, she's so on edge at the moment. Tell Alice I promise I will tell her soon.'

With a final smile, Lewis walked past her and up the stairs.

Susan watched him, looking for a dropping of the shoulders, anything to show he was relaxing from a stressful conversation, but he seemed quite at ease, taking the stairs two at a time as usual.

However, she remembered Alice had said to be careful of him, and Alice was usually right. Susan wandered back into the library. There was no one there, so she sat in one of the armchairs looking into the fire.

She looked at the nativity scene Antoine had brought. The crèche... that's what Lewis called it. The French name for nativity. Why did that feel odd?

Susan shook her head, she couldn't work it out. As it was, the guests would soon be down for the next meal. Because, although life at the manor had been very far from routine, there was still a sense of the rhythm at Christmas. Boxing Day was a day for leftovers, not that Gary was serving up cold meat and mash. Instead, there was game pie, sauté potatoes and vegetables, lighter puddings: meringues and fruit jellies.

Even Kristen was slightly more dressed down, minus diamonds, although in a silk suit. Susan played quietly in the background, her mind working overtime. She had found motives for all the guests. She knew how the murder could have been carried out. But who was it? Who was the killer?

Bryson seemed to be making a determined effort to keep things light, chatting about the day, with Lewis joining in. Even Victoria tried to help things along. However, Hayley was clearly still on edge. She seemed to be muttering to herself and she was knocking back the wine rather freely.

Susan was not the only one to notice. When Hayley reached out to the bottle to fill her glass once more, Bryson, with a slight gesture, tried to steady her hand. She tried to shake it off and glared at him, but he wasn't giving in, and tightened his grip.

'Leave me alone!' she yelled.

'Hayley, you've had enough,' Bryson said firmly.

'It might be better to stop now,' agreed Lewis.

'How dare you both tell me what to do,' Hayley shouted.

'Trust me: you've had enough to drink,' said Lewis.

Hayley gave a loud harsh laugh. 'Trust you? Now, that would be a pretty stupid thing to do, wouldn't it?'

'Hayley, leave it now,' said Bryson. 'We're just trying to look after you. We're worried about you.'

'God, where have I heard that before?' Hayley started to shake. 'You all think I'm mad, don't you? Maybe you're right. I don't understand anything. How many does two and two make? Maybe four, maybe six, a hundred. I've no idea any more.'

'Hayley, love,' Bryson pleaded.

Hayley gave him a defiant smirk, reached out and started to fill her glass, staring at him the whole time. Susan watched as the red wine crept up the glass. The wine started to lap over the edges and flood on to the tablecloth but still Hayley didn't stop.

'For God's sake, Bryson, stop her,' hissed Victoria.

Bryson, who had been sitting opposite Hayley, stood up and started to walk round the table to her. As he did this, Hayley jumped up, held on to the wine bottle by the neck and before anybody could stop her, she smashed it against the edge of the table. The wine splattered, blood red on the white napkin, and large pieces of sharp glass fell onto the floor and the table. Hayley held up the jagged edge threateningly at Bryson, who held both hands up. 'Hey, take it easy now.' Keeping his gaze, Hayley lifted the jagged bottle and dug it deep into the flesh of her left arm. Blood soaked through the sleeve of her dress.

Hayley gasped as if the pain for a moment was so shocking it sobered her. Lewis jumped up, snatched the remains of the bottle from her hands, grabbed a napkin and wrapped it around her arm.

Hayley burst into tears, screaming, 'I'm not crazy. It's better I kill myself than wait for someone else to do it.'

Lewis, regardless of the blood that was going all over his

shirt, gently kissed her head. 'It's okay, cariad. I'm going to get a doctor. He'll make you better.'

Hayley slumped back and collapsed.

'We need an ambulance, straight away,' Victoria said and, grabbing her handbag, she walked out through the library and out of the front door.

Meanwhile, Lewis, who seemed to know basic first aid, laid Hayley down gently in the recovery position and continued to apply pressure to her arm.

Susan rushed to get Meera, who was talking to Robert in the office. They both went back to the Great Hall with her, just as Victoria returned.

'They are on their way,' she told them.

Susan was relieved.

Hayley was very white now. The blood flow had slowed down but not stopped.

'I'll go and meet the ambulance,' Robert said, 'show them where to come.'

Lewis remained next to Hayley. Victoria went and kneeled the other side, speaking quiet, comforting words to an unconscious Hayley.

It felt an eternity to Susan but it wasn't long until the ambulance arrived. The relief in the room as the paramedics took over was palpable. Hayley, unconscious, was taken to the ambulance, and Lewis travelled with her.

Bryson sat with his head in his hands. 'My poor Hayley,' was all he could say.

Victoria put her arms tenderly around him. 'They'll take care of her. They know what to do.'

Meera arranged for coffee to be taken to the guests in the library where they sat stunned.

Meera spoke to Susan. 'Could you just quickly go and check

the rooms? At least make their beds look welcoming when they go up? God, what else can happen?'

Susan went upstairs, opened Kristen's door, turned down the bed, put on the bedside lights, and pulled the curtains. Looking around, she felt at least it looked welcoming as Meera had asked, not that she expected anyone would notice much this evening.

She did the same in Antoine's room, quickly in case he returned. She was avoiding him, knowing he was waiting for that phone. She then went over to Hayley and Lewis's room. She doubted somehow that Lewis would return that evening, but she would try to tidy it a bit.

It wasn't so easy in there with so many clothes and belongings strewn around, but she did her best.

Finally, she went into Bryson and Victoria's room and as she tidied the books on Victoria's side, she remembered that business of Isabelle's cookbook. It had been odd it being under the mattress, and Victoria had looked distinctly put out when Susan spoke about it. Maybe she should look at it again, just to make sure she hadn't missed something?

Susan slipped her hand under the mattress. At first, she couldn't find the book. She leant down, picked up the mattress properly, then she saw the book, placed far more centrally. That was even odder. It was properly hidden now.

Susan reached under, picked up the book, and let go of the mattress. She was slightly out of breath: it had been heavy.

She flicked through the book: nothing. She went through it again, more slowly this time. Then she found it. So this was why Victoria was hiding the book.

The book had been signed by the author, and it was dedicated to Victoria but it was the words that gripped Susan.

To Victoria, friends are the sisters we choose, with many thanks, Isabelle x.

Isabelle had called Victoria her sister. The word sister on the photograph had been in inverted commas, 'sister', and it had been in English, not French. Why hadn't Susan noticed that? Was it possible that the photo had been Victoria's and that she had written those words? Isabelle viewed Victoria as a sister and presumably the bond went both ways.

Victoria had been so incensed and upset by the treatment of Isabelle, so it had to be possible that she had killed Duncan out of anger. She might even have hoped to save her friend from any more attacks by the paper. Antoine had said Victoria was relieved when Duncan was dead, perhaps relieved that her friend wouldn't suffer any more, relieved also that the family were free of a man who she saw as controlling and trapping them all.

Susan sighed, she couldn't be sure. Suddenly, she was exhausted. She replaced the book and went back downstairs where the remaining guests were all still in the library. Susan made her way to the flat.

From a side room she could hear a radio. She realised Robert was in there working, and went in. Her thoughts turned back to what had happened with Hayley.

'It was awful, Robert. The way she deliberately cut herself. She was as white as a ghost by the time she left. Oh, my God. Is she going to die?'

'She's in safe hands now. Don't worry,' Robert said, and put his arms around Susan.

He quickly packed things away, then guided her into the flat's sitting room, where he poured her a glass of wine.

'You stay there and I'll find out what's going on.'

As she sat on her own, Susan had time to think about Hayley screaming. Was somebody really trying to kill her?

When Robert returned, he reported that everyone was settled down. Meera was in control. 'Look, do you fancy a little walk outside? We could take the dogs through the garden. I'll bring my big torch. We can just get some fresh air. It's been a terrible day.'

So that was exactly what they did. Susan walked close to Robert and he put his arm around her. Most of the snow had melted away. They walked up and through the gate, up the steep path on to the downs. Susan breathed in the air. She could taste the saltiness of the sea this evening for the first time since her arrival.

Later, after they'd returned to the flat, Robert put some nonsense on TV. Susan fell asleep without realising it and was only dimly aware of Robert picking her up gently, taking her into her bedroom, tenderly brushing her hair away from her face, removing her shoes, and pulling the duvet over her. 'Thank you,' she whispered, and fell into a deep sleep.

35

Waking early the next morning, Susan crept out of bed, dressed, and took the dogs out into the garden and up on the downs to see the sunrise. She passed the Longstone, and walked on, up to the place where the downs looked over to the sea.

Her timing was perfect. The sky was on fire with streaks of reds and yellows, a dramatic start to the day but, as she watched, the colours became gentler. The fire dampened, softening into lighter pinks, paler yellows.

She couldn't stop thinking about Hayley. How had her night been? How was she this morning?

She called the dogs to her. It was time to make their way back to the manor. However, as she approached the Longstone, she noticed someone sitting on the lower, flat stone.

'Good morning, Bryson.'

He shook his head. He looked so lost.

'How are you?' she asked.

'I got it all wrong. I thought I was helping Hayley last night, but she didn't believe me. I've made everything so much worse.'

He looked at her, his eyes shining with tears.

'Are you talking about the accident up here all those years ago? Alice told me about your mother's fall and the drinking.'

He nodded slightly but grimaced as he did, as if it hurt to move. 'It was a nightmare. I was out of the house with friends and so was Dad. Mum drank a lot, cut herself on a smashed bottle. It was a very frightening experience for Hayley.'

'Yes, I'm sure, but what was it you told her last night?'

'The whole truth. You see, what actually happened was my father came home, saw how drunk Mum was and tried to get the bottle off her. The bottle smashed against the stones and in the tussle, Dad accidentally cut Mum. That's how she sustained that terrible gash on her face. Hayley saw it all from her bedroom window.'

Susan gasped. So Duncan had been involved. 'Hayley has talked about the accident. She never mentioned your father.'

'No, Mum told her Dad hadn't been there, that she'd imagined it.'

'That's very confusing for a child. She was torn between believing what she actually saw and what her parents told her she saw.'

'Exactly. It's been so hard for her. I think coming back here dragged it all up for her. She's been trying to untangle these two accounts. We talked last night and I thought it would help her, knowing she was right about seeing Dad there, but then she said she didn't believe Dad had been trying to help Mum. She has always secretly been scared he'd attacked her and I'd confirmed that.'

Bryson's voice broke. 'I'd never intended her to think that. I hadn't realised, but this aunt she spoke to told Hayley she believed Dad attacked Mum. But the aunt had never liked Dad.

It meant Hayley came away with so much hate in her heart for Dad. And yet he was innocent. I'm sure of that.'

Susan watched Bryson. He might be convinced of his father's innocence. She wasn't so sure.

'The really sad thing,' continued Bryson, 'was that Dad was going to tell the full story in his autobiography. He'd written the story of Mum and the accident. He'd so far omitted the detail of being involved in how she sustained that terrible gash on her face.'

'But you said Hayley came away not knowing this.'

'He hadn't made the changes, and was planning to talk to Hayley this weekend. I wish he'd had the opportunity to talk. She'd have accepted the truth better from him.'

'Why had it taken your father so long to tell the full truth?'

'Mum hadn't wanted him to. He'd never been a popular man. She said people would claim he'd attacked her. Dad had gone along, but hated hiding behind a lie. He'd had to fill in forms at the hospital. It was anathema to him knowingly to print a lie to cover his back. I know he had an awful reputation from his papers, but he honestly believed that whatever he did was to ultimately expose the truth. I'm sure being unwell had affected him. He didn't want to leave this world knowing he'd lied in this way.'

Susan sighed, and asked tentatively, 'And so, do you know how Hayley is now?'

His answer surprised her. 'She's coming back today.'

'Oh, goodness. She's okay to come out of hospital?'

'She has a long way to go, but the recovery she needs is to her mental health rather than her physical health. Her arm has been stitched and she's stable. Her collapse was the result of a combination of alcohol and opioids.'

'Opioids?'

'Yes, painkillers. They found them in her system. Lewis told them she must have taken some of his. He hurt his shoulder a while back and had some pills left from that. He takes one occasionally if the pain returns.'

'Oh, my God. Poor Hayley.'

'Yes. Fortunately, it wasn't a big overdose. She'd come round by the time I arrived at the hospital last night.'

'But she needs help.'

'She does. I've assured the hospital that she will get the best I can get her. We're lucky. We have the money.'

'It's awful, but I'm relieved she's able to return home.'

'Lewis is bringing her back here, and of course she'll come home with Victoria and me tomorrow.'

'It's good she has you both.'

'Of course. We're family.'

Bryson stood up. It was nearly completely light now and he held his hands up to the sky. 'It's a new day, as Hayley would say. We must greet the dawn, have hope.' He smiled at Susan. 'Thank you for listening. Unless Hayley says anything, please keep this to yourself.'

'Of course.'

Susan watched him walk away before she called the dogs. They made their way back down through the woods into the gardens. There were more snowdrops and now some late yellow aconites, colour returning to the woodland floor.

Susan couldn't move on from her conversation with Bryson. She was not completely convinced about Duncan's innocence, and the fact there had been rumours in the village about him assaulting Nancy added to her suspicions. If he had attacked Nancy so viciously, it showed the depth of this man's anger and rage. Was she really to believe this had been a one-off?

Another aspect that worried her was that Hayley had come

to this weekend with a seething hatred of her father. Had that hatred led her to murder? She'd lied about going into Duncan's room, and what could be easier than taking Lewis's hip flask to swap for Duncan's?

Hayley seemed so vulnerable, but she had a steely determination and insight. It had to be possible she had killed her father.

And of course there was Bryson. He had seemed genuinely convinced by his father's story and she'd seen the way they had been together. She couldn't see Bryson killing his father over the accident. However, she had to remember the only time she saw Bryson at odds with his father had been when he was defending Victoria. He was prepared to fight his father for his wife and the future he had with her. His father had threatened that. Bryson still had a very strong motive. Would Bryson have been prepared to murder Duncan to stop him ruining his life with Victoria and then his career? It had to be a possibility.

Susan returned to the flat but Robert had obviously got up and was out, so she sorted out the dogs and went to have breakfast.

She met Meera to plan the evening.

'I talked to Bryson, and we have decided to go ahead with the farewell party this evening. It's only six to nine. We'll prepare the room after lunch, pulling back the wooden partition between the Great Hall and the library, to make one big room. Gary and the staff will lay out a buffet at one end. A small medieval quartet are coming to play and teach a few dances to anyone who wants to learn. Tomorrow, everyone will be off in the morning, and that will be the end of what has to be one of the most eventful hotel openings I've ever presided over.'

Robert came in to join them, holding a plate of hot food.

'Thanks for walking the dogs. I've just checked on the room I was working on. I have to say it's looking good.'

Meera got up and spoke to Susan. 'The guests will be having a hot lunch at one. I don't think there is much else on this morning.'

After she had left, Robert broached an idea with Susan. 'I wonder if we could get Meera out somewhere this morning. She's hardly seen the island since she arrived, and she's so stressed with everything.'

Susan felt in need of getting out to clear her head and agreed to the plan.

Later that morning, Robert and Susan took Meera and the four dogs out in the car. They drove along the military road, and she saw the stunning views over the sea, which had finally stopped looking grey. They drove to the Isle of Wight pearl shop and were delighted to find the café open. They managed to help Meera in and sat close to a window with wonderful views over the sea.

Meera smiled. 'Thank you so much. I didn't realise how much I needed to get out. It's been so intense, hasn't it? Thank you both for keeping me sane. It's good to come out and be reminded how beautiful the island is. I'm looking forward to Easter here.'

'This hasn't put you off the project then?'

'I've had the odd second and third thought, I have to admit, but I've put so much into the manor. I have to see it through.'

After coffee and scones, feeling much refreshed they returned to the manor.

Susan was about to go back to the flat when Victoria, who was sitting alone in the library, asked if she could have a quick word. Victoria looked paler and more upset than at any time since she had arrived.

'I hear Hayley is coming back later,' said Susan, sitting next to her.

'I hope she's ready. I'd rather she stayed there longer. I'm very worried about her. Look, I need to talk to you about something. Antoine told me you've got hold of Duncan's phone. He was pretty smug about it, which was beyond annoying, as you can imagine.'

Susan was about to apologise about going into her bag, when Victoria held up her hand. 'It's okay. You're trying to find answers like all of us. I hear you actually worked out how to get into the phone.'

Susan nodded. She waited to see where Victoria was going.

'I understand you saw the photo of me and this man, the hacker.'

'I did, but Antoine told me that it's a fake.'

Victoria shook her head. 'I don't know why he said that. It's real enough. I was naïve. I didn't know who he was, but he rang me, asked to meet, saying he had information about Zac Ledger. We talked, and then I realised he had nothing to tell me. I saw the photographer and realised what was happening. Duncan was simply getting ammunition to use against me for a future date. Call it insurance. He knew that however hard I tried to explain away the photo, it was likely that my reputation would be tarnished.'

Susan could see the terrible dilemma she had been in. 'Well, you don't need to worry about it any more, do you? Duncan can't use the photos now, and Antoine wants to dispose of the phone. It can't hurt you now.'

Victoria grabbed her arm. 'Hang on, you haven't given the phone to Antoine yet, have you?'

Susan shook her head. 'No, not yet. He seemed keen to have it, though.'

'I bet, honestly, Susan, I don't think he has any intention of destroying it. He was lying. He knows that photograph is real. He wants the phone so he can have it to blackmail me one day if he feels the need.'

Susan felt she was caught up in some complicated TV drama she was failing to keep track of.

Victoria, however, was still talking. 'You need to give me that phone. I can keep it safe. I promise, I'm going to my editor. I'll get this all out in the open.'

'I'm not sure—'

'Please, Susan.'

Susan stood up. 'I need to think about this, Victoria, but I promise I shall not be giving it to Antoine.'

To her surprise, Victoria nodded in acceptance. 'The important thing is not to let Antoine get hold of it. I hope you have hidden it somewhere?'

'Of course.'

'Good. God, I'll be glad to get out of this tangle of lies and secrets. I've had enough of it all.'

Suddenly her face broke into a smile. 'Talking of secrets, I know Lewis has told you the big secret. He went running to Bryson, worried because he'd told you and that you might mention it to me. Bryson was able to reassure him I've known for a long time.'

'Ah. I didn't think you knew.'

'Bryson told me soon after we first met. I thought it was very open of him. Of course, if Hayley had any qualms about being kept in the shadows, I'd have wanted him to tell people about her role as ghost writer, but it's clear she's happy as it stands.'

'Oh, right. I'd been wondering about that threat Duncan made during the meal, about knowing something that would destroy him. I'd assumed it was about Hayley writing the books and that Duncan would destroy him by telling you.' Susan smiled. 'I was completely wrong about that, wasn't I?'

Victoria nodded. 'I'm afraid you were.' She stood up. 'Look, I'd like to have that phone of Duncan's back.'

Susan could understand why, but wasn't sure she was ready to surrender it yet. She simply replied that she would return it soon and, apparently satisfied, Victoria walked away.

Susan walked back to the flat, thinking about the phone, which suddenly seemed to have taken on such importance. She really ought to look at it properly. In the flat she locked the door, opened the kibble bag, fished out the phone and began to trawl through the files again, noticing one she had missed before. Opening it, she saw a number of photographs, and gasped. She hadn't been sure that Antoine had been bluffing about thinking the photograph of Victoria was fake, but seeing this, well, now she knew why he was so desperate to get this phone back.

The first photo was of Antoine and Kristen in a restaurant together. Duncan knew that they were having an affair!

Susan stared at the photo in disbelief. Why hadn't Duncan confronted Kristen or Antoine about this?

She scrolled through. There were more photos of Antoine. One was of Antoine in the office studying a document on his desk. Susan made the document larger. It was headed: 'Isabelle Dumont. Medical Record. Confidential'. There was a date on the letter next to it, a week before the story about Isabelle's abortion.

There were several similar photographs taken, through glass, presumably by a member of staff at the newspaper office. Duncan must have arranged this.

How did this sit with the photo of Antoine and Kristen? Then it came to Susan. She had thought what a deadly enemy Duncan would be. This was about him planning to ruin Antoine in revenge for him having an affair with his wife. Had he simply used Isabelle as a pawn in a bigger game?

Susan didn't think she could feel angrier with Duncan after hearing what he'd done to his first wife, but she was white hot with rage now. The man had been despicable.

She was sure now that Antoine had an idea of what had been going on. No wonder he wanted that phone.

Susan replaced the phone in the dog food. It was lunchtime. After that, the big operation of clearing the Great Hall and the library ready for the party would begin. Gary and the staff had been working hard in the kitchen and a wonderful smell was wafting through the manor.

Susan was aware time was passing. She had until this evening to complete her investigation, then that was it. Everyone would be gone. She needed to make the most of every minute she had now.

Meera told her that Hayley had returned so going to see her seemed a good place to start.

Susan found a pale-faced, exhausted Hayley sitting up in bed, looking very young in white and pink pyjamas.

'How are you?' Susan asked gently.

'I don't know,' replied Hayley. She spoke slowly, softly and Susan guessed she had been given some strong pain relief. 'I don't remember taking pills or pouring those drinks. Life is out of control. One minute I think I understand, and then find I'm wrong. I'm scared all the time.'

'There has been so much to cope with, in particular, losing your father so suddenly. You've been through a very difficult time.'

'Yes, it's been a nightmare, hasn't it? But it hasn't ended yet, has it? I can't trust anyone, not even Lewis now. I'd been suspecting affairs, but I was confused that first time Antoine told us about Isabelle's death and Lewis said about her dying alone... and then when Antoine showed us the photograph, I knew where it had come from.'

Susan gasped. Hayley had given her vital pieces of the puzzle about Lewis.

Hayley, as Susan had known for a long time now, was bright. She put things together. Susan was sure Hayley had worked out who Lewis was and must have realised what a strong motive he would have to kill Duncan. If she suspected Lewis had worked out she was onto him, no wonder she was afraid.

Susan was suddenly afraid for Hayley.

'You need to be careful,' she said as calmly as she could. 'Only drink sealed bottled water. I'll get you a fresh one now.' She took a new bottle from the fridge and put it next to Hayley's bed.

Hayley looked at her with large, scared eyes. 'I understand.'

'Where's Lewis?' Susan asked.

The door opened. Susan started, but it was Bryson.

'Lewis is, of course, in the gym,' explained Hayley, smiling at Bryson.

He came over and touched her hand. 'How are you doing, sis?'

She shrugged.

Bryson spoke. 'Look, you don't need to talk, not heavy stuff, but well, I've told Susan here about what Dad did to Mum.'

Hayley's eyes were wide in alarm. Bryson's face creased with pain. 'I'm so sorry. Forget I mentioned it.' The words rushed out in panic. 'Look, all you have to do is rest. Um, you said Lewis is in the gym? Victoria offered to come and sit with you. Is that okay?'

Hayley smiled and Bryson left her to find Victoria, who had clearly been waiting outside, as she came in straight away.

'Hi, Hayley,' she said, drawing up a chair. 'We don't need to talk. See, I've brought a book. Just thought you'd like some company.'

Susan got up. 'Give me a call if there's anything you need.'

Susan made her way along the corridor. She urgently needed to talk to Lewis.

36

Lewis didn't hear Susan enter. To Susan's surprise, he wasn't using any of the equipment but rather was sitting with his laptop on the floor.

She stayed close to the door, and already had one hand on her two-way radio in her bag.

Seeing her enter, Lewis quickly turned the laptop away, and stood up.

'I've just come from Hayley. Victoria's with her now,' said Susan.

'Oh, good.'

'Lewis, I need to talk to you.' She hesitated, felt her mouth go dry. 'I'm afraid I don't believe the explanations you gave me about why you kept being Catholic a secret and pretended to go to Swansea University.'

'I don't know what you mean—'

'I am saying you haven't been simply trying to cover up a few details of your life. No. You, Lewis, are not, well, Lewis at all, are you? You are someone completely different and have been frantic to keep that a secret from Hayley and the family.'

'That's ridiculous.'

'No, it's not. I've slowly put the pieces together. You not only didn't go to Swansea University, you're not even Welsh. I believe you're French. Calling Antoine's nativity a crèche should have given me a hint. You hid being Catholic because you didn't want anyone to start putting a picture of you together. French, Catholic... but Hayley did.'

His eyes were wide with panic now. 'What does Hayley know?'

'When Antoine showed us the photograph with *My "sister"* written on the back, Hayley recognised it. She knew where she had seen it before. I saw Antoine come out of your room. I should have seen it as well.'

Lewis cringed. 'That's absurd,' he said, but the words were lacking conviction now.

'No, you're a French Catholic and you're Isabelle Dumont's brother. You gave yourself away when Antoine first told us about her death. You said, "No one should die alone," but how did you know that Isabelle had? Antoine at that point had no details of her death.'

He opened his mouth to speak, but then took a beat. His shoulders fell, and he closed his eyes, held on to the bar at the side of the treadmill.

'There's no way out, is there?' He sighed. 'I'm so tired of all the lies. I was actually planning to tell Hayley this weekend. It's why I brought the photo.'

'Why hadn't you told her before?'

'Look, I didn't set out to meet Hayley as part of some vendetta. We met accidentally at a gym and I fell for her. Now I knew her father's paper was after my sister, but to be honest we weren't that close. I was pretty angry at the way she'd upset

Mum and Dad. But I was scared it would put Hayley off if she knew who I was, so, well, yes, I made up a few stories.'

'You must have known she would find out the truth.'

'Of course. I just wanted her to get to know me first. That was the real reason I didn't tell her about being a Catholic or French, I didn't want to give her any hint of who I might really be, but I was going to tell her.'

'And then Duncan died.'

'Exactly, and the police were everywhere. Well, I knew how it would look if they found out not only who I was but that I'd kept it a secret from everyone.' He picked up one of the weights, ten kilograms of solid metal. Susan stepped back, she watched him move the weight from hand to hand. 'But I didn't kill Duncan. I didn't put the newspaper by his bedside. I didn't hate the man. I should have, but I didn't. My sister brought a lot of her problems on herself. She made our parents' lives hell. We'd never been close. We were nothing alike. It's why I wrote *My "sister"* in English and with inverted commas. She'd sold out. She'd become someone different. I was certainly not going to put myself in jeopardy of eternal damnation for her.'

He put the weight carefully back with the others. 'I have an alibi. I went out of the house soon after two. I came downstairs. You were talking to Hayley. I went out through the back way, and actually stayed in my car all night. I couldn't go back inside in case they tried to call me, so I grabbed a bit of sleep in the car. In fact, I saw you as I was coming back.'

'You looked dishevelled,' said Susan, but she was struggling to believe he'd spent the whole night simply in his car on the phone to his parents.

'That's not surprising, is it? But the point is, I was in the car park. I could have proved it to the police if pushed, but obviously I didn't want to.'

'Hayley told me you'd lost your hip flask?'

He blinked, clearly confused at what sounded like a random question. 'It just got lost. I wasn't bothered. Who uses those things any more?' He glanced at the door. 'Look, I ought to be getting back to Hayley. I know you may not rate me as a particularly nice guy now, but I promise you I'm no killer. I love Hayley very much. That's all I care about.'

Susan sighed. 'Thank you for telling me about Isabelle and, well, even if you weren't that close, I'm so sorry for your loss.'

'Thank you,' he replied and, quickly pushing past her, he left the gym.

Susan looked down to the floor, saw the laptop. She was curious: why was he using his laptop in the gym? Susan decided to find out. She wondered what she would find. Slowly, she turned the laptop around, revealing the screen. She stared. It was a gambling site, which was all she could tell. So, was that what Lewis had been secretly doing all this time? Was it gambling, not women, that had been taking him to his phone so often? Was this what Duncan had seen when he looked over Lewis's shoulder that day? Was he worried the partner of his only daughter had some kind of gambling addiction?

Susan remained for a few moments, gathering her thoughts, then left the room.

As she entered the corridor, she saw Bryson disappearing down the stairs in front of her and as she passed his room she saw he'd left his bedroom door open. Peeping in, she could see Victoria's handbag on the chair and she remembered that envelope she had seen before. She was desperate to check it.

She crept in. Her hands shook as she opened the bag and searched for the right pocket. Finally, she found the envelope and pulled out its contents. As she had suspected, it was a death certificate, but what an odd thing to carry around.

Susan quickly replaced it and glanced around the room. She saw the coffee and tea tray, the books by the bed, the hip flask, bottle of whisky and the non-alcoholic spirits. And then she saw something she'd been missing all this time, a vital clue, hiding in plain sight. She went over, slipped an object into her pocket, and left the room. However, as she was closing the door firmly behind her, she was startled by a sharp prod on her shoulder.

She swung round. 'Still snooping around?' asked Antoine.

'Just doing my job,' she said, her voice shaking. Her hand reached for her small bag; it was still unzipped from when she was talking to Lewis.

'Have you got that phone for me?' he asked, threat in his eyes.

Her heart was racing. She stumbled over her words.

'Sorry, I'd forgotten to ask Robert. I'll go and ask him now.' She walked away as quickly as she could and went back to the flat.

She shut the door, shaking, and locked it. She turned to the dogs and fussed over them. 'My protectors,' she said to them as they wagged their tails.

She carefully hid the item she'd taken from Victoria's room in her bedside cabinet, then collapsed on the sofa, closed her eyes and before she knew it was in a deep sleep.

She was woken by Robert. 'Wake up, sleepy. It's not long till the party. I'll take the dogs out for a quick run, give you time to get ready.' He opened the patio doors, and they were gone.

Susan had not been thinking about getting ready at all, but realised she needed to get on with it.

She looked at her dresses hanging up, then pulled out the bag Alice had given her. Inside was a dress, but one unlike any she had ever owned. It was blue, made from silky material: the colours of the ocean, a kind of shift dress but more fitted.

There was no harm in trying, she told herself, and put the dress on. She went into the bathroom and tried jumping up so that she could see it in the mirror. What she could see looked okay, but she wasn't sure.

She knew who might be able to help. She grabbed her coat, threw it on, and ran along to the office barefoot. As she entered, Meera turned.

'Susan, everything okay? You look quite flushed.'

'Um, yes. The thing is, I need an honest opinion, and I trust you to give me that.'

Meera grinned. 'Sounds interesting. What is it?'

Susan took her coat off. 'What do you think?'

Meera's smile was so warm and generous, Susan nearly cried. 'You look absolutely wonderful. It's gorgeous,' she said.

'You're sure?'

'Of course. I hope this is for the party?'

Susan nodded.

'Excellent. Look, come back in half an hour. I'll pop up, get changed, and we can have a drink before the guests arrive. Let's hope we can have one evening without any drama.'

Susan threw her coat back on and returned to the flat. She showered and washed her hair. She heard Robert shout hello as he returned and panicked. Maybe she should play it safe, wear one of her old dresses? The thought of facing Meera after that, though, was too much. No, she'd have to stick with this. After drying her hair, putting on a tidy pair of shoes and even some make-up, she felt ready to go into the living room.

Robert was coming out of his room, having put on his grey suit and blue tie. He was lucky. He was one of those men who really did look good in a suit.

'Wow, Cinders. Is this for the party?' he exclaimed. Susan

looked to see if he was laughing at her but, no, he looked impressed.

'Don't you like it?'

'You look lovely,' he said, now with his usual smile. 'Sorry, you took me by surprise. You look fabulous.'

'I promised to call in for a drink with Meera before the party so why don't you come as well?' said Susan.

They made their way down the hallway and went into the office.

This time Meera was dressed in a beautiful red sari. 'You look gorgeous,' Susan said to her.

'And so do you,' said Meera. 'I have a gift for you,' she said, holding out a beautiful silver necklace with blue stones.

'But I can't.'

'Please. I have to be able to thank you and look, it goes perfectly with your dress.' She grinned.

After swift drinks, they went into what was now the Great Hall and library combined. The quartet had started playing and guests were arriving. Susan recognised quite a few of the faces from the local paper, where they had been pictured opening various functions or meeting royalty as they came over for Cowes week.

She was pleased to see, though, that there were other people from the village invited. Tracy was there with her husband and she greeted Susan enthusiastically.

'Wow, isn't this exciting?' she said. 'It's amazing in here. Don't you look gorgeous?'

'Thank you.'

Susan helped herself to some food from the buffet. There was a lovely atmosphere with people chatting and even a small group of people being taught some basic dance steps by the group who had come to play.

It was surprising how quickly she became hot, and Susan went to stand just outside the open front door to cool down.

Robert came out to stand next to her and put his arm around her and this time she let him. She looked up but as he was bending to kiss her, she heard someone shout.

'Susan? Is that you?'

Her stomach turned over. It couldn't be. She looked over and saw to her horror that it really was.

37

Steve was walking across the courtyard towards her. Susan felt Robert's arm tightening on her shoulder.

Steve ignored him and spoke directly to Susan. 'I'm sorry. I have to talk to you. This is important.'

She felt Robert releasing his grip. He walked away.

'What are you doing here, Steve?' she asked.

'It's about the house.'

'Oh, for God's sake. That can wait. You had no right to come here.'

He waved his arms towards the party, at the same time dropping the car keys he was clasping in his hand. He picked them up, mumbling, 'Oh, they're soaking wet.' Wiping them on his trousers, he continued, 'Obviously, I had no idea there was a do going on. I happened to be on the island and wanted to see you. I hadn't realised you'd be dressed up partying like this. I thought you'd come here to work.'

'I have, but tonight is the farewell do before the guests leave tomorrow.'

'You look different. I've never seen you in a dress like that before.'

'It's a new dress, that's all.' Susan cringed, thinking, *Please don't be rude about it; please don't make me feel stupid.*

However, he just scowled and asked, 'Did Robert give you that necklace?'

'No. That was a gift from someone else. Steve, you need to go.'

'Look, it's freezing out here. Can I come inside? This won't take long.'

Reluctantly she let him in, and took him to Robert's flat.

The four dogs, who had all been asleep, leapt up, excited. They ran over to him, and he made a fuss of them. He always was good with dogs, and they loved him.

'I've been asked to make a decision about the house,' Steve said. 'The estate agent said they've had a few offers.'

'You could have asked me this on the phone. Did you come over on the ferry? Where's Hester?'

'I did come over on the ferry. There are some things that we need to speak about face to face, Susan, and this is one of them.'

'Look, if you must know, I don't want you buying the house next door to me. I'm making a new life for myself now, Steve.'

'With Robert—'

That was the wrong thing for Steve to say. Susan felt the anger bubble up inside her. 'No, not with Robert, with myself. I'm making a new life with myself. For the first time in my life, I have the time and space to think about me, what I want to do, find out who I am. Robert and I are close but we're not about to move in together or anything like that. But you left me, Steve. I don't need you living next door to me, even if it's just for the odd week. I need to be free of any fear that one day I'm going to walk into my garden and see you on the other side of my fence.' She took a breath. Steve raised his eyebrows.

'I see. You've given this some thought. You don't fancy the trips to the beach—'

'Those dreams are from the past. Everything is different now.'

'You can't actually stop me.'

There was that threat again.

'I know that,' she said, as calmly as she could. 'Look, it's up to you if you buy somewhere else to live on the island, or just keep on the flat. I don't own the island, but I would like to hold on to my village.'

He suddenly looked very sad and defeated, but Susan wasn't tempted to relent. He let out a very long sigh, then stood up. 'Okay, I'll pull out. Zoe said it was a stupid idea.'

'Did she?'

'Oh, yes. You know our daughter, ever blunt, but often right. Right, I think I'd better leave you to your party. If I step on it, I'll catch the next ferry.'

After he left, Susan sat down and Rocco and Libs ran over to her. She cuddled them and cried with relief. As she did, though, that line she'd shouted at Steve echoed back: 'I finally have the time and space to think about me...' She needed to give that some more thought, but that would come later. Now she wanted to get back to the party. She got up and washed her face, thinking how lucky it was that she hadn't got layers of mascara and make-up on.

Going back into the party, she grabbed a full glass of sparkling water and wandered over to a group of people standing with Bryson. One man was holding his phone. They were asking each other random general knowledge questions, and it was clearly Bryson's turn. Bryson was laughing with an exaggerated shrug.

Susan stood watching him, remembering Gary saying how good Duncan had been at quizzes. Obviously, Bryson didn't take after him.

Susan glanced over to one side where she saw Kristen, wearing that same white sequinned dress she had worn the first night they had arrived, but like last night she had fewer diamonds on, which seemed odd. Surely, this was the time to wear them all? Looking at those photographs of her had made Susan see her in a different light. Kristen was a clever woman. What was she playing at?

To her surprise, Lewis came over to her. She asked politely how Hayley was and he replied she was resting.

He lowered his voice. 'I hope we are okay after that chat earlier. I'm sorry I've been so secretive. I was thinking about that old lady we saw yesterday. She had me completely fooled, you know.'

Susan smiled. 'I can imagine. She looks very sweet, doesn't she?'

'Yes, but she doesn't miss much. I heard what Alice said to Hayley. She's like a human lie detector.'

A roar of laughter came from the group playing the quiz. Susan looked at them, over at Kristen, and then caught Antoine's eye. He wanted to come and speak to her, she could tell. Looking back at Lewis, she replied, 'You're dead right about Alice. She's seldom wrong.'

'I'm relieved it's out in the open now. I've told Hayley. She understands.'

'I'm glad she knows the truth. She needs you to be honest with her. She worries with you being on your phone so much.'

'I know. It's just work. She'll get used to it. She knows how much it means to me. One day, I'll have my own gym. I'll be the one in charge, telling all the other trainers what to do. It's my dream and I will do whatever I need to achieve that.'

She saw the light burning in his eyes. He was clearly a very determined man.

'I hope you achieve your ambition,' she replied.

'Oh, I shall. Right, I'd better go and check on Hayley,' he said and left her.

Susan wandered over to the buffet table. It was an amazing spread. She picked up a mini quiche and began to nibble on it.

'Enjoying the buffet?' She turned and saw it was Gary asking.

'It's delicious, of course.'

'Victoria came to see me; she was full of praise.' He blushed with pleasure.

'That's wonderful. You deserve that. It's been such a difficult few days, but you've kept the standard of the food top rate.'

'Thank you.' He looked around and then lowered his voice. 'I had a phone call from Dad. He told me you're friends with Alice from the home and have been talking about Nancy's accident all those years ago.'

Susan suddenly remembered that first hint about the accident had come from Gary on her first day at the manor.

'We have. I remember when you mentioned it to me in the kitchen. You told me about your father and Duncan being friends, the quiz, chatting at the garage – then there was the accident. You said your dad knew things.'

She watched him closely. He shifted from one foot to another. 'Well, yes. I guess he did.'

'I have been told a few things about Duncan that night—'

Gary opened his mouth, but then seemed to change his mind and said, 'Look, as I said, it was a long time ago. I think I'd best get back to my kitchen.'

She watched him walk away. He might be wanting to dismiss their conversation but Susan had a feeling it had been far more important than she realised.

Susan looked over and was surprised to see Hayley coming down the stairs with Lewis. She walked over to Hayley, who was in her long purple dress and holding herself very upright.

'Okay?' Susan asked.

'I can't stay up there waiting.' She looked sideways at Lewis. 'I'll go and talk to the stones later, but first I must see Victoria.'

Susan watched her go over to Victoria and slip an arm through hers.

It was clear the party was starting to come to an end: it was never going to be a late night. Susan watched as people started to gather their coats to leave before heading back to the flat: she needed time to think.

Robert came in and offered to take the dogs out. She was grateful: there were so many pieces to put together. It was as if someone had taken several complicated jigsaws and mixed them all up. The picture she wanted to make was the one which resolved who killed Duncan, and yet so many other pieces were getting in the way. She went into her bedroom and was thinking about getting ready for bed. By her bedside table she saw her copy of Bryson's book and remembered Alice saying something about re-reading it. Susan wondered why she wanted her to do that. She flicked through the pages, then stopped, looked down at the page. Her mind was turning this over when she noticed the security light come on. Why had someone left through the back door, when the front was still open? They must be hoping to slip out unnoticed. Susan remembered Hayley's words. Maybe she was going up to the stones as she said she would?

Susan frowned. Hayley should not be out there alone. She had to go out and find her.

38

Susan knew it would be dark and cold up there, so she grabbed her coat. On the side she saw Robert's two-way radio. He must have taken it out of his pocket before the party. She groaned. She really wanted to let him know where she was going. She'd try his mobile once she was outside.

She tried to ring Robert, but he didn't answer.

She knew he had to be out here somewhere. She shone her phone flashlight around the garden but there was no sign of him. He must already be up at the Longstone, which was where she was heading anyway.

She rushed up through the garden, pushed open the gate and clambered up the path, now muddy from the melted snow, up to the Longstone.

When she reached the top of the path and stepped into the opening, though, she paused, shocked at the scene in front of her.

There was a ring of candles on the stone and Hayley was sitting, holding a bottle to her lips. Susan ran over to her, hitting the bottle away.

'Leave it alone, don't drink from it. Why are you here?'

'He told me to come. I'm so tired, Susan. I just want this to be over.'

'No, don't say that. Come back with me.'

'You don't mean to Lewis, do you? You know who he is and what he has done?'

'I know he's Isabelle's brother, but he didn't kill your father.'

'I know, but he's lied to me about so many things. Not just about Isabelle either.'

'He gambles?'

'Yes, and by the way, I am that jealous girlfriend who checks his phone. I know he's gambled with the money I gave him for the gym. It's all gone. But I know it wasn't him who killed my father. I think you know who it was—'

'I do. This was a meticulously planned murder inspired by your book. The first thing the killer did was to arrange for Kristen to provide the hip flasks. They set the stage. I'm guessing they stole some of your father's pills before you all came here. The killer crushed up the pills, and put them in their own hip flask with some whisky. When it was safe and they were sure Duncan was asleep, they went into his room and swapped his hip flask for the one containing the crushed pills, knowing there was a high likelihood of Duncan drinking from that flask and being dead by the morning.'

Susan stepped forward. She thought she heard a twig break in the woodland and hoped it was Robert, waiting, close at hand.

Hayley looked searchingly at Susan. 'Only two people are thought to have gone into Duncan's room: Victoria and me.'

'Victoria was not the killer—'

'But it wasn't me. I'm being set up. I never went in. Bryson made that up.'

Suddenly a figure rushed at them out of the darkness. 'Leave her alone. Get the hell away from her.'

Susan turned, and stepped between the person and Hayley.

'I'm not going anywhere,' she shouted. 'It's time to stop. You've told so many lies, but now I know the truth. You killed your father.'

Bryson threw his head back in a wild laugh. 'I never even went into his room. Hayley wouldn't let me.'

'I didn't,' screamed Hayley.

'You don't know what you're doing,' sneered Bryson. 'No one can believe a word you say.'

'But they can, and I do,' said Susan firmly. 'The lie has been useful for throwing suspicion on Hayley, but you made that up initially to stop Antoine going into Duncan's room. Just before you came downstairs, you'd checked on Duncan, seen he was asleep and swapped the flasks. You didn't want Antoine going in and waking him up. You didn't want anyone going in there, although of course Victoria created a lot of stress for you by unexpectedly going in later. You'd given her a sleeping pill, but it took a while to act. Fortunately, she didn't notice anything amiss. She grabbed that phone and left.'

Bryson was close to Susan now, but she continued.

'In the early hours, it was time for part two of your plan. You returned to Duncan's room and could see straight away your plan had worked. Your father had drunk from the hip flask. He was dead.' Susan paused. 'Of course, if he hadn't drunk from the flask, or the pills hadn't worked, as long as you removed the flask you were covered. If you failed that night, you could try again the next. Like when you pushed me down the steps in the car park. That failed to get rid of me so you tried to drown me in the sea. Neither paid off, but then neither cost you anything. I've no doubt you would have tried again.'

She watched his face. In the darkness she saw that half-smile, a smugness that made her want to hit him. How dare he feel so pleased with himself?

Susan made herself continue. 'You added a touch of drama, the opened newspaper. If there were to be any questions, you would rather the police were looking in Lewis's direction. You returned your father's hip flask and, not wanting to be caught with yours, threw it out of the window. At this point you made a mistake, leaving the window open. Then you returned to bed.'

'Oh yes, and what happened to the hip flask then?'

'You went downstairs early the next morning, let yourself out the front door, taking the key, and found the hip flask by the door behind the bush. You took the flask and hid it in the shack. If the police became involved, you didn't want it found in your room. When you returned to the manor, you let yourself back in.'

Susan watched his mouth drop open with disbelief. 'No, you saw me. I was just leaving the manor when we met.'

'Oh, no. When we met, you had to pretend you were just leaving. When my ex dropped his keys earlier and they got wet in the snow, it jogged my memory. From the outside, the lock would be snowy and wet. You handed me a wet key to hang up. It should have been dry. I should have noticed it at the time.'

'This is all conjecture. You have no proof.'

'I found the hip flask.' Susan saw him step back. Yes: that had scared him. 'It will be interesting to see if you have left any traces of the medication inside.' In the torchlight, she saw his eyes now widen in panic.

'Oh, so you didn't have time to wash it out,' she said, and saw his face freeze. 'And you drank from that, didn't you? I saw you the first night when I was showing you to your room. If you didn't wash it out, simply poured whisky in—' She paused. She was sure he was going through those steps with her... and she was sure that was exactly what happened.

'So, your DNA will be on it as well. You stole Lewis's hip flask, thinking you'd protect yourself, but it proves nothing.'

Again, she saw a look of alarm: she was right. She tried to stay calm.

'You're crazy but, just say you had that right, you don't have anything else—'

'Oh, I do. You needed a way to grind the pills very small, and you thought ahead on that one. You brought all your coffee-making materials. I have your coffee grinder, which I have removed from your room. With even a cursory look, I could see some white powder on it. I should have realised when I noticed it was damp and none of your other coffee-making materials had been used. I'm not sure how you will explain how traces of your father's medication came to be on the grinder?'

Bryson walked over to her. His face, lit up by the torch from below his chin, looked menacing now, reminding her of the game they played as children in the darkness. But this was no game. 'This is madness. You've been reading too many of my books. In any case, why would I have killed my father, who I clearly loved?'

'Bryson, I don't think that you truly love anyone apart from yourself. Your father was planning to write his autobiography. He told you he was going to put things straight about your mother.'

'Yes, he was going to confess to being with her when she had the accident.'

'Oh, no. He was going to tell the world that the accident happened not because his wife drank, but because her own son attacked her.'

'That's a hideous lie. If anyone was responsible, it was my father.'

'But he couldn't have been. The accident happened on the first night of your holiday, a Saturday. Hayley told me she looked out the window and saw her mother as she watched the sunset. That would have been somewhere around nine. There was still some light. Duncan was out, and I know he was at the quiz as this took place on the Saturday night. He was in the pub until closing time. The truth is your father came back and found your mother had been attacked by you and you had run off. That is what Hayley saw. Your parents told her she'd imagined it, tried to protect you. She was so confused.'

'I was never there.'

'You were. Your writing testifies against you. Alice told me you always signed off Hayley's stories with a fancy "The end", and the story she wrote the night of your mother's accident was signed in that way. You were there, with her. I'm guessing you looked out with her, saw your mother and then went out and attacked her. Hayley took that story into Alice's shop the next day. When we visited the nursing home, I'm guessing she put that piece of the puzzle in place. She told me to re-read the ending.'

'Why would I have attacked my own mother?' he sneered.

'Because you were very angry with her for not letting you go on that expensive gap year. You complained to Alice in the shop. You even told Victoria about it years later. Her refusal obviously bit deep. You hated the fact your mother kept you short of money.'

'You think I'd attack her over money?'

'I believe drink actually led to the violence. Those empty bottles found in the house were not your mother's, they were yours. I believe your father had concerns about your drinking.

He went to the garage and shared his worries with Gary's dad. Now Gary told me his father knew things. I thought he'd meant Gary's father knew about your mother drinking, but it wasn't that, was it? No, it couldn't have been, because Gary used the words "so young" and Nancy had been in her early forties. No, it was you. Your father was worried you were drinking too much and, I'm guessing, becoming violent with it. I think you know that about yourself and that is the real reason you no longer drink. You know you lose control.'

Bryson shrugged in the manner of a teenager. 'Well, I've sorted it out. That's to my credit.'

'But your mother—'

'Okay, so I regret that, but you have to understand, I did have a point. You have no idea how frustrating it was always being short of money. I looked a fool at school. And that wasn't any old holiday. It was an amazing opportunity that I deserved. It would have been the making of me. Dad would have let me go, but she put her foot down. My mother was jealous. That's all. She'd never done anything with her life, and she wanted to spoil mine. I wanted her to remember the day she'd ruined my life—' He paused.

'And so, you attacked her. You slashed her face with glass. You wanted to scar her for life.'

He lowered his face and Susan saw the whites of his cold eyes.

'She was always stopping me getting what I wanted. I was right to stand up for myself. Anyway, I had a lot to cope with because of her behaviour. Have you any idea what it's like living with an alcoholic? I've spoken about the heartbreak—'

'You have, and that has all been lies. Your mother wasn't drunk that night.'

'Of course she was. My mother admitted it.'

'They were lies your mother was prepared to live with to protect you. She didn't want people knowing what you'd done. In fact, your mother was not an alcoholic at all.'

'She died of liver failure,' Bryson protested.

'But she didn't. I know she died of a brain tumour. Nothing to do with alcohol.'

'No one knows that. Only Dad—'

Susan took a breath. 'Alice said she had never suspected your mother had addiction problems. Her instincts had been right. I saw it for myself in black and white on her death certificate this evening. I'm guessing your father bought professional silence and then you wrote the obituary because your father couldn't bear to write the lies.' Susan stood back. 'At least he had his limits, but not you. You've profited by this lie. Your life is built on it.'

'Dad understood.'

'He may have but, as you said, his illness changed him. He was tired of the lies. In his autobiography, he was going to tell the world his wife was never an alcoholic, that you had hurt your mother in an accident and she wanted to cover things up.'

'He wouldn't do that to me.'

'Oh, he would. I heard him say he knew you were resilient. He thought you'd weather the storm.'

Bryson shook his head. 'I couldn't believe that he, of all people, could be so naïve. He told me people would understand, that he'd write it sympathetically, explain I was young, and hot headed. But he should have known they would destroy me. I had attacked my mother, cut her face, lied about her being an alcoholic. Who was going to employ me with that CV? Certainly not anyone looking for a friendly chat show host. He had no right to do that—'

'So, he deserved to die?'

Bryson shrugged. 'He probably didn't have long left anyway. I just brought things forward.'

'So, you killed him and then you were going to kill your sister.' Susan turned to Hayley. 'The reason your world has been out of control is because he has been spiking your drinks with strong alcohol and Lewis's opioids. What happened tonight?'

Hayley glanced at the candles. 'He told me to come up here and he would tell me the truth. You see, when he talked to me after I was so drunk in the garden, when he tried to persuade me I'd seen Dad up here that night, I told him I knew it was him. My aunt had told me Mum never drank. She'd also told me Mum was worried about Bryson's drinking and his temper.'

'And you believed her?'

'I wasn't sure. That was why I wanted to talk to Alice. Then Dad died. I was suspicious, scared. Bryson lied about me going into the room. If he lied about that, what else would he lie about? I saw the way he looked at me. When you had the accident on the beach, I was sure it was him. I've been so scared, waiting for him to kill me.'

Susan turned to Bryson in anger. 'You're a wicked man. You've tried your best to drug and discredit your own sister. You were arranging her death to look like suicide, all to protect yourself, because she is an eyewitness to what really happened that night. You've repeatedly lied to her but she knows the truth now.'

Bryson screamed at the sky. 'No one understands me. This chat show is my big chance, my break in life. I didn't write those stupid books, but this is finally all me. I'm going to be brilliant. I'll be a star. I couldn't believe my own father was going to ruin my life for my mother and for her.' He pointed at Hayley. 'Her life won't amount to anything, but I matter.' He paused and then a kind of wild half-smile spread across his face. 'It can still happen. They'll forgive me. I was young. People will love me.'

Susan looked at him. Was he so deluded? He shook his head, spoke to himself. 'I can't chance it. I need her dead.'

Bryson lunged towards Susan. She braced herself, but he pushed past her and grabbed Hayley. He took a bottle from his pocket and tried to force it into her mouth, but then a voice screamed at him to stop.

39

Susan turned and was shocked to see Victoria. 'Leave Hayley alone. You won't hurt anyone else.'

Bryson stared in disbelief, as if Victoria was a ghost. He walked towards her. 'I can explain. It wasn't my fault. It was all my father. You said it was a relief he'd gone. Forgive me.'

Victoria shook her head. 'How could you assault your own mother, write those lies in the obituary and lie to those charities? And now you're a killer, someone who would murder his own father so he can be famous, someone who is trying to destroy his own sister. No, Bryson. No one is ever going to forgive you.'

Bryson collapsed in a heap and started to howl, but no one went to comfort him.

At that moment, Robert arrived with the dogs. As soon as Susan explained what was happening, Robert took control. He phoned the police and stood close to Bryson but there was no need to restrain him. Bryson was in pieces.

It was a long night of statements and by the time Susan returned to the manor in the early hours, she was exhausted.

She walked in to find Victoria sitting by the fire with a cup of tea.

Seeing Susan, Victoria put her tea down, got up and, to Susan's surprise, hugged her. Quickly she pulled back, looking embarrassed. Susan followed her over to the chairs, and sat close to the fire.

'I know you must be ready for bed, but it would be good to talk.'

'Of course.'

'When you told Bryson you had read in black and white that his mother had not died of liver failure, I'm guessing it was this.'

Victoria leant down, took the white envelope out of her bag, and handed it to Susan.

Opening the envelope, Susan found the certificate which she had read the evening before:

Certified copy of an entry of death.

The name below was Nancy Fern.

'That's right. I did wonder how you came to have this?'

'I sent for this before we came here. Bryson had always told me his mother died of liver failure, brought on by her addiction. Then Hayley hinted to me that she wasn't sure what caused her mother's death. Without consulting any of them, I thought I'd just check for myself. When this arrived, I started to wonder why Duncan had allowed this lie to go unchecked, and why in her lifetime Nancy had been complicit. I thought she might have been protecting Duncan. I was planning to challenge him while we were here but, of course, he died.'

'When did you start to work out the truth?'

'When Duncan died, I was scared. I didn't like that newspaper being there. I'd seen it when I went to bed, but it had disappeared by the morning. Only Bryson could have put it there.'

'You should have told the police.'

'I thought it was a silly game, something to spook his father. I didn't think he'd killed him, but then I started getting worried about Hayley. Why was Bryson saying she had money problems when I knew she didn't? I checked again, after the beach. I'd seen Bryson get into her accounts. It was frighteningly easy. Lewis told me Bryson had said she had a drink problem but I'd never seen evidence of it. I was convinced it was made up. But why? Then I saw how scared she was, how confused, all this business about the accident. I was building a picture, but then, last night when everyone was watching Hayley, lying there, unconscious, I caught his eye, and you know what? I saw him smile. It was a horrible grin, and he knew I'd seen it. A thought came to me, that I was next. I heard him leave the manor after the party and I didn't know what to do. Eventually I followed, I heard your conversation. I've been very foolish, Susan.'

'No, he was a liar, and the only foolish thing you did was believe him. But you know there is still one question I don't know the answer to.'

'And that is?'

'Who were you speaking to that Thursday night? Who did you say the words "If only he could die?" to?'

Victoria smiled. 'Ah, that fateful conversation. I was actually talking to Kristen.'

'Kristen?' Susan's eyebrows shot up.

'Yes. She asked to speak to me because she was concerned about me noticing her jewellery going missing. She didn't want me to alert Duncan. I insisted she tell me what was going on and, to be honest, I think it was a relief for her to tell someone. She was so upset, and I was so angry with Antoine. When I said

'If only he could die" I was talking about Antoine, not Duncan. I remember a noise disturbed us and we walked away. And no, we didn't plan on killing Antoine, although I'd have been more than glad the next morning if it had been his body we'd found and not Duncan's. You see, Kristen really did love Duncan. She didn't want her marriage destroyed.'

'But she was having an affair with Antoine. He told me she was infatuated with him.'

'No, that was a lie too. Kristen hated Antoine. He was blackmailing her. When Duncan met Kristen, Antoine recognised that she was in a position of power, and he wanted to control her. He began digging, eventually finding she'd had a friendship with a young man during her last marriage, even found some old photos. This didn't seem enough, so he got her drunk, set up a compromising photo and then he confronted her with the evidence. Asked for money to keep quiet.'

'She should have gone straight to Duncan.'

'She could have, but Duncan was a cynical man. He might not have believed her. And so she paid up, a small amount at first, but of course once she'd paid that first amount, Antoine could use that as proof of guilt. The demands grew bigger. She was selling her jewellery and belongings to pay him off.'

Susan sat back. 'I don't understand. Antoine is a wealthy man.'

'Ah, but he likes control and power. It's why he had her come out to the shack every night. He liked being the puppeteer. Sometimes he'd get her to transfer money, sometimes he made her just sit out there in the cold.'

'What a cruel man. What was all that business about the alibi?'

'Before the police came, after Duncan's body was found, Antoine told Kristen she was going to be a suspect and offered to provide her with an alibi if she'd do the same for him. She agreed. It was simply another thing to hold over her... she'd lied to the police.'

'That was just weakness on her part.'

'It was, but he'd manipulated her. She was scared.'

'Like Bryson frightened Hayley.'

'Exactly. I'm afraid neither Antoine nor Duncan are or were good men.'

Susan shook her head. 'The interesting thing is they both thought they were so clever and yet they were making such a mess of things. Duncan thought his wife was having an affair and was wrong about that. Antoine thought he had all that control and yet the whole time Duncan was setting him up.'

Victoria frowned. 'Sorry. What do you mean?'

Susan told Victoria about the photos of Antoine on the phone.

'So, Duncan thought Antoine was having an affair with his wife and was planning his revenge?'

'That's what I think.'

'That makes sense now you say it. You're right. I'm sure of it. I could do with seeing that phone, you know. I reckon I may be able to make a story out of this. I don't see why Antoine should get away with everything. I'll do this for Isabelle. She deserves this.'

EPILOGUE

A month later, Susan was sitting in the nursing home with Alice. One of the staff had just arranged the daffodils she had brought Alice and the sun was shining through the window.

'Tell me all the news,' said Alice, stroking Princess on her lap.

'Well, Bryson is in prison awaiting trial. Your instincts about Nancy were right. She never did have an addiction.'

'Poor Nancy. I'm sorry it was all such a sad end for her, but it's good Bryson is finally being brought to justice.'

'I agree. His wife Victoria is back at *The Informer* but branching out into investigative journalism. She did do a wonderful write-up of Gary's cooking.'

'His dad showed me. He was so proud.'

'Antoine has been suspended from *The Morning Flame* following accusations of corruption and he's under investigation. Kristen has offered to back Lewis's gym but is on her way back to America.'

'He's persuaded her to do that?'

'I know, she's mad. I found out, by the way, that he had

gambled away the money Hayley gave him for the gym. The reason he was in his car on the night Duncan died was not just because he was speaking to his parents. No, he was online gambling, desperate to try and win the money back. Now, Hayley – she has plans to move to Scotland, to live with her cousin and to write novels under her own name. Oh, and Meera is moving to return to India to open a new chain of hotels.'

Susan reached into her bag. 'Before she left, Meera gave me this, but I want to pass it on to you.' She handed Alice a white envelope. Inside was a postcard and on it a quotation which Alice read out loud.

'"When I despair, I remember that all through history the ways of truth and love have always won. There have been tyrants and murderers, and for a time, they can seem invincible, but in the end, they always fall. Think of it – always." Gandhi.'

Alice smiled. 'Thank you. I shall keep it next to my bed. And what next for you, Susan?'

'Ah, well, I shall enjoy getting my garden ready for the spring and summer. Zoe, Fay and Jamari are coming to stay for half term. It'll be lovely to spend some time with my granddaughter. By the way, I shall be getting new neighbours soon. Apparently, an offer on the house was made in the past few days and has been accepted. It's all happened so quickly.'

'Any idea who will be moving in?'

'I haven't seen anyone, but I spoke to the estate agent who was putting up a sold board this morning. He said that it's a man from the mainland with his teenage daughter. The estate agent said he found him rather reticent so couldn't tell me much more.' Susan laughed, adding, 'I'm guessing this man isn't used to sharing the details of his life with strangers.'

'He'll soon learn things work differently in a village,' said Alice. 'I have to say, he sounds quite intriguing; it'll be good to know more about him. Oh, Tracy came to visit. She told me that a vets' practice is taking over the vacant business premises up from the shop.'

'Now a vets' will be handy. It'll save me driving into Newport with Rocco and Libs.'

'Indeed. One of the vets went into the shop and of course Tracy got them chatting. Apparently, they're going to be looking for a part-time receptionist. I wondered if you'd fancy applying?'

Susan blinked. 'Me?'

'Yes. You're very good with people and animals. I'm sure you would be well suited. I get the feeling you're ready for a new challenge.'

Susan bit her lip. 'It sounds exciting, but would I be able to cope? There would be a lot to learn.'

'Of course you could do it. People do degrees, run marathons, even at my age. You need to believe in yourself. Let's face it, a year ago you wouldn't have imagined you'd be off solving murders, would you?'

'That's very true,' Susan grinned, 'but then I don't suppose you ever dreamed you'd be sitting here quietly chatting to me over a cup of coffee about means and motives, weighing up evidence, working out who may be our killer.'

Alice smiled. 'We make an unlikely but very effective team. And, who knows, maybe we'll have another case one day.' Her eyes twinkled behind her glasses, and she added, 'All these changes in the village: well they must be full of possibilities.'

AUTHOR NOTE

Although Bishopstone is a fictitious place it was inspired by the beautiful village of Brighstone. The people in the book are entirely fictitious.

Bishopstone Manor is inspired by Mottistone Manor, now owned by the National Trust. To date only the gardens have been opened to the public. The interior of the building in the story is completely the product of my imagination as is the idea of the manor being some kind of hotel. However, the details about the history of this stunning building, the gardens and the shack are based on historical fact. If you visit Mottistone Manor, you will find the gardens and shack as featured in the story. You can pass through the gate, walk through the bluebells in the Spring and up onto the downs and see the amazing Longstone for yourself.

One final thing I should add is that in my thirty years on the island I have never experienced a white Christmas, indeed heavy snow fall is a very rare event. However, it was lovely creating one for the story!

ACKNOWLEDGEMENTS

Ever since I read Agatha Christie's 'Hercule Poirot's Christmas' many years ago, I have wanted to write my own Christmas murder and am so excited to realise this dream. I am so grateful to be working with a very special and truly inspirational publisher, Boldwood.

A book of course, is not the work of an individual but a team. Firstly, I would like to say a huge thank you to Sarah Ritherdon. I feel enormously privileged to work with such an outstanding, kind, and gifted editor.

Thank you also to everyone in team Boldwood including Nia, Claire, Ben, Megan, Marcela, for your dedication and hard work, for endless patience and professionalism.

In addition, thank you to everyone else who has worked on this book, online and proof editing, cover design. Thank you everyone who has helped bring this novel to life.

As always, I want to say a huge thank you to my gorgeous family. My husband, Andrew, always my first reader and invaluable critic, and children, Thomas and Emily, for their unending support, humour and encouragement.

Thank you to you, my lovely readers. I hope I have kept even those who read with notebook and pen (you know who you are!), guessing to the end. I really have the best readers; I appreciate and am so grateful to you all.

I have to say a massive thank you to the bloggers who work

tirelessly in supporting writers like myself and to Rachel Gilbey for organising the amazing blog tours.

There are quite a few dogs in this story, and I'd like to thank all the owners for allowing me to use the names and descriptions of their very special dogs. Thank you, Diane Lister, for allowing me to mention Libby (Libs), Pat Pearson for Rocco, Pauline Trimmings for Gemma (Gem Gem), Fiona McGregor for Dougie and Wendy Coates for Lottie. All these people are members of the fabulous group, Cocker Spaniels on Facebook.

Thank you so much Karen Cass for again adding a touch of magic with your wonderful narration of the audiobook.

ABOUT THE AUTHOR

Mary Grand writes gripping, page-turning suspense novels, with a dark and often murderous underside. She grew up in Wales, was for many years a teacher of deaf children and now lives on the Isle of Wight.

Sign up to Mary Grand's mailing list here for news, competitions and updates on future books.

Visit Mary's website: www.marygrand.net/

Follow Mary on social media:

 x.com/authormaryg

 instagram.com/marygrandwriter

 facebook.com/authormarygrand

 bookbub.com/profile/mary-grand

ALSO BY MARY GRAND

The House Party

The Island

Good Neighbours

A Christmas Murder

The Isle of Wight Killings Series

Death at Castle Cove

Death at St Jude's

Poison
& Pens

POISON & PENS IS THE HOME OF
COZY MYSTERIES SO POUR YOURSELF
A CUP OF TEA & GET SLEUTHING!

DISCOVER PAGE-TURNING NOVELS FROM
YOUR FAVOURITE AUTHORS &
MEET NEW FRIENDS

JOIN OUR
FACEBOOK GROUP

BIT.LYPOISONANDPENSFB

SIGN UP TO OUR
NEWSLETTER

BIT.LY/POISONANDPENSNEWS

Boldwood

Boldwood Books is an award-winning fiction publishing company seeking out the best stories from around the world.

Find out more at www.boldwoodbooks.com

Join our reader community for brilliant books, competitions and offers!

Follow us
@BoldwoodBooks
@TheBoldBookClub

Sign up to our weekly deals newsletter

https://bit.ly/BoldwoodBNewsletter

Printed in Great Britain
by Amazon